The Secret of Elephants

The Secret of Elephants

VASUNDRA TAILOR

This is a work of fiction. Names, characters, organizations, places, events, and incidents are either products of the author's imagination or are used fictitiously. Any resemblance to actual persons, living or dead, or actual events is purely coincidental.

Published by Lake Union Publishing, Seattle

www.apub.com

ISBN-13: 9781542038201
ISBN-10: 1542038200

Cover design by Heike Schüssler

Printed in the United States of America

For Kaushal and Priyanka who light up my life
For Mahendra who keeps me grounded
For my parents who gave me so much

In family life, love is the oil that eases friction, the cement that binds closer together, and the music that brings harmony.

Friedrich Nietzsche

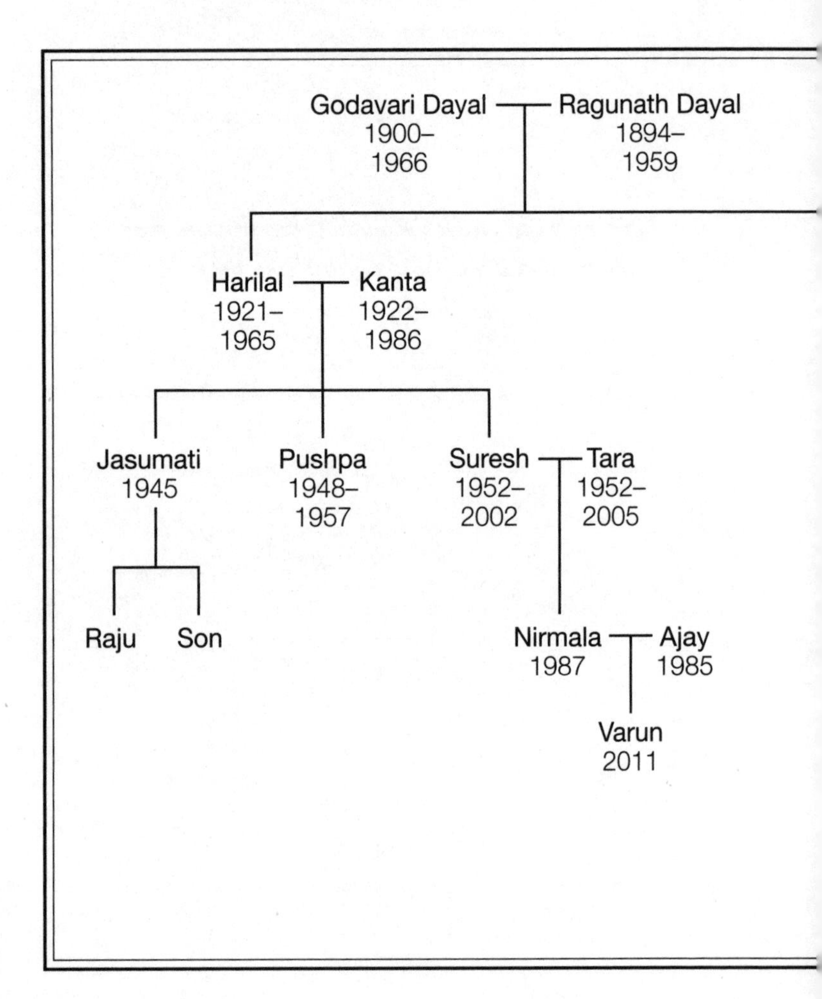
Godavari Dayal
1900–
1966
Ragunath Dayal
1894–
1959
Harilal
1921–
1965
Kanta
1922–
1986
Jasumati
1945
Pushpa
1948–
1957
Suresh
1952–
2002
Tara
1952–
2005
Raju
Son
Nirmala
1987
Ajay
1985
Varun
2011

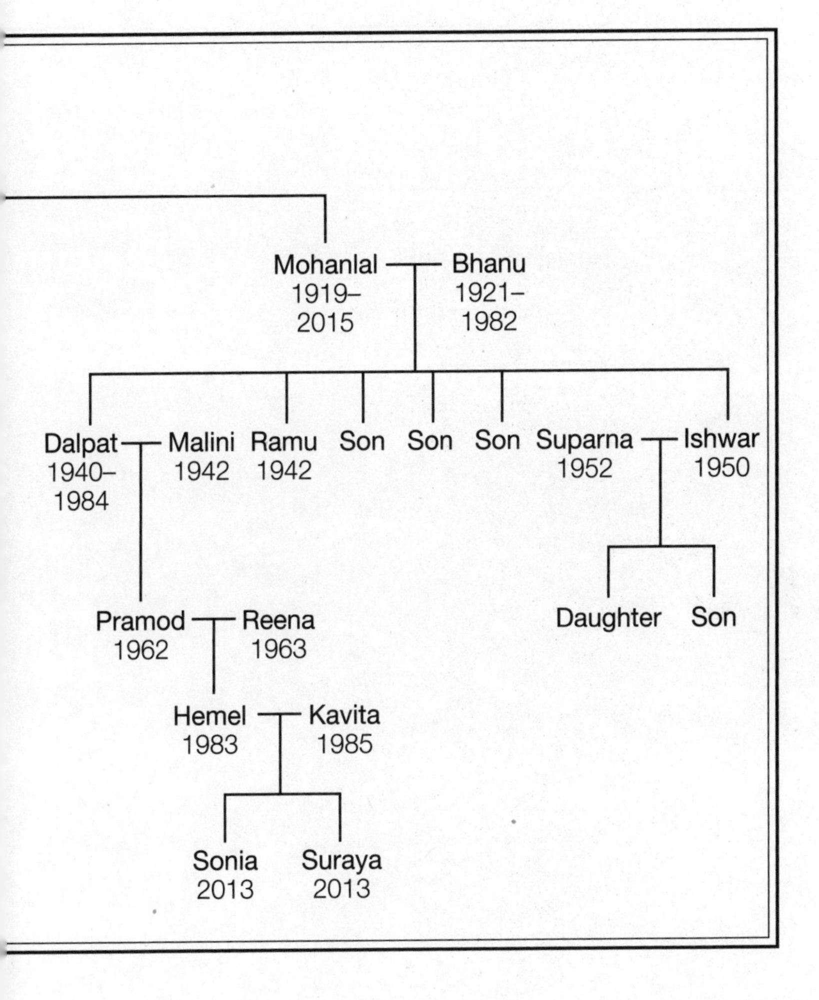
Mohanlal
1919–
2015
Bhanu
1921–
1982
Dalpat
1940–
1984
Malini
1942
Ramu
1942
Son
Son
Son
Suparna
1952
Ishwar
1950
Pramod
1962
Reena
1963
Daughter
Son
Hemel
1983
Kavita
1985
Sonia
2013
Suraya
2013

FAMILY RELATIONSHIPS – HONORIFIC SUFFIXES

Most languages in the Indian subcontinent have honorific suffixes added to people's names to show respect for those who are older. Family members are given specific suffixes to denote specific relationships. Often, friends or people not related are also shown this respect. The list below includes some of the suffixes used in this novel:

Ba – Mother
Bapuji – Father
Foi – Father's sister
Fua – Father's sister's husband
Kaka – Father's younger brother
Kaki – Father's younger brother's wife
Masi – Mother's sister
Masaji – Mother's sister's husband
Mama – Mother's brother
Mami – Mother's brother's wife
Bhai – Brother
Bhabhi – Brother's wife

Ben – Sister
Jija – Sister's husband
Dada – Grandfather
Dadima – Grandmother
Mota-dada – Great-grandfather
Ji – Gender-neutral honorific suffix

PROLOGUE

March 2016 Navsari, India

Her eyes burned with unshed tears. She fought to keep her emotions in check as she held him close, rocking gently on his tiny bed. He felt limp in her arms, tired after being poked and prodded in the doctor's surgery. The words kept rolling around in her head. *Epilepsy. My son has epilepsy.* Visions of him suffering debilitating seizures flared across her mind. It was too much to bear.

'Nirmala! What is the matter with you? Can't you hear me calling you?' She flinched at the acidity in her husband's voice and the boy woke up with a start.

'It's all right, my *dikra*,' she whispered. Clearing her throat, she turned to her husband: 'Ajay. The doctor says Varun has a very serious condition. He is having epileptic fits and needs special medicine. He might need it his whole life!'

She watched him frown as he took this in. Then he spluttered, 'What nonsense is this? The doctor is talking rubbish. Varun has never had a fit. He is just a lazy five-year-old good-for-nothing boy who doesn't want to talk. That's all.'

Nirmala reached for a single sheet of paper. Unfolding it, she read the three words written in neat block letters. 'The doctor called it Childhood Absence Epilepsy.' She looked at her husband pleadingly, hoping that for once he would listen and try to understand. 'You know how he stops what he is doing and goes into a trance. That is a type of epilepsy. We have to get his medicine today.' Trying to stay calm, she asked him for some money.

'You think rupees grow on trees?' His nostrils flared. 'How much do you think I earn stitching sari blouses for the snotty-nosed women of this town? You want rupees?' He leaned forward until his face was level with hers. 'Well, you know where you can get them from.' With eyes narrowed, he glared at her for a moment before whirling around and marching out of the room and house.

Varun trembled and buried his face in Nirmala's chest. She stroked his back and cooed softly in his ear. Not for the first time, she wondered what she had done in her previous life to deserve such an unreasonable husband. If only she had not rushed into marriage.

Stop that, Nirmala told herself. What was done was done and she had to make the best of things. She must not let him intimidate her. But that was easier said than done, especially when it came to matters of money. She remembered how quickly he had flown into a rage when she'd last asked for some. The topic always brought out the worst in him because they never seemed to have enough, even to feed their small family properly.

Varun felt hot and clammy in her arms. She wished the room was cooler and more comfortable, as it used to be when she was little. The ceiling fan had broken down years ago and it had never been fixed. She looked around the small, dark windowless room. On one side, it led to the kitchen, and on the other, it opened out to the front room. The only air and light that came into the house was from this room, which doubled up as Ajay's sewing room and their bedroom. The window and front door opened out to their small porch, which housed her treasured *jhula* swing. Nirmala decided to carry Varun outside.

'You love this *jhula*, don't you, my *dikra*?' she crooned as he lay on the cushions with his head on her lap. As always, she thanked her late father for having the *jhula* built all those years previously. Most people had these at the entrance of their homes, but hers was special, made of solid wood, suspended from the ceiling on four heavy chains. She used to love sitting there as a child, her beloved parents on either side of her.

The afternoon sun was scorching. The porch roof afforded a welcome shade at that time of day. February was meant to be a winter month, but here in the state of Gujarat, Nirmala felt that most days of the year were either hot or unbearably hot. She kicked off her slippers, removed the *odhani* from her neck, and re-tied her long brown hair into a knot further up the back of her head. Even in a thin cotton *salwar kameez*, she was sweating.

There were very few people in the street and Nirmala was glad of it. She was in no mood to return greetings from cheery neighbours or respond to hawkers and street vendors. She watched the few auto rickshaws and scooters buzzing by, leaving behind a trail of dust which tickled her nostrils. There was the usual steady stream of cows and calves strolling along without a care in the world, happy in the knowledge that no one would hurt them. They were a nuisance on the busy roads, where everything had to stop for them. But here in Golwad Street, they were a soothing sight.

Several women walked past carrying bags full of fresh vegetables from the market up the road. They looked at her enviously as she sat in the shade while they sweltered under the blazing sun, wearing brightly coloured saris with the ends tied neatly around their waists. A food seller pulled his stall on wheels in the opposite direction, no doubt on his way to trade at the market. The smell of spicy onion bhajiya and khaman dhokra came wafting through from his wagon, making her mouth water. She considered what she might cook for their evening meal. With a sigh, she knew it would have to be daal and rice again.

Varun twitched in his sleep. Nirmala looked at her beautiful little boy with his curly brown hair, smooth dark skin and perfect features. He was small for his age and thin. A quiet, sensitive child; full of curiosity about the world around him. But recently he had shown signs of something being not quite right. She had noticed that occasionally, right in the middle of a sentence, he would suddenly freeze and stare blankly into space. It was worrying how he would not respond for up to a minute, and afterwards, not even be aware that he had gone into a trance.

Nirmala was terrified that without proper care and treatment, this might develop into full-blown seizures. She could not bear the thought. Somehow, money would have to be found to pay for the treatment. If Ajay would not help, what was she going to do? Her heart began to race. Realising she was beginning to panic she took a deep breath. Think logically, she told herself, and consider what could be done.

She mulled over what Ajay was alluding to. She knew only too well what he meant. Whenever they were short of money, he would put pressure on her to go cap in hand to her father's rich sister, who lived across the road. But Nirmala knew she would get no help from her Aunt Jasumati. Only humiliation. The memory of Jasu-*foi*'s scathing attack flashed through her mind.

'Don't come to me for handouts, Nirmala. Tell that lazy husband of yours to get off his backside and do some proper work.'

That was the first and last time Nirmala asked her for help. She had too much pride and self-respect to ask again. But Ajay had no such feelings. He had gone to her himself several times, but always returned with hands empty and a face distorted with fury.

'You are a stubborn donkey. Go and get some money from your high and mighty Jasu-*foi*. For God's sake!' He always spat out Aunt Jasu's name as if it tasted bitter in his mouth.

Nirmala stroked Varun's hair absent-mindedly while they rocked back and forth. She looked up at the magnificent four-storey mansion standing opposite her house. It was a brick building, painted a soft sky blue, with balconies on every level stretching across the width of the mansion. Colourful ornate decorations embellished the front of the balconies. Once again, Nirmala marvelled at the words etched in an elegant font across the facades of the second- and third-floor balconies: SUPARNA MANSIONS 1952.

'When it was built, it was the tallest and most iconic building in Navsari,' her father had told her when she was a child swinging on the *jhula*. 'Your grandfather Harilal-*dada* was very proud of it, you know.'

'But why is it all broken now?' she had asked. He had never given her a proper answer. The building looked even worse now.

Why was her aunt letting it go like this? It was in an appalling, dilapidated condition, with paint peeling, walls crumbling and stonework looking dirty and decayed. There must be more than enough money to pay for the building's maintenance. The apartments on the top two floors where Jasu-*foi* lived with her family were testament to this. They were lavishly decked out with expensive furniture and fittings. There was also the regular income from the rent paid by all the tenants living below.

Nirmala remembered her father saying he had been very happy living there when his father Harilal had been alive. It was he who'd built the mansion that was now owned by Nirmala's aunt. Her father had often told her that he had been a kind and generous man who would have been a loving grandfather to her.

'Did you have a lot of money, Pappa?' Nirmala had asked.

'Yes, *beta*, but money isn't everything. It doesn't always make you happy. Remember that.'

As she gazed at the mansion, Nirmala could not help wishing she did have some money. A worm of resentment worked its way into her heart and she swallowed saliva that tasted warm and sour. Why couldn't she have a small share of the family fortune? Jasu-*foi* had plenty and could afford to be a little generous. But she was mean and unfeeling, very different from her one and only brother, Suresh, Nirmala's father.

The thought of her father made Nirmala smile. He had doted on her, always bringing home special treats when she was little. Her mother's gentle chiding came to mind.

'Suresh! You must stop spoiling her.'

Nirmala wished she could spoil her own child from time to time. Looking up at the mansion, she pictured her father playing happily with his siblings in lavish surroundings. Why had he turned his back on such a life of luxury and privilege? All she knew was that he'd argued with his mother just before his wedding and walked out of the house forever.

Varun stirred and reached up to touch her cheek. 'I'm thirsty, Mumma.'

She kissed his hand briefly before getting up to fetch a cup of water from the kitchen. He sat up and drank it all in one go. Nirmala was relieved to see that his face was no longer flushed, and he seemed altogether better than before.

'I saved some jalebi for you.' She laughed when she saw his face light up. Her friend Hema had dropped by the day before with a bag full of sweetmeats for them. Nirmala gave Varun the bag and watched him pick out his favourites: yellow jalebi, pink coconut barfi, green halva and orange laddus. He took small bites with relish.

Her thoughts returned to the problem at hand, and she wondered if she might borrow money from Hema yet again. She knew her friend would never deny her a loan, as they had grown up together and felt more like sisters. They'd helped each other out countless times. She remembered how, when they were little, Hema's family had battled with money worries. But now the tables had turned and Hema was earning a good salary as a schoolteacher.

Nevertheless, Nirmala did not like to ask her. Reluctantly, she looked down at her mother's diamond-encrusted gold ring on her finger. Perhaps she should pawn it again. It always fetched a lot of ready cash. But could she really risk losing this precious memory of her parents? Nirmala felt sick at the very idea.

Another thought flashed through her mind, unbidden, which made her catch her breath. *I will always be there for you.* That's what he had said: her dearest love. Not a day went by without her remembering how it used to be. But no. Nirmala pushed all thoughts of him away. She would not allow herself to go down that painful road again.

'Mumma, shall I leave the last ones for Pappa?'

'No, *dikra.* This is all yours.' She watched him hesitate, before dipping into the bag for more. Her beautiful and generous son. He deserved so much more. It broke her heart to see him go without. Tears were beginning to prickle behind her eyes. She fought them away and forced herself to be strong. I will get through this, she told herself firmly.

A sudden thump on the porch startled her out of her despair. Ajay was leaning against the door, staring at them grim-faced.

'You're back.' Nirmala forced a smile on her face.

For a moment, he stood silent and motionless; statue-like. Then he walked forward and thrust a wad of notes into her hand.

'I got this from people who are owing me. Don't ask me for any more.' Bending down to look his son in the eye, he frowned and said in a stern voice, 'You must get better quickly. Rupees don't grow on trees, you know.' Then, making no attempt to soften his words, he walked away to his sewing machine.

Nirmala gave Varun a reassuring smile. She counted out the rupees in her hand and felt immense relief. He could start his treatment today. But even as she enjoyed this happy thought, she felt a nagging tug in her stomach. With all their expenses, how were they going to afford the long-term costs? She looked up at the mansion again and whispered to herself, Why did you give it all up, Pappa? Why is Jasu-*foi* so selfish? What happened between you and your mother?

PART 1

April 1957 Navsari, India

Chapter 1

Harilal watched his children jumping up and down with excitement. They were begging their mother for permission to go to Dudhiya Talav, the local lake. He knew how much they loved to swim and paddle in the cool waters. Suresh, their five-year-old son, was on his knees with palms pressed together in prayer position. Jasumati was their eldest child. At twelve years old, she was quite capable of looking after her younger siblings, so he was happy to let them go. But Kanta was having none of it.

'You can't go on your own. You have to stay home until we get back from Surat. We are going for a few hours only to see *Masi* in hospital.'

'Please, *Ba*.' Suresh was pleading. 'I want to go swimming.'

'No. You can't. Now stop pestering me.' Kanta turned to walk away, only to find Suresh clutching the bottom edge of her sari.

'Stop it, Suresh.' She pulled her sari out of his grasp. 'Don't be a baby.' The boy drew back quickly at her sharp tone, and the girls moved away without a word.

Harilal took pity on them and decided to intervene. 'Jasumati and Pushpa will take care of the little one and it's a very hot day. Why don't we let them go?'

Kanta gave him one of her withering looks. She never argued with him, but he always knew when she was displeased. She stood before him, ramrod straight and chin up. He wished she would speak freely with him. But even after thirteen years of marriage, she was reticent and restrained in his presence. Not cold or rude, but remote. As a dutiful wife and mother, he could not fault her commitment. But he longed to see her smile and relax around him. With deep regret, Harilal knew that Kanta was haunted by past events from which she was still struggling to surface.

'We'll be fine, *Ba*, I promise,' said nine-year-old Pushpa, their middle child, who rarely asked for anything. Quiet and considered, Pushpa always thought of others first. Harilal felt that she was the glue that kept the whole family together. Everyone was drawn to her, but there was no doubt in his mind that Kanta had a special place in her heart for Pushpa.

'Do you really want to go, *dikra*?' Kanta's tone was soft and gentle. When Pushpa nodded, she smiled, and that was it. The battle was over. Suresh jumped up and began to dance and sing at the top of his voice.

'Stop that, Suresh. And get your things ready for the lake. You have all had lunch, so you need to take water only.' Kanta strode away to lock the doors and windows.

Harilal rubbed his hands. 'See you by the car, *chokrao*. We will drop you off on our way out of town.'

He made his way down the four flights of stairs to the front of their beautiful, newly built home. He paused for a moment at every level on the winding stairwell to look out from the open balconies. Suparna Mansions was the tallest and most prepossessing building in Navsari. He was immensely proud of it.

People came from all around to view and admire their home, with its wide balconies and colourful, ornate decorations across the blue facade. There were two apartments on each floor, occupied by families who were pleased to be the first tenants. Harilal had no complaints about any of them, but he was happy to have the whole of the fourth floor and the large open roof terrace at the very top for the private use of his family.

'*Bapuji!* I'm coming down,' shouted Suresh from their balcony.

Harilal looked up and waved. All he could see was a mop of curly brown hair atop his son's beaming face. One minute he was there and the next he could be heard running down the marble stairs with his red sandals slapping against the pearl-white steps. In no time at all, he was standing beside his father, grinning up at him.

'*Bapuji*, you look like Dilip Kumar today!'

Harilal laughed. He knew he looked nothing like the famous film star, though he did dress like him by wearing the best western clothes available. He also kept his hair in a similar style: neat and short with side-parting and quiff. His facial features were not as sharp as the popular actor, and he did carry more weight around the middle. But it pleased him to know that his son thought him a hero.

He ruffled the boy's hair and looked into his beautiful grey-green eyes. *Those with light eyes cannot be trusted.* It made him laugh when people quoted the old adage to him. But it always made Kanta angry. He remembered the time she had lashed out at her brother.

'That is a stupid thing to say! Just keep your comments to yourself.'

Suresh was gazing with excitement at the shiny magenta-coloured Ambassador car: his father's pride and joy. Harilal was delighted to see his own passion reflected in his son's eyes. He loved the look of this four-door sedan with its grand, bulbous shape. Its design exuded class and money. He had placed an order well in advance of the launch earlier that year by Hindustan Motors. Ten years after independence from British rule, this was the first car to be built in India, and he was proud to be supporting his country.

He took great delight in the appreciative looks he got when out driving.

He was not someone who liked to flaunt his material assets, but he had to admit that he enjoyed the good things in life. After Independence, when Indians were offered economic benefits, Harilal had taken full advantage. He had invested wisely in a number of up-and-coming Indian companies and was pleased to find himself reaping the rewards of his efforts.

'Can I sit in front, *Bapuji*?'

'Of course you can. Hop in before the others come.'

He opened the front door and lifted the boy onto the bench seat. He watched him slide along to the middle and sit still, staring entranced at the black all-leather interior. He took in the wood trim, the shiny Nardi steering wheel and stylish dashboard instrumentation.

'Are you going someplace nice?'

Even before he turned around, Harilal knew that it was Mr Saleji, their ground-floor tenant. He was a popular man in the neighbourhood, especially with children. He was often found with a group gathered around him on his porch, listening to him read or tell stories from Indian legends and folklore. He had a habit of laughing when he spoke, and his laugh sounded like a horse neighing, earning him the nickname *Ghoda-kaka*, Uncle Horse.

'We are going to Surat for the afternoon, dropping the children off at Dudhiya Talav.'

'Nice hot day for a swim,' neighed Mr Saleji.

The rest of the family was now piling into the car with their cloth bags filled with towels, a change of clothes and drinking water.

'Have a good time, *chokrao*.' Mr Saleji neighed again, making the children giggle.

'What are you doing in the front, Suresh? Get back,' ordered Kanta.

'No, it's okay. I told him to sit there. I will let him out when we reach the lake.'

Kanta pursed her lips and walked regally to the front passenger side of the bench seat. Harilal watched her with admiring eyes. She was wearing a russet-coloured silk sari with a wide black border. Her matching blouse was long-sleeved, as was currently in vogue. He noticed that she was wearing her gold marriage necklace and bangles. As usual, she had applied the vermillion powder on her forehead in a large round *chandlo.* She had kohl-rimmed eyes and her hair was twisted into a bun at the nape of her neck. So correct and proper, he thought.

She had kept her slim figure even after three children and always managed to look elegant and sophisticated. To him, she was beautiful, with her unblemished dark skin, high cheekbones and full lips. But there were many who did not agree with him, simply because of her dark complexion. It was maddening how obsessed people were with fair skin. He hated the general belief that only light-skinned people could be attractive.

His own mother had objected to him marrying Kanta, even though she came from a well-respected and wealthy family.

'Look how *kali* she is, Hari. You can't marry her. There are so many *gori* girls you can choose from.'

But Harilal had insisted that she was the one. He often thought of their first meeting. Wearing a pastel-green sari with a contrasting puff-sleeved blouse, she had accompanied her parents when they had come with their marriage proposal. He had been intrigued by her direct eye contact and calm confidence, unlike other potential brides who looked at him surreptitiously or not at all. She had charmed him with her quiet demeanour and elegant poise.

If only she didn't look so severe these days. It hadn't always been like that. She used to be warm and affectionate towards him and friendly with the people around her. But that was before things had changed.

Harilal felt his chest go tight as he remembered the events that had caused so much distress and unhappiness. With all his heart he regretted the part he had played in the decisions taken all those years previously. Sadly, there was nothing he could do to make things right. But he was determined to try everything in his power to make Kanta happy and approachable once again. There was a certain haughty dignity about her. But underneath all that, he knew that Kanta was kind and compassionate, keen to help those in need.

Harilal reversed the car out of the space in front of the mansion and began to drive slowly towards Dudhiya Talav. Situated right in the middle of town, the small lake was a real haven of peace and tranquillity for the residents of Navsari. He would have liked more green space around the water but was glad there was a paved pathway which people could stroll along. Shady trees and stone benches made the walk more pleasant and people flocked there at weekends and on religious holidays.

When they reached the lake, they were pleased to find it quieter than usual. Normally the area was buzzing with people. It was a popular stop for those wanting to rest, cool down or simply relax. The scorching heat of the day had obviously encouraged many to stay cool at home. Harilal saw a number of local residents in the surrounding apartment blocks, sitting in their shady balconies looking out at the water.

Further ahead, he could see the walkway that stretched out to Navsari's famous open-air fruit and vegetable market, where their cook did the daily shopping for their meals. Across the distance, he could hear the clamour of the buyers and sellers: voices shouting and calling to one another. The fragrant smells of the fresh produce came wafting over.

'Shall we buy some fruit for your sister?' he asked.

'Okay. But we should drop the children off first.'

He found a parking spot by the three-foot stone wall that separated the lake from the busy street. Several vendors on bicycle carts were parked along the wall, their shiny hoods fluttering in the breeze in green, blue, bright orange or yellow. They enticed children and adults alike with their loud cries of 'Kulfis, faloodas, ice cream! Come and get it.'

Just beyond the walled section, there was a purpose-built beach area which was the children's favourite spot. A gradual downslope filled with sand, grass, stones and cement inclined towards the shallowest part of the lake. Here, the water lapped gently against the man-made shore.

'We are going swimming! We are going swimming!' Suresh was bouncing on the seat, singing at the top of his voice.

Harilal laughed as he slipped out of the driving seat and helped his son jump to the ground.

'Calm down, *dikra*, and be careful on the slope. Girls, hold his hand and stay together. Jasumati, you are in charge, okay? Do you have everything you need?'

'Yes, *Bapuji*,' they all chimed as they waved goodbye. They had been there many times and knew the drill.

'I'll walk them down to the water while you get the fruit,' said Kanta.

'Let's go together. The *chokrao* are quite safe, and you'll only get your sari dirty.'

He watched her hesitate before deciding that his advice made sense. 'Don't stay at the beach too long,' she shouted at the children. They turned and waved again before continuing on their way.

Harilal made sure all the windows were wound up, then locked the car doors. After one final admiring glance, he followed his wife to the market. They both enjoyed going to the marketplace where they could walk along the aisles just to soak up the atmosphere with its sights, smells and sounds. It was good to see the friendly bartering and haggling that went on. Harilal was always pleased and surprised to see how Kanta joined in with everyone. She could raise her voice and hold her own like any woman doing her daily shop.

'Two rupees for five guavas! Are you mad? You think because I am wearing a nice sari you can rob me?'

'No, madam. That is the right price. You will not find it anywhere cheaper.'

Harilal loved the bright colours: people's clothes, the canopies above the stalls, the mats on the ground and the huge variety of fresh fruits and vegetables. Being vegetarian, like so many Gujaratis, it pleased him to see the enormous selection of vegetables in different shades of green, heaped in little mountains around the sellers. He saw okra, gourd, marrow, various beans such as papdi valor, tindora, saragvo and plenty more. It was good to know that they were all grown in the nearby villages by local farmers in their smallholdings.

Kanta was gazing at the mangoes: the nation's favourite fruit. It was considered the fruit of Gods; perfect in red, orange or gold. It was the right season for mangoes, with every variety on sale: alphonsos from Maharashtra, chaunsa and dasheri from the north, mulgoba from the south and, their favourite of all, kesar from western Gujarat.

Harilal watched his wife select half a dozen of the best. She knew which ones would be sweet and juicy just by their aromatic fragrance and soft fleshy feel. Naturally, she haggled over the price. But finally, they paid up and walked away with the mangoes wrapped in old newspaper.

'Do you think your sister will be able to eat them?'

'I don't know. Her TB is getting worse and she's not responding to the new treatment. Let's see how she is today.'

When they reached the car, Kanta said she wanted to check on the children.

'Be quick, Kanta. The sooner we go the sooner we return.' He took the mangoes from her and watched her walk along the roadside. Within minutes, she was back, looking satisfied.

'*Chalo*. Let's go.'

Harilal reversed the car and headed north to begin the twenty-five-mile drive to Surat. He had to concentrate on the roads, which were packed with scooters, rickshaws, cyclists, pedestrians, and the inevitable stray dogs and cattle. He felt more at ease when they reached the outskirts of the town. His thoughts turned to Surat and their plans to support Kanta's family. He stepped on the accelerator and his Hindustan Ambassador picked up speed. For years to come, Harilal would think back to this moment and wonder how different their lives would have been had they not gone to Surat that day.

Chapter 2

Pushpa struggled to hold on to her brother as he ran for the water's edge. She pulled him back with both hands to restrain him.

'Let me go! Let me go!'

'No, you must wait. First we have to find a place to sit.' Pushpa held him firmly while their older sister Jasumati looked for a shady place to park their few belongings. There was a cool breeze coming off the lake, but at two o'clock in the afternoon, the heat of the summer was fierce. She pointed to the concrete pathway at the top end of the beach where leafy arjun trees provided some protection from the blazing sun.

Pushpa shook her head. 'It is too far from the water. And there it is crowded.' She looked around at the scattering of hardy individuals sitting on the beach under the full glare of the sun. In small groups, they sat on straw mats, keeping an eye on their children playing in the water. A few were holding up umbrellas, but most had nothing but *odhanis* or scarves covering their heads.

Pushpa inclined her head towards a space between two groups of people. 'We can sit there.'

'No. We'll die in the sun.' Jasumati insisted on walking upwards, away from the water. 'Come. Someone will give us room.'

With Suresh squirming between them, they made their way up. A young couple with two small children moved closer together so that the trio could squeeze in. The girls quickly sat down on the hard ground. Pushpa smiled and thanked the parents who were feeding their toddlers. The mother returned her smile with a friendly nod.

'Can I go in the water now?' asked Suresh, who was already barefoot and jumping up and down with impatience.

'All right! All right!' Jasumati tutted and rolled her eyes. 'You do one thing. Take off your shorts and shirt. Pushpa, you go with him first.'

Pushpa wobbled her head in acquiescence. She took off her sandals and dropped her cloth bag in which she'd been carrying the dress she would wear over her wet clothes to walk back home. Pulling down her blouse over her long black shorts, she held out her hand to Suresh.

'Let's go!' he screamed, tugging at his sister's hand. She laughed as they ran down the beach, weaving their way around the people watching their children frolicking in the lake.

They both squealed with delight when their feet touched the water. It was colder than they were expecting. They jumped up and down, watching the water splash around them. Pushpa imagined that the droplets were colourful splashes of paint dancing at their feet. They waded in until the water was up to Suresh's waist. He was not allowed to go any deeper, yet he tried to push forward.

'Stop!' Pushpa blocked his way. 'You know what *Ba* said.'

Suresh giggled. He loved to tease his sisters, pushing at the boundaries all the time. 'Then teach me how to swim. Please.'

Pushpa had only mastered the art a few months earlier. She was proud of herself for learning how to float, then swim so fast. But she wasn't yet confident enough to go any deeper.

'Let's just paddle and splash. It's more fun than anything!'

They laughed as they played together, cupping their hands, scooping the water and throwing it at one another. With flat palms, they smacked the surface and shrieked with excitement when the water hit their faces. Holding hands, they jumped in and out of the small waves. Further in, the surface of the lake was as smooth as glass.

'Pushpaaaaa,' a voice called from further along the shore.

It was Gopna, one of her school friends, out with her older brother to enjoy an afternoon at the beach. Waving to one another, they soon joined up to play together. Gopna had made some paper boats to float on the water. The four of them began to enjoy a new activity: boat racing and riding the tiny waves.

Pushpa was having enormous fun, but she was conscious of the fact that her sister would also want to swim. 'Come, Suresh. We must fetch Jasu-*ben*. It's her turn now.'

'No. I want to stay here!'

'You have to come. I can't leave you here.'

'We can look after him,' said Gopna. 'Leave him with us.'

Pushpa insisted she could not do that. Her brother was her responsibility. But Suresh was beginning to throw a tantrum.

'Please Pushpa-*ben*. Let me stay. I won't go in too far. I promise.'

'Don't you trust us?' asked Gopna.

Not wishing to offend her friend, Pushpa agreed with reluctance. She wobbled her head and said, 'Jasu-*ben* will be here in one minute.' Giving Suresh a stern look, she turned and began to run up the beach.

It was a fairly straight run to the trees because there were fewer people around. Some of the stalwarts had gathered up their children and abandoned the sweltering heat. She could see her sister and called out as she ran. But Jasumati was busy talking to the young mother, or rather, listening intently. She looked up only when Pushpa reached her.

'You have to go to Suresh right now, Jasu-*ben*. He's in the water.'

'What! On his own?'

'No. My friend is looking after him.'

'Then there's no rush, is there? I will go in one minute.' Jasumati turned back to the woman who immediately resumed her story. She was clearly upset about something and was offloading onto Jasumati, who seemed willing to lend an ear.

Pushpa wished her sister was less interested in gossip. Biting back a sigh of irritation, she bent down and spoke with urgency: 'You have to go now! *Ba* said we can't leave Suresh with other people.'

The woman stopped in mid-flow. She turned her attention to the child on her lap. Her husband and other child were nowhere to be seen.

Jasumati was not pleased. She glared at Pushpa but stood up slowly. 'Is *Ba* watching us right now? Can she see us? Why must you be such a goody-goody? Always doing everything she says!' She spoke through gritted teeth. Even though she spoke quietly, the aggression in her tone was unmistakable, and a few people began to stare.

Looking daggers at her sister, Jasumati nevertheless took off her sandals and walked away unhurriedly. Pushpa watched her go, shading her eyes with one hand. Not until her sister was in the water with Suresh did she sit down. With a sigh, she rummaged in her bag for a towel to place round her shoulders. She also pulled out their water flask, tipped her head back and took a swig without touching the rim with her lips. Their mother had taught them this trick which she said was the only hygienic way to share drinks.

'What is your name?' asked the woman.

'Pushpa.'

The woman tilted her head and smiled. 'This is Ram. His brother has gone home with his father.'

Pushpa smiled at the little boy and tickled him under the chin, making him chuckle.

'You see how good he is? He is no trouble at all. Yet my mother-in-law complains about him all the time. I was telling your sister how nasty she is.' With that, she launched into an angry tirade about how wonderful her husband was, but how terrible his mother was.

Pushpa pursed her lips and looked away. She knew what was to follow and prepared herself for a long, one-sided conversation. Politely, Pushpa listened, nodding every now and then to indicate sympathy. In truth, her mind was somewhere else and her eyes were on the children having fun in the water. For nearly thirty minutes the woman ranted, keeping her voice low. She only stopped when Jasumati and Suresh both came up for a drink.

'Look, Pushpa-*ben*.' Suresh was holding out a paper boat, still folded and unused. 'They are gone but they left this for us. Can we go and play?'

Pushpa shook her head. 'We have to go home too.'

'No, no, no. Just one more swim. Please?' Suresh's hands were in the prayer position once more.

'I don't think so. *Ba* said we shouldn't stay long.' Pushpa caught her sister's eye and realised this was the wrong thing to say.

'Go in with him one more time, Pushpa. It's only four o'clock.'

'Yesssssssss!' Suresh clapped his hands with excitement. 'Let's go, let's go, let's go.'

Reluctantly, Pushpa agreed and allowed her brother to drag her down to the water. She would keep him amused for ten minutes, then insist on returning. They waded in and began to play with the paper boat. Suresh moved it along the surface by splashing water behind it.

'Don't let the water get inside. It will sink.' Pushpa pushed his hands away and showed him how to move it by making gentle waves on either side of it. He soon learned how to manoeuvre it. With great concentration, he floated the boat around Pushpa as she stood still in one place.

'Now you!' he commanded, as he stood for the boat to go around him.

They played this game several times before Pushpa said they should go. She was getting bored and anxious to head home.

'Come on, Suresh. Let's go. We can buy ice-cold faloodas now.' But her brother was not so easily distracted. She looked towards the trees and could just make out Jasumati's head inclined towards the young mother. She seemed engrossed.

She noticed that the beach was now almost empty and the crowd under the trees had thinned out. She waved her arms to attract Jasumati's attention. Suresh might make a move if their older sister walked down to take charge. But all she managed to do was to attract vacant looks from the strangers sitting around her.

If only people didn't stare so much. She hated that. Her father had told her it was a national pastime, and she should just ignore them. Turning her gaze away from them, she tried to catch Jasumati's eye again. No joy. Glancing back to make sure Suresh was all right, she moved closer to the shore. Taking a few steps out of the water, she waved both hands and called out to Jasumati as loudly as she could.

The folk who'd been staring at her started to wave back, as if they knew her. Silly people. Jasumati was finally looking her way. She stood up and began to walk, then hurry down the slope. Pushpa heard her shout something but couldn't make out what it was. A few men near her also stood up and began to follow her down.

Pushpa began to feel uneasy, the first fluttering of anxiety in the pit of her stomach. Something was wrong. They were all pointing at her. All at once, it hit her. Suresh! She whipped around to call him. But he was not there. With her heart in her mouth, she spun around, hoping to see him on the sand, but he wasn't there. Fearfully, she looked further into the lake. Still nothing. Then she saw it: the white paper boat, bobbing up and down.

'Suresh!' she screamed, her eyes searching the area around the boat. He was nowhere to be seen. 'Suresh!' She screamed again and again. Frozen with fear, she stood motionless.

Suddenly, she sensed some movement to the left of the boat. With a shock, she saw her brother's head shoot out of the water. He coughed and spluttered as he gasped for air, thrashing his arms in complete panic. The water was too deep for him and he struggled frantically to keep his head up. Pushpa saw him go down again as the water pulled him in.

With her heart in her mouth, Pushpa flew into action. She rushed into the water and began to swim towards him. Moving fast, she soon reached the spot in the deeper part of the lake. Treading water, she looked around in panic, screaming out his name again and again. Taking a deep breath, she submerged completely into the darkness and silence, searching for him with her eyes and arms.

Almost immediately, she felt something hard. It was him, frighteningly still. She put her arms around him from behind and pulled him up. They broke through the surface together. Breathing in deeply, she sucked air into her lungs. He was very still, hanging limp in her arms. He felt very heavy, but she tried to shake him, crying into his ear as she held on to him.

Suddenly she felt strong arms around her. 'Let him go,' she heard a muffled voice say. 'No!' she gasped, fighting for air. 'He's going to be okay,' the voice insisted. Pushpa would not let go. She held Suresh tightly, willing him to breathe as she struggled to stay afloat herself.

He was being pulled away from her. Someone strong, a man, took hold of Suresh. She heard him ask if she was okay, and then he began to swim to the shore, holding Suresh's head above water. Helplessly she watched them move towards the crowd waiting on the beach. She saw Jasumati standing in the front, pressing her mouth with both hands, eyes wide with fear.

Pushpa was exhausted, drained of all energy. Looking around, she realised she was in deep water. Deeper than she was used to. Panic set in. The water was beginning to tug her away and down. Desperately, she tried to pull herself up. But her arms and legs had given up. She opened her mouth to scream.

'Jasu-*ben*! Help! Help me someone!' Her voice came out as a whimper and no one was listening. All eyes were on Suresh. She cried for help again and again. This can't be happening, she thought as the water dragged her further down.

Every time she opened her mouth, water gushed in, making her cough and choke. Panicking, she pushed her head back and tried to breathe. She made one last desperate appeal for help, but she swallowed more water and her lungs began to fill up. Exhausted, Pushpa was defeated. Hopeless. It was all hopeless. She closed her eyes and gave in to the darkness that engulfed her.

Chapter 3

Kanta was pleased it was still daylight when they arrived back from Surat. It was 6.15 p.m. when Harilal turned the car into Golwad Street. As they drove up, she was surprised to see a small crowd of people outside Suparna Mansions. Her first thought was that someone was throwing a party or having a religious function in one of the apartments. But when they came closer, their cheerless faces belied these possibilities.

'Maybe someone has died,' said Harilal as he cut off the engine. It was not unusual for neighbours to pay their respects in this way.

For a moment, his words had no effect on Kanta. She was looking out of the window, annoyed at having their entrance blocked. Then, as if in slow motion, she registered his meaning. Suddenly, she felt a queasiness in her stomach. Her chest began to feel tight. She jerked her attention to Harilal. At the same moment, he turned to face her. She saw a shadow pass over his face before he gave her a weak smile, attempting reassurance. He opened his door.

'Let's go in.'

The crowd parted to let them through. Kanta looked straight ahead, as they walked to the front gate. She heard Harilal greet a few people. Some murmured *namaste*, wobbling their heads, while others stared silently.

On the other side of the gate, they found their ground-floor tenants, Mr and Mrs Saleji, waiting for them. The queasiness in Kanta's stomach became a tight knot.

'Hari-*bhai*, Kanta-*ben*, please come inside.' Mr Saleji spoke with urgency.

Kanta looked from him to his wife, whose eyebrows were knitted together in a frown. Nervously, she smiled at her. But Fatima Saleji did not smile back. That was the moment Kanta knew her fears were going to be confirmed. Her scalp prickled and a feeling of dread took hold of her. Terrified, she looked at her husband. But he was following Mr Saleji, keeping his head down. Kanta walked behind him, the feeling of dread intensifying with every step.

Fatima shut the door as her husband seated Harilal and Kanta on their settee. She went into her kitchen to fetch them a drink of water.

'What is it? What has happened?' Kanta heard the alarm in her husband's voice. She held her breath. Mr Saleji cleared his throat.

'There was trouble at Dudhiya Talav.'

'The children?' Harilal was on his feet. Kanta felt her gut twist in fear.

Keeping his voice low, Mr Saleji continued. 'Suresh nearly drowned but he was rescued and taken to hospital.'

Harilal moved towards the door. 'We must go there right away!'

'Wait! Please wait. I am sorry. Suresh is okay, but . . . I'm afraid . . .'

Harilal grabbed Saleji's arm. 'Jasumati? Pushpa?'

Fatima came in with two glasses of water, but she stopped at the door when her husband uttered the words that no parent wants to hear.

'Pushpa went to rescue Suresh, but then got herself into trouble. I'm afraid . . . I'm afraid . . . Pushpa did not make it.' He paused. 'I am so sorry. She was in deep water and she drowned. She is no more.' His voice cracked.

For a moment, there was no sound. Saleji's words hung in the air, bearing down on their heads, on their shoulders; unbelievable, unimaginable.

'No!' Kanta stood up and screamed. 'It's not true!' She covered her ears with both hands, as if by blocking out the words she could erase the truth. Fatima put the glasses down on a side table and ran to comfort her. She put her arms around her and held her tightly while she screamed.

'She can't be dead!' Kanta looked up, her eyes burning with fury. 'They've made a mistake.' The image of her daughter waving cheerfully just a few hours previously was imprinted in her mind's eye. Pulling away from Fatima, she looked deeply into her eyes, frowning half in anger, half in fear.

Fatima gave a little sob as she nodded her head, her eyes full of pain. Kanta stood motionless, rooted to the spot. Then she dropped her shoulders and let out a loud wail of despair. She felt Fatima's arms around her again. This time, she clung to her, sobbing uncontrollably.

Harilal was still gripping Saleji's arm. 'Where is Jasumati? What has happened to her?'

'She is with Suresh in the hospital. She told the staff to telephone me so I could let you know. Straight away I sent my son Altaf to the hospital on his bicycle.'

Kanta was inconsolable, heart-wrenching sobs shaking her body. Saleji looked towards her and shook Harilal's arm. Harilal stepped forward, as though sleepwalking, and tried to prise her away from Fatima. But Kanta would not let go. 'Come, Kanta. We have to go. We have to go.'

With soothing words, Fatima persuaded Kanta to go to her husband. But when he tried to fold her in his arms, she shrugged him off and moved away. Taking quick steps, she walked to the front door, then stopped. Abruptly, she whirled around and looked at Harilal. With eyes blazing, she screamed, 'This is your fault! All your fault! Why don't you ever listen to me?' Then she crumpled to the floor, weeping hysterically.

It was many minutes before Kanta realised Fatima was crouching beside her, rubbing her back. She heard Mr Saleji speaking to her husband.

'You mustn't take it to heart, Hari-*bhai*. It is her grief speaking.'

But it was more than grief, and Kanta knew her husband would understand that. Only the two of them knew. Buried deep in their souls were terrible memories, and on this day of unbearable pain, those memories were rising to the surface. His face was etched in agony, and as their eyes met, she knew that he was remembering the past, the torment, the mental suffering. This only served to increase her anger.

Ignoring his anguish, she stood up, holding on to Fatima's arm. With shoulders drooping, she wiped her eyes and face with the end of her sari. Straightening her shoulders, she faced the front door. Her voice trembling, she said, 'Let's go.'

The four of them made their way to the car. The crowd was still standing in sympathy outside. Without a word, the foursome walked past them and Harilal slid into the driver's seat. He drove the few miles to the local hospital. In the reception area, Mr Saleji made enquiries and following directions, led them to a private room on the ground floor.

Kanta entered anxiously and felt a crushing pain in her chest when she saw two, and not three of her children. Jasumati ran to her, sobbing in spasms. Suresh lay on the hospital bed, looking pale and lifeless. Twelve-year-old Altaf Saleji sat at the bedside. How could this have happened? The children had always been so careful in the water. Jasumati was a strong swimmer, and Suresh knew the rules about staying in the shallows.

Kanta's anger returned. Why did Pushpa drown? Why her? She was the sweetest and most lovable child possible. Holding Jasumati to her chest, she stared at her son on the bed. Her thoughts flew to her best-loved child, smiling and waving, running and laughing, hugging her tightly at bedtime. How was it possible that she was not here?

Harilal sat on the bed and began to stroke Suresh's cheek. Smiling through his tears, he looked at Jasumati, whose whole body was shaking as she clung to Kanta.

Mr Saleji entered the room with a slim young man in a white coat, wearing a stethoscope round his neck.

'*Namaste*. I am Dr Mistry. Your children were in my care when they arrived by ambulance. Your son is very weak, but he will be fine after a few days of rest.' When no one responded, he continued, 'It was lucky that the man who rescued him knew what to do.'

The doctor spoke imperiously, without any emotion in his voice. He had his hands in his pockets and looked only at Harilal. Kanta felt a wave of outrage rise up her chest. He was ignoring her just because she was a woman. Like water bubbling over a pot, her anger boiled over.

'And what about my daughter? Was she in your care? What did you do for her?' Her voice was a high-pitched, penetrating sound that made everyone jump. The doctor looked at her in stony silence for a moment. Then his whole body-language changed. His shoulders dropped and his eyes softened with sadness. Taking his hands out of his pockets, he addressed Kanta.

'I wish I could have done something for your daughter. But she was dead on arrival. I could do nothing for her. I am sorry.'

Kanta stifled a sob and sat down heavily on a chair. Harilal rose from the bed and went to hold Jasumati. She wrapped her arms round his waist and buried her face in his shirt.

'The man who rescued your son is still here. He came with the children in the ambulance and has been waiting to see you. I will go and call him.'

The doctor left the room but returned almost immediately with a tall, well-built man who walked in with hesitant steps. He scanned the room then dropped his gaze to the floor. Kanta looked at his thick, greying hair, thin moustache, broad shoulders and strong bare arms. His short-sleeved shirt and trousers were old and brown, still damp from the afternoon. The tatty leather *chappals* on his feet exposed toenails that needed some attention. Kanta felt an immediate affinity with this man who stood so humbly before them.

'This is Feroz-*bhai*. He will tell you what happened.'

Kanta watched the man lift his face to look first at Suresh, then Jasumati. His expression was so sorrowful, it made her throat contract and an involuntary sound escaped from her. The man immediately turned to her.

'I was thinking your daughter was following me,' he said in a low voice. 'She said she was all right. Please forgive me.' He looked troubled.

Harilal stepped forward and put a hand on the man's shoulder. 'You saved our son. We can never thank you enough. God bless you.'

The man looked at Kanta. With tears pouring down her face, she smiled weakly and nodded her head. He looked once more at the children, then took a few steps towards the door. Mr Saleji moved to lead him out.

Dr Mistry confirmed that the police had been called and all the necessary details had been taken. 'But now, we need to do one thing. We . . . er . . . We have to go to the mortuary to identify the . . . er . . . body.'

Kanta let out a low moan of anguish.

'It's all right, Kanta.' Harilal's voice was low and strained. 'I will go with the doctor. You stay here.'

Kanta closed her eyes and leaned against Fatima. No one moved or spoke until Harilal returned with Mr Saleji. Kanta looked up and saw that her husband's eyes were red and swollen. He sat down on a chair by the wall. Mr Saleji was visibly shaken. His wife went to him and touched his arm. His eyes welled up and he gripped her hand.

Kanta stared pointedly at Harilal, forcing him to look. He seemed unable to meet her eyes. When he did look up, he tried to speak, but broke down. Great sobs racked his body. She knew she should go to him. They should comfort one another. But she could not. This was his fault. Why did he let them go to the lake? If he had listened to her, they would not have lost Pushpa. Her beautiful baby. Kanta was overcome with grief. The room began to spin and go dark.

She must have fainted because she realised someone was shaking her by the shoulders. It was Fatima, trying to tell her something. It took a few moments before she understood that her son was calling for her from the bed.

'Go to him, Kanta-*ben*. Suresh needs you.'

Kanta saw her five-year-old boy sitting up and screaming for her. She could not move. Harilal went to console him, but he kept screaming and calling her name. When she did not get up, he began to shout for his lost sister.

'Pushpa-*ben*! Help me. Pushpa-*ben*!'

Something snapped inside Kanta and she stood up abruptly. The scene in front of her froze like a tableau. She clamped her hands over her ears and ran out of the door.

Rushing down the corridor, she found an open doorway leading to the hospital grounds. She hurried to an area with lawn, trees and flowers. Spotting an empty wooden bench in one corner, she slumped down. Burying her face in her hands, she bent forward and began to cry, her shoulders shaking as she wept.

She remained like that for a long time, oblivious to everything around her. She cried until she thought she could cry no more. She sat up slowly and with a start, realised she was not alone. Jasumati was sitting beside her, looking at her with ineffable sadness. She touched her arm tentatively. Kanta saw the concern in her eyes. But there was also fear.

'*Ba*. I'm sorry. I should have looked after her.'

Kanta visualised the scene by the lake, with Jasumati watching the unthinkable unfold before her. She understood her need to be exonerated from any blame. With a grimace, Kanta put her arms around her and held her close.

'It's all right, *dikra*, it's all right.'

Rocking gently, they sat looking at the giant peepal tree in front of them, with its roots exposed above ground. There was a small shrine dedicated to Lord Vishnu at the foot of the sacred tree. The soothing and fragrant smoke of incense floated over the shrine, creating a serene, peaceful atmosphere. Kanta breathed in deeply and allowed the ambiance to envelop her, calm her and steady her emotions. Her anger spent, she stared at the shrine and spoke to Lord Vishnu, preserver and protector of the universe.

'Where were you when my Pushpa needed you, oh Lord? Where were you? You should have protected her. You should have.'

Chapter 4

Pushpa's lifeless body lay in an open casket in the front room. Kanta sat cross-legged on the white sheet covering the floor, staring fixedly at her daughter's calm and peaceful expression. Numb with shock, she half listened to the murmurings of the people around her who had come to say their last goodbyes. A priest dressed in a white dhoti and long shirt chanted holy mantras and sprinkled consecrated water over Pushpa's body.

Someone had dressed her in her favourite pink frock. Matching ribbons adorned her braided hair. Kanta imagined that any minute now, Pushpa would wake up, stretch her arms, and smile in that way that always made her heart sing.

Wake up, Pushpa, wake up! Kanta's lips did not move but inside her head, she screamed the words. People sniffled around her and when she glanced up at the priest, she saw that his eyes were also filled with tears.

Soon, they would take her away to be cremated. She was never coming back. Kanta knew she was going to have to accept that. She was not going with Harilal to the crematorium. The sight of the funeral pyre firing and burning would be too much for her to bear. She wanted to drink in the vision of her beautiful Pushpa sleeping peacefully and keep that image imprinted in her mind forever.

Eventually, Kanta felt the air shift around her, and the sound of chanting grew steadily louder. People began to sing *Aum Nama Shivaya, Aum Nama Shivaya* over and over again. Someone, she didn't know who, moved her gently to one side and several men stepped forward to lift the casket with care. Everyone, except Kanta, stood up. She felt panic rising up her throat, threatening to burst its banks. She tried to swallow it down. Willing herself to hold back her fear, Kanta watched the men carry her precious child away. A piece of herself was lost that day and despite so many kind friends, neighbours and family supporting her, she felt desperately alone and isolated in her grief.

~

Every day for the next two weeks, Kanta dressed in a white sari for the mourning period and sat on the floor of her front room. People came and went to offer their condolences, sitting with her in solemn silence, listening to one of the elders read verses from the Bhagavad Gita, the holy book.

Every so often, someone touched Kanta's shoulder and whispered *Jai Sri Krishna* in praise of the Lord, before sitting down. Others stood up to leave so that there would be room for newcomers. Everyone's attention was focused on the little shrine arranged beside Kanta: a framed photograph of Pushpa surrounded by fresh flowers, incense and one small *diva* lamp, its dancing flame creating an ethereal field around it. The smoke of the burning sticks carried a sweet, woody smell across the room.

Kanta kept her eyes on the floor and tried not to think of Pushpa. Pushpa laughing; Pushpa singing; Pushpa skipping. The ache in her heart was so great that she found herself struggling to breathe at times. She felt a deep sense of loss; piercing, ripping loss.

'Can I get you something to drink?' asked her brother's wife, Umagauri. Her whole family had come from Surat to help her get through this difficult time. As she shook her head, she felt a hand on her knee. It was Jasumati, her twelve-year-old daughter. The tender gesture brought Kanta back to the present, reminding her she was not the only one grieving. Kanta squeezed her hand and gave her a brief smile.

At midday, the reading from the scriptures ended and people began to take their leave. Kanta watched them join palms and bow their heads towards her before leaving to reclaim their *chappals*. She heard them make their way down the stairs. Some of them would be back later for the evening prayers.

Umagauri, who had taken over the kitchen, called Jasumati and Suresh for lunch.

'I'll eat with *Ba*,' said Jasumati, who had taken it upon herself to look after her mother. Kanta wondered at this role reversal but realised that her older daughter had always been a strong child, unlike Pushpa, whose gentle nature had needed greater nurturing.

Suresh sat beside his father Harilal, clinging to him and refusing to engage with anyone else.

'Go, *dikra*.' Harilal tried to move Suresh, but he shook his head and clung on even more tightly.

'Come here, Suresh,' Kanta said, trying not to sound too firm. She saw him glance at her timidly, then bury his face in his father's arm. A flash of irritation crossed her gaze as he disobeyed her. She found it hard to feel close to him, but she was trying to show some sympathy. He refused any attempt from her to comfort him and this was beginning to wear her down.

'Go to *Ba*, Suresh,' said Harilal.

Suresh stuck out his lower lip and began to whimper while nestling even closer. Harilal gave Kanta a resigned look.

Lunch was a simple meal of potato curry, moong daal and rice. They ate from individual stainless-steel thalis placed on small rectangular mats on the dining room floor. Suresh accepted a few bites from Harilal, but only when he was fed hand-to-mouth like a baby. Kanta felt her irritation increasing. He was a stubborn child. So unlike her sweet Pushpa. *She* should be sitting here, not Suresh.

Biting her lip, Kanta turned away from the boy. She found him infuriating at the best of times, but when he behaved like a baby, it was hard to be patient. Somehow, she managed to restrain herself from making a cutting remark but made a mental note to tackle the issue when the mourning period was over.

The evening prayer *bhajans* were led by a local group of musicians. They came with their harmonium, tabla and *manjira*, small hand cymbals that tinkled in time to the music. The sound of their soulful melodies comforted Kanta and soothed her aching heart.

'Are you okay?' asked Harilal when they retired to bed. This was a question he asked her every night. Wasn't it obvious she was not okay? If he expected her to open up to him, tell him exactly how she was feeling, he was mistaken. Her anger towards him had not abated in the slightest.

A week later, when her family returned to Surat, Kanta was surprised at how distressed she felt. Her father urged her to accept Pushpa's *neseeb*, her destiny to die young. But this seemed impossible for Kanta. Her grief was deep and her sadness as vast as an ocean.

It was Jasumati who helped her regain some of her emotional strength over the coming days and weeks. She stayed close, encouraging her to return to her daily routine. It was a painful struggle, but after a few weeks, Kanta felt able to do some of the things that interested her, such as reading and sewing. When Jasumati returned from school, she sat with her on the *jhula* and updated her on the events of the day or the charity activities that she was missing.

In time, Kanta was able to mention Pushpa's name. She began by sharing a few happy memories of her with Jasumati, smiling at some funny moments or conversations. The two of them developed a close connection with one another: a strong mother-daughter bond. While doing so, Kanta began to build a wall between herself and her husband and son. She avoided having conversations with either of them. But Harilal kept trying. He was especially concerned about helping Suresh deal with his grief.

'You need to talk to Suresh,' Harilal told her. 'He is so scared of you.'

'Why should he be scared? I'm not doing anything to him. There's nothing I can do if he won't loosen the rope that is tying him to you.'

'No, Kanta. That is not right. He is still in shock. He feels the loss more than any of us.'

Kanta was incensed. 'How dare you say that? You know how hard this is for me.'

'Be reasonable, Kanta. He's only five years old.'

For a moment, she stood still, glaring at him. Then she pulled her sari *chedo* tight over her shoulder and walked away.

Later that day, Harilal tried to explain why he thought Suresh's grief was so deep. He told Kanta and Jasumati that even though no one was holding him responsible for Pushpa's death, Suresh was clearly blaming himself.

'He doesn't believe me when I tell him it was not his fault. He needs to hear it from you, Kanta. It's very important you do that. If not, he will carry this guilt all his life. Who knows how much damage that will cause.'

Kanta knew that what he said made sense. But how was she going to convince him he was blameless, when she was not convinced herself?

'Kanta, talk to him. Please.' Harilal was pleading. Kanta saw the anguish in his eyes as he continued. 'It was a tragedy. A terrible tragedy. Suresh was not to blame.'

Kanta forced herself to see things through the eyes of a five-year-old child. His sister had died while saving his life, and for that he felt totally responsible. Although she had not accused him of causing Pushpa's death, she knew he could sense her hostility and he was afraid to be anywhere near her. A small part of her felt sorry for the boy, but only a small part. She would need to hide her true feelings.

'Fine. I will talk to him tonight.'

Harilal's relief was imprinted on every feature of his face. Jasumati slipped her arm round her mother's waist. 'I'll come with you, *Ba*,' she said.

That night, outside Suresh's room, they could hear Harilal comforting Suresh. 'You must never blame yourself. It was no one's fault. And *Ba* is not angry with you so don't be scared of her.'

To announce her entry, Kanta shook the bangles on her wrists, making them clink and jangle. With the swish of her sari and further jangling, she walked in, followed by Jasumati.

'There is no need for you to be scared of me, Suresh,' she said with a fixed smile. 'I am not angry with you and I am not blaming you for what happened.'

She saw the fear in his grey-green eyes, mixed with confusion and disbelief. Open-mouthed, he stared at her. Softening her voice somewhat, she continued: 'It was God who decided to take Pushpa-*ben* away. It was not your fault.'

Suresh's lower lip began to quiver, his face contorted and he began to cry. Tears rolled down his face as he looked up at her. She knew Harilal would expect her to comfort the boy. But she stood still, her face impassive. Harilal stroked his back.

'You see, *dikra.* I told you *Ba* doesn't blame you. Now you do one thing. Stop crying and think of all the good things that are going to happen. You'll be going to school soon and you'll make new friends. Everything is going to be all right.'

Kanta stood listening to her husband trying to cheer up her son. She watched them all as if from afar. Her thoughts turned dark as her mind wandered to Pushpa. She replayed the events of that fateful day as she saw them: Pushpa swimming out to save Suresh; disappearing underwater; pulling him up and gasping for air; being pulled back in, kicking and struggling. So much noise. Then, complete silence.

All at once, another painful memory sprang to mind. It came unbidden, reminding her of the trauma from years before. Harilal again. Why did he never listen to her? A wave of bitter resentment surged through her veins and she stepped back. Her mouth filled with saliva, warm and metallic. Swallowing a rush of nausea, Kanta fled from the room.

20 YEARS LATER

December 1977, Navsari, India

Chapter 5

Suresh walked up and down the college hall, invigilating final-year examinations. He took turns with his colleague Iqbal, watching over the students. The nervous tension in the room was palpable.

He remembered how anxious he had been when he had taken his finals in Agricultural Studies. Was it only five years ago? Mercifully, he had passed. Inspired by his uncle, who had a farm just outside Surat, Suresh was passionate about improving farming practices in India. He was determined to do more for local farmers. But right now, he wanted these students to do well. Looking at some of their blank faces, he felt their pain. Their whole futures depended on these exams.

Suresh cared about his students and loved to see them grow and flourish. But lecturing was not what he wanted to do forever. He would soon be saying goodbye to the students and all his colleagues. Looking around the hall, Suresh knew he would miss the college where he had spent many happy years both as a student and member of staff.

Smiling to himself, he thought about the main reason for his happiness. Tara. He had been attracted to her from the first moment of their meeting. She had looked so small beside her moped, which she had parked beside his scooter. Slim, petite and pretty with delicate features and enormous brown eyes.

In the pin-drop silence of the exam hall, Suresh allowed his mind to roll back the years. The first time he had asked Tara to join him for a cup of *chaa* at the students' canteen, she had lowered her gaze and shaken her head. When she'd tried to move away, he had blocked her path.

'My name is Suresh. What's yours?'

Looking startled, she had turned around and walked away quickly. After that, she had avoided him, keeping close to her girlfriends. But he had persisted, always looking friendly, making sure she understood that he meant her no harm. Eventually, she had rewarded him with a shy smile and a nod. After that, they had spent as much time together as they could.

Tara would be waiting for him outside when the exam was over. Their plan was to go to her house for lunch with her family. Suresh glanced at the clock at the far end of the hall. Nearly time.

In due course, he called out to the students, 'Five minutes left. Make sure you have answered all the questions and get ready to put down your pens.'

When all the papers had been collected, the students were allowed out into the bright sunshine. Suresh handed over the exam sheets to his colleague.

'Can you take these to the office? I am in a hurry.'

'Yes. Yes, I know. Always you are in a hurry when your lady friend is waiting,' Iqbal teased.

Laughing, Suresh gave him a friendly pat on the back and walked out through the main doors. Immediately, he saw Tara standing beside her white moped, wearing a maroon-coloured *salwar kameez.* She waved when she saw him, then began to remove the moped stand in readiness for the ride. He strode towards her, feeling the wind blow his fringe away from his face. He had chosen to wear his green jacket because Tara had told him she liked the way it brought out the green in his grey-green eyes. He wore it over his sand-coloured bell-bottoms.

'Hi, Tara. Were you waiting a long time?'

'Not long.' She looked up at him with large smiling eyes. Being a foot taller than her, he bent his head to look into her face, moving as close as he dared. His hand reached out to touch the soft skin of her cheek. Arching her eyebrows, she pushed him gently away with one hand. Then she gave him that tender look which never failed to make his heart flutter. Her whole face radiated with the warmth and love she felt for him.

She turned to get the moped started and Suresh hopped on behind her, placing his hands lightly on her shoulders. Riding slowly, she wove her way through the town's traffic. Her house was in the busy area of Juna Thana, northeast of the college. On the smaller, quieter streets, she sped up, her long brown hair flying across Suresh's face. He moved his head closer to hers and breathed in the perfumed fragrance of her hair. He shifted his hands to her hips and leaned in, wishing he could put his arms around her. But he knew better than to embarrass her in public.

When they reached her home, Tara parked in the small, cemented area in front. Before they could alight, her father opened the door and stepped out to welcome them. Grey-haired and portly, he beamed with pleasure at seeing them.

'Come in, come in. We have been waiting for you.'

He ushered Suresh into the small front room. Immediately, the mouth-watering aromas of home cooking enveloped him.

'The ladies have cooked all your favourite things. I hope you are hungry.'

Tara went into the kitchen and returned with two glasses of water. Handing them over to both men, she left them to have a chat. Suresh enjoyed talking to her father as he always had a lot to say on a wide range of subjects. He had worked all his life in a local store selling books, stationery and objects of arts and crafts.

'I wish I could go to help in the shop, but these ladies won't let me out. Everyone wants to keep me prisoner here.'

Suresh laughed. 'You worked there long enough, *Kaka*. You need to look after your health.'

'Nonsense! I am fine. My diabetes is well-controlled. It is a curse in our country, isn't it? I don't know why so many people suffer from it.' He shook his head, looking troubled.

Tara's sister-in-law came in to say lunch was ready.

'*Namaste*, Suresh.'

'*Namaste, Bhabhi*. I am back again to eat your delicious food.'

'*Arey*, you are always welcome. You are practically family.'

Suresh's smile froze. The path to being part of this family was filled with thorns and he would have to tread very carefully. Breathing deeply, he followed them through the back room and into the kitchen. A small square table at one end of the room was set with four *thalis*, each filled with at least three different vegetarian dishes: onion bhajiya, ragda patties, and kachoris filled with peas. On the side were slices of lemon and three chutneys: green coriander, red tomato with tamarind, and yogurt with green chilli and coconut flakes.

As always, Suresh enjoyed the spread and relaxed atmosphere round the table. He could not help comparing it to mealtimes in his own house. His mother did not approve of noise at the table. They usually ate in sombre silence: his mother, his older sister Jasumati, her husband Manoj and he. Sometimes, Jasumati's two boys ate with them, which he preferred because at least then there was some conversation.

His mother Kanta was firm with her grandchildren, though not as firm as she had been with him and his sister Jasumati. She had mellowed over the years, but she still ruled the roost. They were all intimidated by her, even her son-in-law.

'How is everyone at home, Suresh?' asked Tara's father.

'*Ba* is well, but Manoj-*jija* is back in hospital. He's under treatment for his back problem.'

Suresh omitted to say that together with his painful back, Manoj suffered from regular bouts of depression. It was a taboo subject, and he was under strict instructions from his mother to keep the illness a secret. She believed this malady was a sign of madness.

Suresh felt sorry for Manoj, who had little or no control over any family decisions. Jasumati's forceful character had ground him down over the years. Kanta had arranged Jasumati's marriage to him and had been trying to do the same for Suresh ever since he had finished high school. He wondered when she would accept that he was never going to agree to an arranged marriage. He had told her many times that he was going to marry for love, but she always dismissed the subject with an angry shrug.

'Is everything okay?' Tara asked with concern. 'You are miles away.'

'Sorry. I was just thinking about home. Everything is fine.' Tara gave him a knowing look.

After lunch, the two men returned to the front room, while the women cleared up. The window was open and the ceiling fan whirred noisily overhead. The afternoon sun poured in and the air in the room was stifling. Suresh opened the front door to let in some fresh air. Straight away, the noise level went up: car and rickshaw horns hooting, bicycle bells ringing and hawkers clamouring to sell their wares. Hastily he shut the door, instantly muffling the noise.

'Sit down, Suresh. I want to ask you something.'

Suresh's heart skipped a beat. *Not now*, he thought. *I'm not ready*.

'I think it is time for me to visit your mother. I need to talk to her about the wedding. If your father was alive, I would be speaking to him.'

Suresh's face clouded over. Even after twelve years, the memory of his father's sudden death was a nauseating pain. Tara's father touched his hand. 'You were only a boy when he had his heart attack. How old were you, *dikra*?'

'I was thirteen.'

'Too young. Too young. I know what a shock it was for you. But these things are not in our hands.' He raised his palms and eyes heavenward and sighed. 'I am sorry to remind you like this. But it is my duty as Tara's father to see her settled. You understand?' When Suresh did not reply, he continued, 'You do one thing. Ask your mother if she prefers to come here. Do you think she will come?'

'I think . . . No, I'm sure she will,' Suresh lied.

The older man looked at him thoughtfully. Then he nodded and reached for his little stash of *paan,* his betel leaves all made up into triangular parcels. He was addicted to this after-meal digestive made with lime paste, *kaththa* and areca nut. He popped one parcel into his mouth, then offered one to Suresh.

'No, thank you. But I will have some *mukhwas*.' He pointed to the jar containing the seed mixture of fennel, anise and sesame. He was not averse to the taste of *paan*, but he disliked the red juice it produced in the mouth.

When Tara joined them, she reminded her father that it was time for his insulin injection. 'It is ready for you on your bed with the syringe and needle. Shall I help you?'

'No need, *dikra*. I can manage.' Standing up, he turned to Suresh. 'I'm going for my afternoon nap so I will see you next time. But don't forget what I said, okay?'

'*Ji, Kaka.*'

Tara's sister-in-law came in to say she was going out to the market. She had changed into another sari, fresh and free of lingering food smells. With a cheery wave, she took her leave of them. Tara offered to take Suresh back to the campus to collect his scooter.

'Not yet, Tara. Let's sit for a while.'

Tucking her feet under her, she curled up against him on the settee. He put his arms around her and held her close, resting his chin on top of her head. Tara snuggled in. Suresh felt a deep connection with her; they fitted into each other's lives like perfect puzzle pieces. With every passing day, he could feel the connection getting stronger.

'She won't listen, you know,' he said. 'I just can't talk to her.'

He felt Tara tense up in his arms. She said nothing at first. Then she spoke without looking up.

'Is your mother against our marriage because we are not of the same caste?'

'No.' Suresh did not want to hurt her with the truth.

'Then because my family is poor?'

Suresh moved her gently so that she was facing him. 'Listen to me, Tara. I don't care what her reasons are. She is not going to stop us from getting married.'

Tara looked unconvinced.

'Believe me, Tara. We *will* get married, with or without her blessing.'

He did not have the heart to tell her all the reasons Kanta had listed for opposing the marriage. Tara *was* of the wrong caste, she *was* from a poor family, their class and social backgrounds did not match, her family was not from their community, not equal to them in the eyes of their own family and friends, and she would never fit in.

'If you refuse to see any of the girls I have chosen for you, then I refuse to meet the girl that you have chosen,' she had declared.

'Do you think she will ever agree?' asked Tara.

'I've been asking her for three years now. She just closes her ears to me when I bring it up.' He paused for a moment, then said, 'What would your father say if we married without her blessing?'

Tara sat up slowly. 'He wouldn't like it. But . . . he does want us to get married.'

Suresh lifted his shoulders, then let them drop, breathing out slowly. He kissed her on the forehead. Then, lifting her chin with one finger, he kissed her softly on the lips. Looking into her eyes, he smiled. 'I will talk to my mother again.'

'Do you think your sister Jasu-*ben* would help?'

Suresh shrugged. 'I doubt it. She never takes my side.'

'Why not?'

'I don't know. She changed after my father passed away.' Suresh closed his eyes and thought of the day his father had collapsed and died. He had been at school when he got the message. His whole world had come crashing down around him.

Tara took his hands in hers. 'You still miss him, don't you?'

'He meant everything to me. Without him, I couldn't see the point in living.'

'But your mother . . .'

'My mother!' Suresh gave vent to a short harsh laugh. 'Yes. I had my mother.' His voice became choked with emotion. 'I've told you what she's like. There is no space in her heart for me. She doesn't like me at all. I know she still believes it's my fault that my sister Pushpa drowned when she was only nine years old. Sometimes I believe that too.'

'Don't ever say that!' Tara's tone was sharp and commanding. 'Don't even think it.' He winced as if in physical pain and she immediately wrapped her arms around him. 'You are not to blame for your sister's death. I can't understand why your mother doesn't see how much this hurts you.'

Suresh buried his face in her hair and squeezed his eyes shut. Kanta's manner towards him was bad enough, but even Jasumati showed him little if any love. 'They make me feel as if I am not part of the family. After *Bapuji* passed away, my mother became even colder towards me and I'm sure it was she who turned Jasu-*ben* against me. I've tried to fight my corner, I really have. But it's hard to fight them both.'

Tara squeezed him tight. 'It's okay, Suresh,' she murmured. 'Don't let them upset you. You are strong and you can rise above all their cruelty. Remember what I always say: my family is your family.'

Suresh pressed his lips together and nodded. Moving back, he faced her and gave her an affectionate smile. He adored her. Kissing her on the lips once more, he stood up. 'We should go now. Before I get home, I need to check on the equipment.'

'Has it arrived?' Tara asked. It lifted his spirits to see how interested she was in his small business venture.

'Yes. It's in my store right now with the other tools. I haven't had a chance to give it a proper inspection. I want to see how good it is.'

Tara checked on her father before they left. She took the same route as before, but the roads were busier, so their journey took longer. When they reached their destination, Tara parked next to Suresh's scooter. It was a Bajaj Super, red and white, still shiny. Suresh was happy with it, but his ambition was to possess an Ambassador car like his father used to have. He hoped that one day soon, he could buy one.

'I'll phone you tomorrow.' He gave Tara a quick hug then watched her ride away. When she was out of sight, he mounted his scooter and made his way out of the college gateway heading for home.

Chapter 6

Suresh parked his scooter in front of the house where his equipment was stored. He needed to inspect the new device that he had recently ordered. Before walking to the front door, he glanced up to the fourth floor of Suparna Mansions on the opposite side of the road, wondering if anyone was looking down. He laughed when he saw his little nephew Raju peering over the balcony wall, grinning impishly.

The boy began to wave. Suresh held up both hands to indicate that he should stay where he was. Turning around, he went up the steps to the porch and unlocked the heavy wooden door to let himself in. The front room was dark and dusty, but cool because the curtains were drawn to keep out the hot sun. As soon as he opened them, sunlight poured in, making the dust motes dance all around him.

The smell of chemicals filled the room: a mixture of tar, phenol and ether. Overriding the acrid smells was the odour of peanut and garlic oil. That was the strange smell of his main product: neem oil. The room was full of neem oil bottles and packets, all boxed and stored along one wall.

Suresh's nose twitched at the overpowering organic scent of this vegetable oil. It was very strong, but he preferred it to the chemical tang of the synthetic pesticides used widely by local farmers. In his opinion, they were dangerous because they left toxic residue behind.

His research on neem oil had convinced him that this was the safest pest control product available for treatment and prevention. It was organic, biodegradable and non-toxic for birds, pollinators and animals. Suresh wanted to encourage safer farming practices and he was aware that local farmers needed help to make the necessary changes.

His latest acquisition was leaning against the back wall. This is what he had come to check. It was a hand granule applicator which would help farmers accurately place neem oil granules around their crops. He examined it carefully and visualised himself demonstrating how it should be used. It would make work easier for farmers in smallholdings.

Suresh looked around at all his other tools and equipment. He had no doubt these would be sold when he took them out to farms. There was a huge demand for them. The most popular were the knapsack cylinders and sprayers which farmers found easy to handle. In addition, some of his customers asked for protective hand gloves, goggles, masks, outer garments and boots. Suresh made sure he had sufficient stocks of all these items.

Turning around, he decided to take a quick look at the back rooms. He walked through the small, dark inner room and entered the kitchen area. Using his keys, he opened the door that led out to a small courtyard, letting in a welcome rush of fresh air.

Suresh walked back to the inner room where he could now see what was in storage. Straight away he felt a pang of nostalgia. This was where his father used to store some of his paintings, books and old furniture. After his death, most of his belongings had been sold or given away by his mother. But he was glad to see some items still there. Their *kaamwadi*, the housemaid, used to live in this house and she had retained some of these things. When she'd moved away, the house had become a small warehouse.

Suresh remembered the day he had asked his mother if he could use the house to store things for his new pest control business. Her response had surprised him.

'Take it. I have no need for it. It's full of rubbish anyway.'

Suresh realised it was getting late and he needed to be on time for supper. This was one of his mother's many rules. Making sure every door and window was locked and the front room curtain drawn, he walked his scooter across the road and parked it inside the gate of Suparna Mansions. A few other scooters and bicycles owned by the tenants were already there, safely stored for the night.

Mr Saleji was sitting on his *jhula*, reading a book. '*Arey* Suresh. You are late today.'

'I won't be if I run.' He took the stairs two at a time.

With relief, he saw that the family had not yet started eating, though they *were* seated round the table. Kanta had modernised the room with an imported table, chairs and sideboard for new crockery and cutlery. No more *thalis* and *desi* products in this house.

'Why are you late, Suresh-*mama*?' asked his younger nephew, as he washed his hands at the sink.

His brother Raju answered for him. 'He was busy in his storeroom.' Suresh stuck his tongue out at him and opened his eyes wide in mock anger, making him giggle.

'No noise now,' Kanta ordered. Suresh waited for his rebuke, but when it didn't come, he sat down and began to pick at his food.

'Aren't you hungry?' asked Jasumati.

'Not really. I had a big lunch.' Suresh was going to leave it at that. But then he saw the smug look on his sister's face. She seemed to be goading him to say more. Normally, Suresh would simply ignore her and like a tortoise, retreat into his shell. But her expression at that moment irritated him. Before he could stop himself, he said, 'Not that it's any of your business but I ate at Tara's house.'

Jasumati now had a mile-wide smirk on her face. Suresh dared to carry on. He fixed his eyes on his mother. 'I have a message for you, *Ba*. From Tara's father.'

Kanta ignored him. Suresh felt a rush of anger. He had to speak out. 'You need to discuss wedding arrangements with him.'

There was a hushed silence. Everyone stopped eating and all eyes were on him. All eyes except Kanta's. She continued with her meal as if he hadn't spoken. Suresh had never mentioned Tara in front of the whole family, but now that he had, he decided to seize the moment.

'He is happy to come here if you want. What do you think, *Ba*?'

Still no answer. Everyone sat completely still, even the children.

'Shall we arrange it for this weekend?' Suresh persisted. He could sense everyone's nervousness. Jasumati broke the silence by kicking him under the table and telling her boys to stop staring.

Suresh was furious. It was as if she had lit a fuse.

'What is your problem, Jasu-*ben*? Why can't you support me on this?'

Jasumati looked at Kanta. 'Tell him what you said to me, *Ba*. Tell him!'

Kanta's head shot up. She glared at Jasumati. 'Be quiet, Jasu.'

Suresh looked from one to the other, then asked his mother, 'Tell me what?'

Slowly Kanta turned to face Suresh. 'We are not going to discuss this now. If you want to talk, come to me later. Right now, do you think we can have some peace and quiet?'

Looking at her closed face, Suresh knew that he would get nothing from her until she was ready. He would pin her down later that evening. There was still unease round the table, and the children were darting nervous glances at him. Feeling sorry for them, he smiled. His sister sniffed. Tutting loudly, she scowled at him, then pointedly ignored him.

It was past 8 p.m. before Suresh could speak to his mother. The children were in their rooms, Jasumati was visiting her husband in hospital, and Kanta was sitting on the *jhula* in the balcony reading a magazine. Suresh took a deep breath and went to join her on the swing, leaving a sizeable gap between them.

After a few minutes, he began: '*Ba*, please try to understand. I am going to marry Tara because I love her. I really want you to be happy about it. Why won't you accept her?'

Kanta put her magazine aside and looked at him impassively. 'I have given you my reasons, so I will not go into that again. But tell me one thing: where do you intend to live with her?'

Suresh was taken aback. He had always believed that Kanta would expect him to follow the tradition of bringing his wife to live with them.

'Isn't it my duty as a son to bring her here?'

'No! I have no place for a girl like that in my house.'

Suresh frowned and shook his head in disbelief.

'Don't shake your head at me! I told you before that you cannot marry out of caste. No one in this family has ever done that. I will not have you lower our status.' She paused for effect, then continued, 'You know very well why people stay within their own caste. It preserves our culture and protects our traditions. That is how our society operates.'

Lost for words, Suresh could only stare at her in dismay.

'Listen carefully, Suresh. If you insist on marrying her, you will marry her without my consent or blessings. Is that clear?'

Suresh felt a wave of anger ride up inside him. With hands clenched together on his lap, he asked her the question that had always tormented him: 'Why do you hate me so much, *Ba*? I really want to know.'

For a moment, she said nothing. She fixed him with an ice-cold stare. Then in a low voice that sent a chill down his spine, she said, 'Okay. I will tell you.' She narrowed her eyes. 'The day you were born, my whole world turned upside down. Because of you, I have suffered. Because of you *and* your father.'

Astounded, Suresh tried to make sense of what he had just heard. 'I don't understand. What do you mean?'

'Just what I said,' Kanta hissed, her eyes blazing with animosity.

It was more than Suresh could bear. He could hear his heart pounding in his ears. He wanted to be as far away from her as possible. But there were things he needed to say; things he needed to hear from her.

'I know you blame me for Pushpa-*ben*'s death. And I know you blamed *Bapuji* for letting us go to the lake. But how could we possibly know what would happen? It was fate. Pushpa-*ben*'s fate to die on that day.'

At the mention of Pushpa's name, Kanta shuddered, as if in physical pain. 'Yes!' she cried out. 'I do blame you both. But your father wronged me long before that!'

Suresh pulled back, stunned. What could she possibly mean? Before he could recover, his mother delivered her final coup de grâce.

'If you marry this girl, I will wash my hands of you. You will not receive a single *paiso* from me. Not one *paiso*.'

Speechless, Suresh looked at her and understood that she meant every word. Nodding his head slowly, he stood up and took a few steps away. Turning to face her, he said as calmly as he could, 'I *am* going to marry Tara so I will leave this house as soon as I can. But are you sure that's what you want? Because once I go, I will never return.'

Kanta's face was a cold mask of indifference.

'You have made your choice, so there is nothing more to discuss.' She began to rise from the *jhula.*

Suresh held up both hands, making her wait to hear him out. With his heart hammering in his chest, he made a huge effort to control his voice. 'Tell me, *Ba*. How exactly were you wronged by *Bapuji*? I need to know.'

She stared at him dispassionately, looking perfectly composed.

'No. You don't need to know. And this discussion is over.' Kanta's words were cold and final. She looked away, then stood up abruptly. Pulling her sari tight around her body, she stepped past him and walked regally into the apartment, leaving Suresh staring after her in disbelief.

Chapter 7

Suresh stood frozen to the spot until his mother's footsteps faded away. Then he sank down on the *jhula* with his face buried in his hands. His mother had just disowned him, accusing him of causing her much suffering. His chest felt tight and his body burned with emotions he found difficult to control. He realised she had never loved him. *The day you were born, my world turned upside down.* How was he going to come to terms with that?

Kanta also blamed his father. What could she have meant when she said he had wronged her long before Pushpa drowned? He could not imagine his father doing anything to hurt her. He had always treated her with love and respect; Suresh was certain of this. He was thirteen years old when his father had passed away, and he could not recall a single occasion when he'd raised his voice at her.

It was Kanta who often expressed annoyance with him. Suresh remembered how frequently she used to purse her lips and glare at Harilal. It always frightened Suresh even though there were never any loud, enraged arguments. Kanta was much too restrained and Harilal was such a gentle soul, he avoided quarrelling at all costs.

Suresh remembered the fog that had settled around him for over a year after his father's death. He had meant the world to him. Kind and loving, he had always made him feel safe and protected.

When his sudden heart attack had taken him away, Suresh had been inconsolable. On that day, he had lost his whole world.

The rattling of the metal barrier at the entrance pulled him back to the present. He looked up to see Jasumati sliding open the bolt on the vertical bars at the top of the stairway. She walked through and paused to catch her breath after climbing up four flights. Suresh's tormented gaze met hers. She frowned at first and then gave him a knowing look.

'So. You spoke to *Ba.*'

Suresh did not reply.

'What did she say?'

'You know what she said!' Suresh's bitterness spilled over. Looking at his sister, he knew he would get no support from her. When Suresh had needed her most, after their father's death, she had turned her back on him, providing no comfort.

Jasumati gazed at him with a watchful expression. For a moment, he thought she was going to say nothing and walk away, leaving him to his despair. But she surprised him by heaving a sigh and stepping up to sit beside him. For a long minute, they stayed silent, rocking slowly to and fro, looking straight ahead.

It was past 9 p.m. but there was still a lot of activity on the street below. The noise of people talking, dogs barking and late-evening traffic floated up to them. Suresh was oblivious to everything except his mother's wounding words swirling around in his head.

Jasumati broke the silence. 'Have you decided what you are going to do?'

Suresh did not reply.

'Are you going to marry Tara?'

He glared at her. 'What do *you* think?'

She tutted. 'You are mad, Suresh. You are going to lose everything. Is she really worth it?'

'Of course she's worth it.' Suresh spoke through gritted teeth. 'If you made the effort to get to know her, you would understand. But all you want to do is suck up to *Ba.* I just don't know why.' Feeling a prickling sensation behind his eyes, he turned away.

Once again, they became silent. After a while, Suresh spoke again, keeping his voice low and eyes straight ahead.

'*Ba* hates me because she still thinks it's my fault Pushpa-*ben* drowned.'

Jasumati did not respond. Suresh continued in the same tone. 'Is that why *you* hate me too?'

'I don't hate you, Suresh.' Jasumati's denial was too quick.

He smiled grimly. His sister was a habitual liar, and he had learned over the years to take what she said with a good pinch of salt.

'I don't believe you.'

'Okay. Don't believe me. I don't care.'

He turned to look pointedly at her. 'I know you don't care. But you might care if you knew what *Ba* said about *Bapuji.*' He saw her look of surprise. 'She told me that he had hurt her long before Pushpa-*ben* drowned.'

Suresh heard her sharp intake of breath. 'She told you?'

Something in the way she said that made Suresh suspect that she knew what Kanta was referring to. He fixed her with a penetrating stare.

'Yes. She told me. She told me everything.'

Jasumati turned away, but not before Suresh saw her half-closed eyes. She was hiding something.

'What do you know about this?'

'Nothing.'

'You're lying. I can tell. What did *Bapuji* do to upset *Ba* so much?'

Jasumati's head jerked up. 'You mean she didn't tell you?'

'Tell me what you know.'

Jasumati became agitated. 'I don't know anything!' She looked down at her hands, cracking her knuckles.

'Whatever it is, just tell me, Jasu-*ben*. Why can't you tell me?'

Jasumati would not look at him. Suresh could almost see the cogs whirring in her brain as she considered what she should say. He waited, watching her carefully. Eventually, she let out a loud, exasperated sigh and stood up. Looking down at him, she shook her head.

'Look. All I know is that years ago, *Ba* was forced to do something for the family that she did not want to do. Something that hurt her very much. And it was *Bapuji* who forced her to do it.'

Suresh frowned, trying to understand what this meant. 'But what . . .'

'Don't ask me what! You have to ask her yourself.' Jasumati began to walk away.

'Wait!' Suresh was on his feet. 'You *have* to tell me.'

But Jasumati simply shook her head and hurried away into the apartment, leaving him in a daze. He started after her, then stopped, knowing it was pointless. It would only disturb everyone and incur the wrath of their mother yet again. He ran his fingers through his hair, staring absently at the door.

After a while, he turned and went to stand at the parapet. He gazed down at the road which was lit up with streetlights, people's homes and moving scooters and rickshaws. Everything was calmer now, at the end of the usual bustle of the day. The smell of cooking drifted up from the kitchens of some of his neighbours, still preparing their evening meals. He recognised several people, standing or sitting in front of their homes, chatting with one another. How could life go on so normally when his own had just been turned upside down? He tried to steady his nerves as he stared down at the street.

Gradually, his eyes settled on the little house across the road where all his tools and chemicals were stored. It was in complete darkness. He allowed his mind to drift towards his business and thought about the new pest control equipment he had inspected earlier that evening. The customers were going to love the new tool. When he showed them how to use it on their farms, he was sure they would place their orders immediately. More stock would need to be bought and his sales were bound to go up.

An unexpected flutter of excitement stirred in his stomach. He could see his business growing. He would work hard to make sure it did. The germ of an idea began to form in his mind. He was going to need more storage space. A proper storeroom for all his products, and he knew just the place to find one. Barely a mile away, near the train station, he had seen a new build of shop fronts with storage facilities behind. There were large billboards advertising these as business units available for rent. The charges had seemed affordable and the thought had already crossed his mind that he should pay them a visit. In spite of all that had just occurred, Suresh began to get excited at the prospect of moving his business to a new location and expanding.

He gazed down at his current storeroom. Not so long ago, it had been a family home for the *kaamwadi*, their housemaid. It could easily become someone's home once again. For the first time that evening, Suresh felt a glimmer of hope. He smiled to himself.

Kanta's cold and forbidding face appeared in his mind's eye, and his smile vanished. He let out a low groan and rubbed his face with both hands, as if by doing so, her face would disappear. He thought of his beloved father, Harilal. *Dear Bapuji. I wish you were here.*

If only God had not taken him away. His heart ached with an intense longing for him. If he was still with them, Suresh was certain that he would have understood what Tara meant to him. He would have accepted her and not allowed Kanta to push him away.

Suresh stood at the balcony for a long time, trying to work out what he should do. All the plans he had made for his future were based on the premise that he would live with Tara in Suparna Mansions. He was the only son and it was his responsibility to look after his mother as she grew into old age. That was the custom. But this was one custom his mother did not want to follow. It was a blow, but Suresh knew he had to move on. There was a lot to think about. Straightening up, he pushed back his shoulders and headed for his bedroom.

~

The next morning, Suresh woke early, ready and prepared to face Kanta. Surprisingly, he had slept well. He'd thought through all his options and made some decisions. Somehow, by forcing him to move out, Kanta had made it easier for him to plan his next steps. Although it pained him to remember her harsh words, he realised that she had simplified things for him.

Knowing that Kanta always let the *kaamwadi* in at 7 a.m. to prepare breakfast for the family, Suresh got ready and joined her at the table just as the housemaid was pouring her a cup of *chaa*. Kanta raised her eyebrows in surprise when he walked in, then calmly reached over for a *poori*.

'Can I have *chaa* too?' Suresh asked the *kaamwadi*. 'But nothing to eat.' He watched Kanta dip her *poori* into coriander chutney before biting into the fried bread.

Suresh waited until the maid had left the dining room before speaking. Clearing his throat, he began.

'I have thought about what you said last night.' He watched her look up for an instant, then continue with her breakfast. 'I will leave Suparna Mansions as soon as possible. I'm going to move into the house across the road.'

Kanta's head jerked up, a frown wrinkling her forehead. 'You want to live in that *kachro* place full of rubbish?'

'Yes. There's nothing wrong with it. I just need to clear out my stock.'

'And where are you going to put that?'

'I'll rent a proper storeroom somewhere else.'

Kanta stared at him, her piercing gaze leaving him in no doubt that she thought he was crazy. He had tried to talk to her about the business and discuss the plans he had for it, but she had shown little interest.

He waited for her to say something, quietly sipping his tea, keeping his eyes on her.

She was gazing down pensively into her cup of *chaa.* He wondered what she was thinking. The little house was part of his father's estate, so technically, it belonged to her. But she had previously told him that he could have it. He was acutely aware that things were different now.

He watched her pour tea into the saucer then lift it to her lips to drink. When she finally spoke, she did not look up. 'I meant what I said last night. You will get nothing from me if you marry this girl.'

'I know. And I accept your terms.' Suresh could not control the tremor in his voice. He suddenly felt very sad about having this conversation with his mother. This should not be happening. He tried to explain his feelings to her.

'I know you are disappointed in me. And I'm sorry. I really am.'

He paused, willing her to say something. Something positive. But she remained stubbornly silent, gazing down at her empty cup. Suresh let out an exasperated sigh. He ran his fingers through his hair, concentrating on pulling all his energy together. He cleared his throat again.

'I have some money saved up from my job at the college. As soon as I have enough, I will marry Tara and we will find a place of our own. Until then, if you have no objections, I will live across the road.'

Abruptly, Kanta stood up and looked directly at him. 'If you want to live in that house, you can have it. Stay in that rubbish heap forever if you want. It makes no difference to me.' With that, she strode out of the kitchen, her sari swishing and her bangles jangling.

Suresh stared at his tea, feeling sick. He took a few moments to bring his emotions under control. Then he walked to the telephone and dialled the number of the one person he knew would give him the strength he needed.

'Tara. We need to talk.'

MARCH 2016

Navsari, India

Chapter 8

Nirmala sat on the *jhula* gazing up at the fourth-floor balcony of Suparna Mansions, her thoughts far away in the past. She was picturing her father, Suresh, walking away from the building and making a home for himself and his wife, Tara, in this little house where she grew up. It was hers now and in time, it would be her son's. Absentmindedly, she stroked Varun's hair, his head in her lap.

With a shock, she realised her aunt Jasumati was standing at the parapet staring down at her. How long had she been there? Tentatively, Nirmala raised her hand in greeting. Jasumati's chin went up, but instead of returning the wave, she nodded her head just once and stepped back, out of sight.

Nirmala sighed. For as long as she could remember, her aunt had been cold towards her and her parents. Throughout her childhood, Nirmala had been aware of the frosty relationship between her father Suresh and his sister Jasumati, but she had never been told exactly what had caused the rift. She had longed for some affection from her aunt, especially after her parents had passed away; first her father when she was only fifteen years old, then her mother just after she had married Ajay.

Nirmala had tried hard to win favour with her aunt, but Jasumati remained aloof, often even hostile. She was the only connection she had to her parents. To be kept at a distance like this was very hurtful.

Varun tugged on her arm. 'Mumma, can we go to see Hema-*masi*?'

'No, *dikra*. She's still teaching at the school. But I have to go out to get your medicine, so you will have to stay home with your Pappa.'

'No! I don't want to stay with him. I want to come with you.'

Nirmala tutted, annoyed with Ajay for making Varun feel nervous in his presence. He was always angry with the boy for no apparent reason. He seemed incapable of showing that he cared. He'd been better when Varun was a baby. After two miscarriages, Varun's arrival had been a very special moment. Nirmala remembered the way Ajay had beamed when he was told he had a son. She knew he would have been disappointed if the baby had been a girl. Like many families in India, daughters were still considered a burden. They would grow up, get married and be part of someone else's family, taking their name, looking after them in their old age. Having a son gave Ajay something to brag about.

But in recent years, he complained constantly about Varun. 'He's got no backbone, this boy. He needs to toughen up. You're too soft with him.'

Nirmala tried hard to make him understand that Varun was a sensitive child. Ajay needed to be gentle. But her pleas always fell on deaf ears. Once, he had even suggested that Varun was not right in the head and that she had given him a mentally retarded child. His words had wounded Nirmala deeply. She'd turned away from him, determined to protect Varun and shower him with love.

Looking down at his bright smiling face, she put the palm of her hand on his forehead. 'You aren't hot anymore, so that's a good sign. Are you sure you feel better?' He nodded, giving her a wide grin. She kissed the top of his head and stood up. 'Okay. Let's get ready. We will get your medicine from the pharmacy. After that, I'll take you to see Hema-*masi* at her school.' She smiled at her son's obvious delight in being with her friend Hema. She helped him down from the *jhula* and took him inside.

Lifting out her shoulder bag from the wardrobe in the middle room, Nirmala put away the rupees Ajay had just given her. Making sure Varun's prescription was also in the bag, she zipped it up and slung the long strap over her shoulder and across her body, letting it hang loose against her hip.

Turning to the mirror on the wall, Nirmala studied her appearance. The *chandlo* on her forehead had moved from the centre position and a few strands of hair had escaped the knot at the back of her head. Big brown eyes stared back at her, looking wistful, as if she was longing for something she couldn't have. The skin on her finely chiselled face was pale, glistening with perspiration from the heat. Nirmala grimaced. I can't go out like this, she thought.

Using the end of her *odhani*, Nirmala dabbed the moisture away. Checking her face again and reflecting on where she was heading, Nirmala decided to take action. First, she reached into the drawer for her small pot of *kajal*. Wiping her little finger across the black paste, she smeared the kohl across the bottom rim of her eyes. Next, she took out her powder compact and lightly touched her forehead, cheeks, nose and chin. Finally, she picked up her tube of lipstick and carefully applied the soft mauve colour over her lips.

Satisfied with the result, Nirmala put her few items of cosmetics away. It wasn't often she wore make-up, but when she did, it always gave her a little boost of confidence. Fixing her hair and *chandlo*, she turned to run a comb through Varun's hair and moved to the front room where Ajay was busy at his sewing machine.

It was an old treadle machine that he had bought second-hand from a tailoring shop having a clear out. The sharp clacking of the machine and the rocking of the treadle made a noisy rhythmic sound. Nirmala waited for him to pause before letting him know they were off. All she got in reply was a loud grunt.

Heading for the main road, she walked with Varun up Golwad Street. The late afternoon sun was still too hot for them to linger in the open, and they made haste towards the shops with awnings which would provide some respite. But before they reached their destination, they heard the sound of running feet behind them.

'Varun! Wait. I have something to give your Mumma.'

It was the boy from the ground-floor apartment in Suparna Mansions. Nirmala was very fond of his great-grandfather, Saleji-*dada*. The boy waved a white envelope at her as he raced to catch up.

'The postman was going to deliver this to the top floor, but my *Mota Dada* saw your father's name on it.'

Nirmala was surprised. Her father had passed away fourteen years ago, and as far as she was aware, none of his mail ever went to Suparna Mansions. She studied the name and address carefully.

Mr Suresh Dayal
Suparna Mansions
162 Golwad Street
Navsari, Gujarat
India

'Yes. This *is* for my father. Thank you. And my *namaste* to your *Mota Dada*.'

She watched him run back and thought about the kind old man who sat on his *jhula* on Friday evenings reading to the neighbourhood's children. They loved to hear his stories, especially when he told them with his peculiar horsey laugh.

Standing at the side of the road, she looked carefully at the white envelope. The top half was covered with one blue air mail sticker and three brightly coloured stamps with black postage marks all over them. On one corner of each stamp there was a small image of a golden bird sitting on a throne. Different animals stood proudly in the foreground: a zebra, a rhinoceros, a giraffe. The country of origin was printed in bold block letters: Zimbabwe.

That's in southern Africa, thought Nirmala. How strange. Pappa had never mentioned any friends in Africa. Who could it be? Her curiosity aroused, she went to open the envelope. But Varun was tugging at her *kameez*.

'Let's go, Mumma. I'm too hot!'

One look at her son's face and she knew she had better keep moving. Dropping the envelope into her handbag, she took his hand again and walked briskly to the end of the street, then left onto Tower Road. They stepped onto the pavement and melted into the heat and dust of the busy road. As usual, they were enveloped by a cacophony of noise from the hooting tooting traffic and bellowing vendors. The pavements were narrow and non-existent in some places, so most people walked on the road, darting out of the way when moving vehicles sounded their horns.

Crossing the busy road was going to be a challenge. Nirmala knew she had to step out in front of the moving traffic with her hand held up to indicate her intention to cross. She tried several times but failed. With Varun at her side, she could not take any risks. A passing stranger saw her predicament and came to her rescue. Fearlessly, he stepped out onto the road, holding up both hands. It was amazing to watch how the traffic stopped to let them through. Nirmala threw the man a smile over her shoulder, as she crossed.

It wasn't long before they were standing in front of the glass-fronted shop with 'Sudhir's Chemist' emblazoned across the top in big red letters on a white background. Nirmala stopped to look through the glass shop front. She could see several people being served at the two counters on the left, but she was more interested in the dispensary at the back. There was only one customer standing in front of the pharmacist with several medicine bottles and packs in front of him.

Nirmala felt her heart begin to race. She waited a moment to collect herself then straightened her shoulders and stepped through the door with Varun in tow. She made her way towards the dispensary. As she drew closer, she heard the pharmacist speaking to his elderly patient in a gentle voice. It was a voice only too familiar to Nirmala. Deep and warm.

Nirmala held her breath. This was Sudhir, the boy she had grown up with. They had grown fond of one another and become inseparable. Sitting side by side in every class at school, they'd made plans about going to university together and beyond. Plans that had not worked out.

Sudhir was speaking to the patient, who was clearly confused about his medicines. Judging from the large array of bottles and blister packs in front of him, he was on at least ten different medications. Sudhir was patiently explaining when and how each one should be taken.

He saw her before she reached the counter. He did a double take before his face broke into a smile.

'Nirmala.'

'Hello, Sudhir.' She lowered her eyes under his gaze.

He cleared his throat. 'Take a seat.' He pointed to a chair. 'I will be with you in one minute.'

Nirmala nodded and moved away. She watched him at his work, helping his patient with professionalism and efficiency. He was confident, assertive and self-assured. All the things *she* had been in the past.

Back then, Sudhir had been shy and reserved, studying hard to achieve top marks. He was not the best-looking boy in class, not in the Bollywood movie star way. But he had a certain charm about him that Nirmala found attractive. She remembered his serious expression when they'd made the commitment to one another, his long fringe in his eyes. How different things had turned out, and none of it of Sudhir's making. She studied him now with his short hair and modish, black-framed spectacles, still looking serious. A white coat over his shirt and trousers finished his look of the competent health professional.

'God bless you,' said the patient as he shuffled away with his bag of pills.

Nirmala walked forward with Varun and placed the prescription in front of Sudhir. She could feel his eyes boring into her, but she fixed hers on the counter.

'Are you okay?' His voice was soft, like a caress.

'I'm fine, but it's Varun.' When she looked at him, the expression on his face was so tender that she caught her breath. An image flashed through her mind, of the two of them watching a movie in the cinema with their friends, and her leaning over to plant a kiss on his lips, surprising him and shocking herself. Their first kiss. Nirmala blinked and turned her gaze away.

'I . . . I need your advice.'

He frowned, then inclined his head to speak to Varun.

'Hello, *beta*. I haven't seen you for a long time. You must be four years old now.'

'No! I'm five.' Varun grinned.

'Really? I can't believe that! Are you sure?'

The boy nodded, delighted. Sudhir laughed out loud, then turned to Nirmala. She gave him a quick smile, then looked down at the prescription. He picked it up and scanned it. Immediately, his face clouded over.

'Have there been seizures?'

'No. But there are other symptoms. The doctor said all the tests confirm a diagnosis of CAE: childhood absence epilepsy.'

He nodded thoughtfully. 'Okay. Wait one minute and I'll get the medicine ready for you.'

He walked up the few steps behind him into his dispensary. Nirmala saw him search along the white shelves lined with mysterious tablets, capsules and blister packs jostling with stock bottles filled with solid and liquid drugs. There was a faint smell of pharmaceuticals, disinfectants and other chemicals emanating from the shelves. It instantly brought back memories of her father's pest control business. As a child, she had spent many happy hours watching him advise local farmers on which products they should buy for their various crops.

'Here you are,' said Sudhir, handing over a small brown bottle containing a clear liquid. 'This is sodium valproate syrup. Give him one teaspoon twice a day, morning and night.'

'With food?'

'Only if he gets an upset stomach. But he should be fine.'

'Thank you. How much do I owe you?'

'Don't worry about it, Nirmala. It's not much.'

'Oh no. I have the money. Please take it.' She held out all the rupees she had. He stared at her for a moment, then shook his head in resignation.

'Okay. I don't want to upset you.' He counted out 60 rupees, then put the rest in her hand, folding her fingers over them with both his hands. He held on for longer than necessary, gazing into her eyes earnestly, until she blinked and pulled away.

'I have to go,' she said, putting the medicine bottle in her bag and reaching for Varun's hand.

'Wait, Nirmala. I have something for Varun.'

He reached into a drawer behind him and brought out three lollipops, each wrapped in different-coloured paper. He leaned over and held them out to Varun. 'Which colour do you like?'

Varun grinned and pointed to the red one.

'That's yours then. And you do one thing: keep this yellow one for tomorrow and the green one for the day after. Will you do that?' He smiled as the boy nodded. Turning to Nirmala, he spoke quietly. 'He's going to be fine. Don't worry, okay? The medicine will take care of it.'

A sudden lump in her throat meant Nirmala could not speak. Looking down quickly, she held open her bag for Varun to put his sweets inside. They walked slowly to the door, but before stepping outside, Nirmala turned and started to lift her hand to wave goodbye. It froze when she saw the expression of profound sadness depicted on Sudhir's face. Immediately, he rearranged his expression and smiled as he returned her wave. Nirmala sighed, wondering why fate had dealt them both such a bitter blow.

Chapter 9

Children were already pouring out of the school gate when Nirmala arrived with Varun. A few rushed out excitedly, bumping into the small crowd waiting patiently on the pavement. Others dawdled as they made their way outside, chatting noisily with one another. Some of them were talking on their smart phones as they ambled along.

The youngest children waited behind the metal railings which enclosed the front courtyard and main building. A few teachers stood with them, making sure they did not stray or run out. When the little ones saw their families enter through the gate, their faces lit up. Nirmala saw them being scooped into loving arms or patted on the head before being taken by the hand and led away.

Varun was looking eagerly through the railings for any sign of Hema. 'There she is, Mumma! There's Hema-*masi*.'

Nirmala followed his gaze and smiled when she saw the diminutive young woman wearing a blue *salwar kameez*. Guarding the small children, Hema waited patiently outside the double-door entrance of the building.

Nirmala took hold of Varun's hand and pushed forward against the tide of children leaving the school. When they reached the group, Varun wrapped his arms around Hema, who he considered the best aunt in the world. She yelped with joy and hugged him back.

'Hi, Hema. Hope it's okay for us to come and see you.'

'Of course it's okay! School's finished. I was going to come over to yours this evening anyway.'

'Were you? Why?'

'Just to invite you both for lunch this Sunday. Are you free?'

'I think so. But what's the occasion?'

'No occasion. Just want to spend some time with you and Varun. And there's something I want to talk to you about.'

Nirmala's attention was on Varun's happy face. She could hardly believe how ill he had been just that morning. She frowned as she thought of the doctor's diagnosis.

'What is it?' Hema asked.

Shaking her head, Nirmala took a deep breath. 'Do you have a few minutes now?'

'Yes, sure. As soon as these little ones are picked up, we can go to the infants' playground to chat.'

It wasn't long before they were seated together on a bench in the play area. Varun was happy on the swings, slides and other outdoor equipment. He was delighted to have it all to himself.

Keeping one eye on him, Nirmala began to give Hema an update of all the news on Varun's condition. She went into detail about the visit to the doctor, Ajay's reaction, and her worries about finding the money to pay for the treatment. When she reached the part about collecting the medicine and seeing Sudhir, she found herself overcome with emotion.

'It's okay, Nirmala. You don't need to hold back when you are with me. Let it all out.' Hema put an arm round her shoulder. Not wanting Varun to see how upset she was, Nirmala willed herself not to cry. But with tears blurring her vision, she could not prevent a huge sob escaping her lips. The enormity of the challenges she was facing, together with her sadness over Sudhir suddenly seemed too much to bear, and Nirmala buried her face in Hema's shoulder and wept silent tears.

It wasn't the first time Hema had lent her a shoulder to cry on, and Nirmala knew she was fortunate to have such a good friend. Her unfailing support always seemed to make things better. When she was feeling more in control, Nirmala checked on Varun. He was still happily at play. Giving Hema a teary smile, she reached for her handbag to find a handkerchief to dry her face.

When she unzipped the bag, she saw the white envelope addressed to her father, and realised she had forgotten all about it. Her curiosity was aroused once again. Pulling it out, she handed it to Hema, before wiping her tears and blowing her nose.

'What is this?' asked Hema, puzzled.

'Someone from Africa has written to my Pappa. I don't know who.'

'And you haven't opened it to find out?'

'I haven't had time!' Nirmala blew out her cheeks. Giving Hema a tight smile, she said, 'Let's read it together.'

Hema was frowning, concern written all over her face.

'It's okay,' Nirmala told her. 'I'm all right now. I was just overwhelmed with everything that happened today.' She stared at the envelope. 'Go on. You read it.'

'Okay. If you are sure . . .'

Hema gave her a final, searching look before carefully tearing open the envelope and removing the sheet of white paper from inside. It was a single page letter written in neat handwriting with a blue ink pen. Hema cleared her throat, then read out loud the sender's details at the top, followed by the contents of the letter.

Dear Suresh-kaka

Please forgive me for writing to you out of the blue like this, but I have only recently found out that we are related. From documents we have been shown, I've learned that my father, whose name was Dalpat Dayal, was your first cousin. My grandfather, Mohanlal, and your father, Harilal, were real brothers.

If this is a shock to you, as it was for us, I apologise. But I had to get in touch. You see, Mohan-dada passed away last year and left us with some surprising information. From his will and other legal papers, we have discovered that not only did he have close family in Navsari, but also property. The documents indicate that he was the owner of the building at this address. And now, as part of my inheritance, Suparna Mansions has been passed down to me.

I understand that although Mohan-dada owned the mansion, he wanted his younger brother Harilal to take care of it by letting it out, collecting the rent and living there with his family free of charge. It was a mutual understanding between brothers.

Naturally, this has come as a huge surprise, and we are keen to know if you are aware of all this. I know that your father Harilal passed away some time ago. When he did, am I right in thinking that you took over the responsibility of looking after the property? If so, please be assured that I have no intention whatsoever of making any changes to the arrangements.

My reason for writing is simply to connect with family that I never knew I had. I am very curious to know why Mohan-dada never said anything to us about your family, his close relatives, and also about Suparna Mansions. I am hoping you will have some idea.

If this letter reaches you safely, please do reply, either by post or email as per contact details above. I am also happy to telephone you directly if you would send me your number.

It would be wonderful to hear from you and I look forward to receiving your response.

With best wishes

Pramod Dayal

For a moment, neither of them spoke. They looked at one another in shocked silence. Hema puffed up her cheeks and exhaled noisily. Nirmala stared at her, dumbfounded. She could feel her heart pounding in her chest. The news was impossible to absorb. She opened her mouth to speak then clamped it shut again. Shaking her head in disbelief, she took the letter into her own hands and read it aloud slowly. But it still made no sense.

'There must be some mistake,' she said at last. 'Pappa never mentioned any family outside India. And he told me that *his* father owned Suparna Mansions which he passed on to Jasu-*foi*.'

'Let me read the letter again,' said Hema, taking it back. Nirmala sat still, watching Varun absentmindedly. Her thoughts were all in a muddle. How could a stranger from a far-away land claim to be her father's nephew? And then to say Suparna Mansions did not belong to her grandfather. It was inconceivable.

Hema was deep in thought. Eventually, she said, 'This is mind-blowing. Just think, Nirmala. If this is true, then everything could change for you.'

'What do you mean?'

'Well. For a start, it means you have more family than you thought. And maybe, just maybe, your horrible Jasu-*foi* is not the landlady that she thinks she is. This letter suggests that Jasu-*foi*'s father, Harilal, your grandfather, was just the caretaker of Suparna Mansions, not the owner. It was not his or his wife's mansion to bequeath to anyone. So your grandmother Kanta could not legally leave it to Jasu-*foi*.'

Nirmala tried to digest this. Could this really be possible? She frowned as she concentrated, then screwed up her eyes as if dazzled by the sun.

'I can't believe it. I just can't. This must be some kind of scam. How can someone come out of nowhere to say he is a distant cousin and that he is the rightful owner of the mansion. It just doesn't make sense.'

They both sat quietly for a while, allowing the contents of the letter to sink in. Then, taking Nirmala's hand in her own, Hema said wisely, 'I think there is a lot more to this story. And you need to find out all there is to know.'

'But how? The only person I can ask is Jasu-*foi*. And if my father didn't know all this, his sister won't know either. Besides, she doesn't really talk to me.'

Hema rolled her eyes. 'She thinks she's so high and mighty, that one, but she's just a shrivelled-up old *daakan*, a witch.'

Nirmala gave her a warning look. Hema held up her hands in surrender.

'Okay, okay. But think, Nirmala. She's not the only person you can ask. There is someone else.'

Nirmala was incapable of thinking clearly. From under furrowed brows, she implored her friend to help her out. Hema held out the letter, pointing at the name of the sender.

'Pramod Dayal. He's the one you have to talk to.'

Nirmala still looked confused.

'You can contact him. He wants you to. He doesn't know you, but he knows of your Pappa.'

Nirmala took the letter and stared at the name: Dayal. That had been *her* surname before she married Ajay.

'You can reach him very easily.' Hema spoke as if talking to a small child. 'Come to my house, use our computer, and send him an email.'

Nirmala blinked and considered her next move. She looked at Varun, who was now sitting on the rails of the merry-go-round which was spinning very slowly. He looked tired and was probably hungry.

'No. I can't do that. I just can't. I don't know this man. How can I email him?'

Hema pursed her lips. 'Come on, Nirmala. You've got to. Why are you so scared? You never used to be like this.'

Nirmala breathed in deeply and looked away. Her friend was always telling her to speak up more and not be submissive, especially with Ajay.

'Are you going to tell Ajay?' Hema's voice was low.

Nirmala hesitated, giving her answer serious reflection. This was undoubtedly news that she should share with her husband. But Ajay was not easy to talk to. She knew he would jump to conclusions and expect her to confront her aunt Jasumati. His first thoughts would be of potential financial gain for the family.

'No. I can't tell him anything about this. You know what he's like.'

'Only too well. That *daaku* will only see how he can profit from this. You mustn't tell him. Why don't you come over later tonight and we can talk. That's if you don't mind Ashvin knowing.'

Nirmala considered before speaking. 'Ashvin might be able to help as he is a lawyer. Maybe he can give me some professional advice.' Giving Hema a watery smile, she returned the letter and envelope to her handbag and stood up. 'It's getting late. I must take Varun home.'

Hema put a hand on Nirmala's arm. 'Please come to ours tonight. There's something I need to tell you. It's about Ajay.'

Nirmala puckered her eyebrows. 'What about him?' When Hema did not reply, she sighed. 'Is this another complaint about him being rude to someone? If it is, I don't want to hear it. I have too much on my mind right now.'

Hema gave her a rueful smile. Nirmala hugged her, then called out to her son. He came running straight away, eager now to get home.

Hema looked fondly at him and said, 'I'm making *pau bhaji* for lunch on Sunday. Will that do?'

'Yay, *pau bhaji*. My favourite!'

Hema laughed as she gave him a quick squeeze. Nirmala headed out towards the gate, but she looked back to mouth the words *thank you*, before disappearing behind the school building.

Chapter 10

Ajay was on his sewing machine when Nirmala arrived with Varun. Silently, they moved past him, knowing better than to disturb him at his work. But he looked up when Varun went by.

'You see how hard I have to work for your medicines? They cost a lot of rupees you know.'

Varun stopped and looked up timidly. Nirmala tutted and drew him close, smoothing back his hair.

'It's okay, *dikra*,' she soothed. 'You go on. Go and rest for a little while.'

She smiled at him, but inside, she was fuming. Her husband's snide remarks were fine when directed at her. But not when he frightened their son.

'Did you have to say that? Look how scared he is. Why can't you be nice sometimes?' She spoke quietly, but with suppressed anger.

'I'm not here to be nice to anyone. You can see how busy I am, working day and night to put food into your mouths.' He scowled at her, then picked up his tailoring scissors to cut off the thread ends.

Nirmala clenched her jaw. She did not want to argue with him but felt compelled to remind him that there was a solution to their problem.

Lifting her chin, she spoke in a low, exasperated voice: 'I have told you so many times that if you would only agree to look after Varun, I could go out to work and bring in some extra money.'

'And I have told you it is not my job to look after him!' Ajay slapped the scissors down on the sewing machine as he shouted, spittle spraying from his mouth. He was a tall man with long limbs on a thin frame. His jet-black hair was slicked back with coconut oil and his bushy eyebrows were drawn together over angry, flashing eyes.

Nirmala stood still. She was not afraid of him, but she knew there was no point in arguing. It only served to increase his anger. She stared back at him and felt her fury drain away to be replaced by frustration and sadness. She wished they could be like other couples who were able to make each other happy. After an arranged marriage, love was supposed to follow. She had seen it happen all around her. But in their case, love had never even made an appearance.

He'd been cheerful enough on the day Jasu-*foi* had brought him to her home with his proposal of marriage. And he'd behaved impeccably. But it had all been an act to impress her. It wasn't long before she realised that his aim had been to leave behind the poverty of his home in the nearby village. By marrying Nirmala, he was not only moving up the social ladder but also moving in with someone who owned her own home.

Nirmala sighed. She couldn't really blame him for wanting to move up in the world. But she wished he would treat her with respect and be kind to his son. It wasn't too much to ask. Shaking her head, she looked away.

'Okay, Ajay. Just forget it. I will find a job in June when Varun starts school.'

Leaving him scowling, she walked into the back room where Varun was sitting on his bed, looking anxious. She smiled broadly and gathered him up in her arms.

'It's okay. There's nothing to worry about. Come on, smile. Food will be ready soon and, in the meantime, I think you can open one of the presents you got today.'

He looked puzzled. 'What presents?'

'Have you forgotten, *dikra*? Didn't you get some presents from the pharmacy?'

His face lit up. 'The lollipops. All different colours!'

Nirmala held her handbag open. 'Here you are.'

Varun pulled out the lollipops with eagerness, taking the one with the red wrapper and putting the other two under his pillow. Nirmala watched the delight on his face as he unwrapped the colourful paper before licking the sweet juicy sugar ball on a stick.

Although they would soon be eating their evening meal, she was happy for Varun to enjoy the treat. He needed cheering up. Putting her handbag away in the wardrobe, she walked through to the kitchen. The window above the sink was open and a pleasant early evening breeze touched her warm cheeks. A faint smell of jasmine wafted in from the climbing vine that was still blooming along the side wall. Nirmala breathed in deeply, happy in the knowledge that there would be more flowers and perfume in the months to come.

She looked over at the sacred *tulsi* she had planted in a large terracotta pot right in the centre of their small courtyard. Although some green leaves had sprouted promisingly, this holy basil was not thriving as it should. Nirmala remembered her mother's beautiful *tulsi* with its aromatic, spicy scent.

'If you care for it lovingly and worship it every day, it will protect us from evil and bring our family good luck,' she had said.

Nirmala was trying hard to do that. Almost every Hindu family she knew had healthy *tulsis* in their homes. She had heard that women grew them to keep their husbands contented. For some reason, her *tulsi* had never been able to flourish. Maybe that's why Ajay never seems to be happy, she thought.

Her eyes wandered to their bathroom and toilet at the back of the yard. They were in dire need of repair and renovation. Built before her birth, they had served the family well. But now the plumbing needed attention and several parts required replacing.

Negative thoughts. Stop it, she chided herself. Another one of her mother's quotes came to mind: 'Remember there is always someone worse off than you.'

With a sigh, she tied an apron round her waist and inspected all the different lentils lined up on her shelf. They were in glass jars of all shapes and sizes. Which one should she cook today? The green *moong* daal was out of the question because they'd had this for two days in a row. The red *mesoor* daal was a problem because Ajay was not fond of it. The yellow split *chana* was her favourite, but Varun was not too keen.

The black *arad* daal would be a good choice. But did she have enough yogurt to go with it? Lifting the lid of her pot, she was disappointed. She had forgotten to make some the night before. Plain yogurt was a staple in her house, and she regularly made it by boiling milk, adding leftover yogurt and leaving it to set overnight. It was too expensive to buy these days; the price had gone up to almost fifty rupees for a litre packet.

She missed her old fridge which they had sold when money was tight after Varun's birth. She reflected for a moment on that painful period in her life.

'Your blood pressure is too high,' the midwife had told her when she was writhing in pain in hospital. 'You have to have a Caesarean section. If you get eclampsia, you and your baby could die.'

The operation and postnatal medical fees had gobbled up all that had remained of her inheritance fund. Nirmala often wondered what her father would have thought of the way his savings had simply drained away after his death. He had intended it for her university fees. But her dream of a career in the IT world had come crashing down around her. Most of the money went on the treatment and care needed for her mother, whose condition had worsened with a second stroke after her father's passing.

Nirmala wiped her face with the end of her *odhani*, as if by doing so, she could wipe away the memory of her mother's suffering. She had cooking to do.

It wasn't long before the house was filled with the pungent aroma of tasty *daal*. Nirmala had learned from her mother how to use just the right amount of fresh ginger, garlic and green chillies. Lured by the smell, Varun walked in to announce that he was very hungry.

'It's ready, *dikra*. Come, help me with the table.'

Pulling the lightweight table away from the wall, they set out two plates with matching bowls. Ajay preferred to eat later, so there was no point in calling him. He also insisted on eating in old-fashioned thalis, not these beautiful plates which were Nirmala's mother's cherished Corelle set, still going strong after nearly twenty years.

'Wash your hands before you sit,' she instructed. Ladling the *daal* into the bowls, she placed one *rotli* on each plate and left the pot of warm rice in the centre of the table. Sitting beside Varun, she watched him tucking in, making no complaints about having lentils again. It moved her to tears to see how resigned he was. Shamefully, she remembered how fussy she had been at his age.

No lentils tomorrow, she resolved. She would buy vegetables from the market with what remained of her shopping money. Normally, the money Ajay gave her was enough to provide them with a reasonably varied diet. But in recent months, there had been a steady decline in the amount of cash handed over.

'It's not *my* fault I don't have more rupees this week,' he had thundered when she questioned him. 'Go and blame all the sari shops selling ready-made blouses. Can't you see they are taking away my business?'

Nirmala had her doubts about this. Made-to-measure sari blouses were as popular as ever and there were plenty of ladies' tailors earning good money from their trade. When she'd pointed this out, Ajay had flown into a rage.

'Do you think I am hiding rupees from you? Huh? Do you think I am spending it on whiskey?' Bringing his face close to hers, he said what he always said when they quarrelled over money: 'If you want more rupees, go and ask your rich Jasu-*foi* across the road.'

Nirmala shook her head, as if to dispel the memory of the argument. She concentrated on Varun eating his *daal*.

'Can we go to Saleji-*dada* tonight, Mumma? I want to hear his stories.'

'Maybe. If you're sure he'll be there.'

'It's Friday. He's there every Friday.'

Nirmala had no objection to him going to sit around the old man's *jhula* while he read or told stories to the children of the neighbourhood. She had often done that herself when she was little. She used to love his fantastical tales about magicians, kings and queens, witches, demons, mystical animals and more. Waving his hands around theatrically, he made funny faces to entertain his young audience. She remembered how he had them in stitches by neighing like a horse whenever he laughed himself.

He was over ninety years old, but it seemed to Nirmala that he was still strong and healthy. His voice was a little wobbly, but he had lost none of his warmth and passion for storytelling. Her father, Suresh, had told her that even when he had been a child, Saleji-*dada* had held court from his *jhula*. Nirmala calculated that he was older than Suparna Mansions, so he must have been one of the first tenants.

With a jolt, she realised that he must have known his landlord, her grandfather Harilal. Was it possible that he knew something about Harilal's mysterious brother in Zimbabwe?

She became excited as she thought about this. She had to ask him. Nirmala knew certain details about her parents' relatives. But perhaps Saleji-*dada* could tell her something new. Turning to Varun, she said, 'Okay. Let's go over together.'

'You want to hear the stories too?' Varun's eyes were wide, surprise covering his beautiful little boy features.

Nirmala laughed and kissed his cheek. 'I just want to speak to Saleji-*dada*. We'll go before seven o' clock, and when he starts reading, I'll come home and you can stay till the end.'

With the meal over, they washed up and got ready to go out. Ajay was now sitting quietly on the *jhula,* drinking his usual evening glass of whiskey and smoking his *beedi* cigarettes. Even though they were short of money, she knew he would not give these up. She also knew that he was drinking more than just one glass each evening, though he took pains to hide this fact from her.

'I'm taking Varun across to Saleji-*dada*,' she told him. Without looking at her, he grunted in reply.

The old man was already chatting with the early birds seated cross-legged before him.

She greeted him with folded palms. '*Namaste Dada*. How are you?'

'I'm fine, *beta*. Is everything all right?'

'Yes. I just wanted to ask you something.'

'Come and sit with me.'

She joined him on the *jhula* and said, '*Dada*. You know the letter addressed to Mr Suresh Dayal, my father? The one you sent with your great-grandson? Well, it came as a very big surprise to me. It is from Africa from someone who says my father Suresh was his uncle.'

He gazed at her with a puzzled expression.

'Do you know if my Harilal-*dada* had a brother who lived in Africa?'

The old man frowned and shook his head. 'I didn't think he had any brothers. Or even sisters. I know your grandmother Kanta had a brother.'

'No. This man from is from Zimbabwe and he says his grandfather Mohanlal was the older brother of my father's father, Harilal-*dada*. Did anyone ever mention we had family connections outside India?'

'No. I can't remember anyone saying that.'

She watched him concentrate, thinking deeply before speaking. 'I can tell you one thing. Yesterday, when I saw the foreign stamps on the envelope, I remembered that Harilal used to receive many of those from abroad. The postman sometimes asked me to hold on to them if no one was upstairs. That was a long time ago.'

Nirmala's heart began to race. 'Were they from Zimbabwe?'

'No.' His eyebrows furrowed. 'Not Zimbabwe.'

'Oh.' Nirmala felt crushed.

'I remember the stamps. They were beautiful. I was a collector at one time. The ones I loved most were large and full of colour.' Saleji-*dada*'s eyes became dreamy.

'What sort of pictures were on the stamps?'

'The ones for your grandfather?'

Nirmala felt a growing sense of impatience. She wanted the conversation to speed up.

'Yes, *Dada*. Can you remember the pictures on the stamps?'

'Oh yes. Wild animals. I remember lions, giraffes, hippopotamuses. And images of the British Royal family.'

A sudden thought occurred to Nirmala. 'Do you still have those stamps?'

'*Na*.' The old man shook his head with a rueful smile. 'Too long ago.'

Disappointed, Nirmala turned away. They sat side by side, rocking gently. The old man was lost in thought. Suddenly, he said, 'Rhodesia. They were from Southern Rhodesia.'

Slowly, Nirmala realised what this meant. 'Wasn't that the old name for Zimbabwe?' She watched him smile as he nodded.

Nirmala let out a sigh of relief. Clearly her grandfather Harilal *had* received letters from Zimbabwe. Surely this confirmed the family connection in that country so far away.

'I just don't understand why no one told us. Why keep it secret?'

He turned his wrist with fingers splayed, the Indian hand gesture which meant *I don't know*. They both became silent as they reflected on the implications of what they had gleaned.

The noise level had risen considerably with more children arriving. Nirmala stood up. 'Your little followers are getting restless.'

He looked fondly at her, then turned away, but not before she saw the cloud that passed over his face.

'What is it, *Dada*?'

The old man shook his head and sighed. 'I can never forget the day little Pushpa drowned in Dudhiya Talav. Your father Suresh was just a boy, and when his sister died, it changed him forever. From a happy, noisy child, he became so quiet, hardly speaking to anyone.'

Nirmala watched his body sag with the memory. She knew all about her aunt's drowning in the lake. Her father's survivor-guilt had never left him. Seeing the old man look so sad, she touched him lightly on his arm.

'You mustn't worry. Look. You have a big crowd tonight.'

He looked at the group waiting eagerly for him to start. 'You know, your father and your two aunties used to come every Friday to listen to my stories. Then you started to come. And now, it's your little boy.' He smiled at Varun and got a shy smile back in return. 'He is a good boy.'

Sensing the old man was ready to begin, the group of children at his feet began to chant loudly: *Namaste Dada*.

'I'd better go.' Nirmala thanked him with joined palms and made her way through the group, touching Varun on the shoulder as she passed. At the gate, she turned around and was pleased to see the old man looking jolly once again.

Walking home, she thought about what she had learned. The fact that there were previous letters from Zimbabwe must mean that the contents of this new letter were true. Her grandfather probably did have a brother living in Zimbabwe. But why keep it a secret? Was there a big fallout between the brothers, resulting in a terrible rift? And were her father and Jasumati aware of this? Maybe there was a link between this secret and the frosty relationship between her father and his sister.

Nirmala wondered about asking her Jasu-*foi*. But if it was true that she was not the real owner of Suparna Mansions, it might be better to say nothing to her at this stage. She had to be sure of the facts, and there was only one way to do this.

Chapter 11

Nirmala woke up to the sound of birds chirping on the electricity lines running along the street. She lay still, listening to the early-morning noises of the town getting ready for a new day. A feeling of anticipation crept over her, filling her with a sense that something important was going to happen. Slowly, her thoughts turned to the astonishing news she had received the day before. Excitement fluttered through her.

Carefully, so as not to waken Ajay, she stood up from the roll-up mattress on the floor. Padding through the house, she stopped at the kitchen window and looked out at the yard, her mind on the events of the previous day. The house was silent. Nirmala began to think about all her tasks for the day. There was a lot to do so she roused herself to have her bath, get ready and begin her chores.

Half an hour later, she was washing down the stonework in the yard when Ajay stepped out. He made a face when his feet touched the wet surface.

'Why must you start your cleaning so early in the morning? Can't you wait till I'm gone?'

Nirmala pursed her lips, sorely tempted to splash some water directly at him. But knowing how that would go down, she gritted her teeth and looked at him with a face devoid of expression.

He clicked his tongue in annoyance, then walked past her to perform his morning ablutions. It was Saturday, so he would be out all day. He spent every weekend with a group of like-minded men, playing cards, going to the cinema, drinking and doing whatever it was that men did when they were out together. Nirmala was only too happy with this arrangement because it kept him occupied outside the house and out of her hair.

When Varun was up, she told him to get ready quickly as she was taking him out. For breakfast, she made *chaa* and *masala thepla*, the tasty flatbread that was quick and easy to prepare. After tidying the house, they were ready to leave just after 11 a.m.

'Are we going to the market, Mumma?'

'No. We're going first to the *mandir* for prayers, then to Hema-*masi*'s house.'

Varun looked puzzled, then burst into giggles. 'Silly Mumma! We are going there tomorrow, not today. You forgot.'

'Very funny.' She reached out to tickle his tummy, making him shriek with laughter. 'I didn't forget. I need to see her today also. Come, let's go.'

She locked the windows and doors and stepped off the porch without looking ahead. In her haste, she crashed into a woman standing right in front of her house, sending her shopping bag flying out of her hand.

'*Arey, arey, arey!*' The woman was waving her arms, trying to keep her balance.

'*Hai Ram!*' Nirmala eyes were on the woman's bag. She rushed to pick it up.

'For God's sake, Nirmala.' The woman was breathing heavily. 'What's the big hurry?'

Surprised at hearing her name, she looked properly at the short, plump woman who was glaring at her accusingly. It was Chanda, one of the mothers she had befriended at the school gate.

'I'm sorry. I didn't see you there.'

'No, because you are in too much of a hurry. Hurry, hurry, and spoil your curry!' She let out a shrill laugh at her own joke, clutching at Nirmala's arm. 'I was just coming to see if Varun would like to come and play with my son this afternoon. Guests are coming for dinner, and I will be very busy cooking. So, I thought it would be nice for my Naveen to have his friend over.'

Varun whooped with delight and pulled at Nirmala's *odhani* excitedly. He loved going to Chanda's house where there was an abundance of toys and games.

Nirmala smiled. 'That's very kind, Chanda. If you are sure he won't be in the way, I will bring him to yours later.'

Chanda was pleased. 'You must stay for lunch; I made ragda patties.'

Nirmala laughed. There was no doubting Chanda's love for cooking and feeding. She took offence if people declined her invitations to eat her food. Her chubby husband and overweight children were testament to her constant feeding. Everything she made was rich in ghee and calories. Giving Nirmala a quick hug, she hurried away.

The morning prayers were in full swing at the *mandir*. Listening to the singers was a small gathering of men, women and children. Removing their sandals, Nirmala and Varun sat down in front of a beautiful statue of Lord Krishna. He stood tall, holding a flute in his hands and wearing a peacock feather in his golden crown. His skin was the colour of the sea and he was adorned with a golden *dhoti* tied round his waist and a matching scarf over his shoulders. To Nirmala, he exuded compassion, tenderness and love. She closed her eyes and immersed herself in the peace and serenity of worship.

When the prayers ended, Nirmala placed a coin beside the single flame *diva* lamp and bowed her head with her palms joined in prayer. In silence, she asked the Lord to make Varun better.

Chanda's house was a fifteen-minute walk away. They had to tread carefully along the congested main road, which was not only busy with traffic, but also strewn with litter. Despite ubiquitous posters and billboards reminding people to 'Keep India Clean', some residents were still throwing their rubbish out onto the streets. Not to mention the dog mess and cow dung left on the side of the road. Nirmala wrinkled up her nose at the nasty smell, making Varun laugh at her grimace.

Eventually, they turned into a quiet street with shady trees and large houses behind gates. Nirmala stopped beside a wrought-iron gate beyond which they could see a small blue car. Lifting the latch, they opened the gate and walked up the small driveway, past the little garden in the front, and up to the porch with the obligatory *jhula.* Nirmala lifted the brass knocker on the front door, rapping it smartly several times. Chanda let them in.

'Come in, come in,' sang Chanda. 'Naveen is waiting for you in the backyard, Varun. Go and find him.' They watched him skip away happily.

Chanda insisted that Nirmala sit down for a chat. As always, she took control of the conversation, voicing her opinion on the current school politics, bad behaviour of some children, and the dilapidated state of so many buildings in Navsari.

'They are all owned by NRIs, you know. These non-resident Indians buy property in India then go back to their countries without making sure they are looked after. Too much money they have, isn't it?'

When Nirmala could get a word in edgeways, she apologised and told Chanda she could not stay for lunch.

'*Arey,* nah! You have to stay. I've made so much food.'

'It smells delicious. But I really have to go.' Nirmala stood up and began to walk to the door. 'I'll let you get on with your cooking and be back for Varun around five.'

When she was finally able to get away, Nirmala headed out towards Hema's flat. Her thoughts were filled with the mystery surrounding her grandfather's secret family. Today, she would be taking the first step towards solving that mystery.

Although not expecting her, Hema and Ashvin were delighted to see her. They lived in a two-bedroom, self-contained apartment on the third floor of a housing block, with a balcony overlooking the street. The furnishings were contemporary in style and the flat was filled with all the latest electrical and electronic devices. Ashvin had a passion for computers and all things digital.

'Bought any new toys recently?' Nirmala asked with arched eyebrows.

'Unfortunately, no. I want to buy a GoPro camera, but Hema won't let me,' he said with a rueful grin.

Hema rolled her eyes, making Nirmala laugh. 'No relatives this weekend? You usually have someone or other staying with you.'

'Thank God everyone is busy.' Ashvin grinned and punched Hema's arm playfully. 'Gives us a chance to be alone, doesn't it?'

'Stop it,' she scolded, pulling away.

Nirmala watched them with affection. They were like two peas in a pod. Both were short, slim and dark in complexion, with thick wavy hair. She had always envied Hema's hair; she was reminded of her father's curly head. She wished she had inherited those curls. Those, and his beautiful grey-green eyes. Her mother, Tara, had told her that it was his eyes that had first attracted her to Suresh. They were such an unusual colour. Nirmala's own eyes were like Tara's: dark brown. She looked a lot like her mother, with delicate facial features and high cheekbones.

What she had inherited from Suresh was his height. Nirmala was taller than most Gujarati women and also some of the men. It was the first thing people noticed about her. 'You should take up modelling,' she was often told. 'You would look great walking up and down the catwalk wearing all those beautiful outfits.'

'So,' began Ashvin. 'You had some surprising news yesterday.'

'Yes. And I need your professional advice. Here's the letter.'

She handed it over and watched him put on his spectacles to read it. His face was inscrutable. When he finished, he placed it on the coffee table and sat looking at it pensively.

'Well? What do you think?' Nirmala asked.

'I think it's very curious.'

'But do you think it's true?'

'Which part?' His face was deadpan.

Nirmala and Hema looked at each other, confused.

'What do you mean, WHICH PART?' Hema almost yelled at her husband.

'I mean which part? The part about the family connection, or the part about the ownership of Suparna Mansions?'

'Both parts!' the women shouted in unison.

Ashvin held up his hands, laughing out loud.

'Calm down, you two. Okay. I think it is possible your grandfather had a brother abroad, but I'm not sure about the property rights. It's a valuable asset. I would have thought that someone with a claim to it would have asserted their rights before now.'

Ashvin looked down at the letter and tapped the coffee table with his fingers. He seemed to be mulling something over.

'What is it?' asked Hema.

'There is something we have to consider here. Under certain conditions, it is possible for people to lose ownership over their property if someone else has been living there for a long time. But it's a long and complicated process for anyone wanting to go down that route.'

Nirmala raised her eyebrows. 'You mean this Pramod-*bhai* might not be able to claim ownership after all this time?' Ashvin nodded. 'But what if there was an agreement, like in this case? The two brothers, Mohanlal and Harilal had an understanding.'

'I'm not sure. Do we know if they really were brothers?'

'I think they were.' Nirmala looked earnest. 'Yesterday I learned something that makes me certain of it.' She explained the details of her conversation with Saleji-*dada* the previous night.

'So there *were* letters coming from Zimbabwe.' Hema looked thoughtful.

'I've been thinking and thinking about this,' said Nirmala. 'They must have stopped when Harilal-*dada* died. The question I keep asking myself is, if this letter had been delivered to Jasu-*foi* yesterday, would she have passed it on to me?'

Her friends exchanged a look. Nirmala was aware they had little time for her aunt.

Hema raised her eyebrows. 'I bet that *daakan* has been keeping a lot of things from you.'

Ashvin frowned. 'Hema, please! There's no need to be rude.'

'You are not thinking of telling her, are you?' Hema asked Nirmala with concern.

'I'm not sure.'

Ashvin cleared his throat. 'If I were in your shoes, I would first try to find out what is true and what is not. The person who wrote this letter has given you his email address. Send him a message, and you will soon know if this is all a big lie. You still have your email address, haven't you?'

'I do. But I haven't used it for years.'

'Then it's probably expired,' said Hema. 'You can use mine.'

Nirmala shook her head slowly. 'I don't know.'

Hema tutted and stood up. 'You are such a scaredy-cat! Come with me,' she ordered. Walking over to a sideboard in her dining room, she picked up a laptop sitting to one side. She placed it on the table, flipped up the lid and sat down in front of it. After logging on, she moved away and insisted that Nirmala took her place.

'Here you are. Start composing your email.'

Still looking doubtful, Nirmala sat down and faced the screen. She thought for a long minute, then hesitantly began typing. Hema patted her shoulder and walked away, leaving her friend to start an email dialogue with her cousin.

Chapter 12

Dear Pramod-bhai

Your letter of 15th January 2016 addressed to my father, Mr Suresh Dayal, came as a big surprise. It was given to me because he passed away in 2002. My mother died in 2006 and I am an only child.

I have no memories of my grandfather Harilal, who died before I was born. If he had an older brother living abroad, it is strange that my parents did not mention it to me.

My father grew up in Suparna Mansions, but he moved out when he got married. His sister, my Jasu-foi, is the current owner and landlady. It is she who inherited the property, not my father. Right now, she does not know about your letter. Before she is told, I think it would be wise to make sure you have conclusive evidence to substantiate your claims.

I look forward to hearing from you.

Kind regards

Nirmala Darzi

'Does this sound too rude?' Nirmala asked Hema, who was reading over her shoulder.

'No. It's just right; short and to the point. Send it off. You can bombard him with questions later.'

Nirmala pressed SEND. In seconds, a text appeared on the screen: *Your message has been sent.*

'Right,' said Ashvin from the front room. 'Now you just have to wait.'

'I wonder what time it is in Zimbabwe?' mused Hema. 'Let's google it.'

Nirmala opened a new tab and typed *time in India and Zimbabwe.* As soon as she pressed *Enter,* they got their answer:

India is 3 hours and 30 minutes ahead of Zimbabwe

15.26 Saturday in India is

11.56 Saturday in Zimbabwe

'It's still early there, so he might reply today,' said Hema. 'Let's check the distance between the countries.'

Google informed them that they were 6,983 kilometres apart.

'That's far.' Nirmala chewed her lower lip as they stared at the screen. 'Why would two brothers want to live so far apart?'

'You are not going to find the answer on Google!' called Ashvin. He looked at his watch. 'I need to go out for a while, so I'll leave you two alone now. I'm sure you have a lot to talk about.'

Nirmala caught a look pass between them and wondered what silent message they were giving each other. She loved them dearly but couldn't help being envious of their intimacy.

'Come on,' said Hema when he was gone. 'Let's go and relax. But leave the computer on, just in case . . .'

She poured two glasses of cold coconut water from a carton in the fridge and they made themselves comfortable on the sofa.

'I'll need to go soon to pick up Varun.'

'There's plenty of time. It's not even four o' clock yet.'

'Yes, but I worry about Varun. I don't like to be away from him for too long. We never know when he will have another fit.'

'Tell me about that, Nirmala. What actually happens?'

Nirmala sighed. 'His body doesn't shake or jerk like a proper epileptic fit. But he sometimes starts breathing very fast, then stops talking or whatever he is doing and just stares into space. When we speak to him, he doesn't answer, like he can't hear us. They call it childhood absence epilepsy.'

'How long does it go on for?'

'Sometimes for a whole minute. When he comes out of it, he feels so weak that he needs to lie down. It doesn't happen too often, but I'm scared it's going to get worse.'

'That's worrying. What does Ajay say?'

Nirmala tutted. 'He makes me so angry! He thinks Varun is just being naughty; deliberately playing dumb to annoy us. He seems to have it in for Varun. And he complains about the cost of the medicines. Can you believe that?'

Hema took Nirmala's hand in hers and stared at it. After a while, she raised her head and said, 'There's something you need to know about Ajay. I've been trying to tell you for a while now, but you keep putting me off.'

Nirmala closed her eyes. She braced herself for one of Hema's pep talks on how she should be more assertive with Ajay.

'You're not going to complain about him again, are you?'

'No. But I wish you would send him packing back to the village he came from.'

'You know I can't do that. Varun needs his father.'

'Not a father like that—' Hema began, looking angry. Nirmala gave her a warning look. 'Okay.' Hema took a long sip before venturing further. 'But you do need to hear this.'

Nirmala's heart skipped a beat. What had Ajay done now, she wondered? He had already embarrassed her enough in front of neighbours, who had seen him come home in a drunken stupor many a night. They had also on occasion complained that he had been verbally abusive to their children. She knew he was not a popular man, and she also knew he was not an intelligent man. But he was not a bad person. Whatever his faults, he *was* doing his best to provide for their family, wasn't he?

'He's been seen going in and out of the house of a widow woman near Indira Gandhi Chowk. It seems he spends all his weekends there.' Hema spoke with kindness, stroking Nirmala's hand while looking directly at her.

Nirmala fixed her eyes on her, steady and unwavering. Then she frowned and pulled her hand away, looking hurt.

'How can you say that to me?' Her voice shook with distress. 'It's a lie!'

'Nirmala . . .'

'No! People make things up. You know that.'

Hema pursed her lips and shook her head sadly. 'I'm your best friend, and I wouldn't do anything to hurt you. But it would be wrong of me to keep this from you.'

Nirmala dropped her head, shocked and appalled. Ajay with another woman. Was that possible? Slowly, with a sinking feeling, Nirmala realised that this was definitely possible. It explained why Ajay had become increasingly difficult to live with over recent years.

'I'm sorry, Nirmala, but there's more.'

With dread settling in her stomach, Nirmala looked at Hema's face filled with sadness.

'The widow has a little boy . . . and there are rumours that . . . that Ajay is the father.'

'What?' Nirmala jumped up. 'No!'

Hema stood up too. 'I'm sorry, Nirmala.' Gently she persuaded Nirmala to sit down again. 'I asked Ashvin to investigate.'

Nirmala's heart was thudding; she knew what was coming next.

'He saw them with his own eyes coming out of the widow's little house together. They didn't see him, but he was sorely tempted to confront Ajay there and then. He didn't because he knows it's up to you what happens next.'

With a cold realisation, Nirmala thought about Ajay's hostility towards her, his cruel behaviour towards Varun, his constant irritability and grumpiness. It made perfect sense. Why hadn't she seen this coming?

'Look, Nirmala. You have to handle this very carefully. Is he likely to get violent if you tell him that you know?'

Nirmala dropped her shoulders. 'No. He has never hit me. But . . .'

She gazed out of the window, trying to take it in. How could he do this to her? A mistress and a child! Was it her fault? Did she push him into the arms of another woman?

Hema nudged her. 'What were you going to say? What will he do?'

Nirmala sighed. 'I'm not sure. When he gets angry, he shouts and swears. He becomes nasty and frightens Varun. I can't let that happen.' She closed her eyes. 'I suppose the whole town knows?'

'No, they don't. And you mustn't worry about that.'

'How can I not? It's so embarrassing! And people will be blaming me because it's always the wife's fault, isn't it?' She groaned and sank her head into her hands. 'A child! Oh God. My poor son.' She spoke through her fingers.

Thinking about Varun brought a lump to her throat. Ajay was always finding fault with him, complaining that Varun was too weak, too lazy, too afraid of everything. He was constantly losing his temper.

She remembered how quickly he had flown into a rage the day before when she had talked about getting a job. He did seem more disgruntled recently, especially when they had to discuss money.

Suddenly, an alarming thought struck her. Was he spending their money on this woman and her child? *His* child? Could that be the reason they were so short of cash? Outrage began to build up inside her.

'I have been such a fool,' she said through gritted teeth. 'He's been giving me so little shopping money recently that we have been eating daal and rice every day. Now I know where it's all going.'

She got up and walked to the window where she stood with her hands balled into fists at her sides. Taking deep breaths, she tried to calm the storm building up inside her. This was outrageous; unforgivable. How could she have been so easily deceived? It took all the strength she had to keep her anger in check.

After a while, when she felt more in control of her emotions, Nirmala rejoined Hema on the sofa.

'I should have known this was going on. I should have paid more attention. But it was easier to manage everything without him in the house. I was glad to see him go out and never even questioned him. I feel so stupid.'

'It's he that is stupid, not you.' Hema was furious. 'Stop putting yourself down all the time. You are better than him in every way. Leave him, Nirmala. Send him away. Why you married him, I will never understand.'

Nirmala expelled a breath. 'Let's not go into that again. I told you how it happened. There was no other option for me.' With a deep sigh, Nirmal slumped down into the sofa. 'I have been trying hard to make my marriage work. You know that, don't you? It was Sudhir I wanted to marry, but when I realised that was not possible, I put him out of my mind and changed my whole way of life to fit in with Ajay's wishes. He wanted to be the man of the house, the old-fashioned way, with him making the decisions and me being subservient. I had to learn his mother's ways and be the dutiful daughter-in-law. I did all that, hoping we could have a happy life together. But look what he's done!'

'He's a bastard! I've always thought he was like a *rakshas*, a monster.'

Nirmala breathed out noisily. 'What am I going to do?'

'Whatever you do, be careful.' Hema was concerned. 'I don't trust Ajay. He might try to hurt you.'

Nirmala closed her eyes. 'I won't do anything right away. I need to think this through.' She glanced up at the digital clock on the wall. 'I have to go now.'

'Will you be okay?'

Nirmala nodded and Hema gave her a resigned smile. She looked at the computer. 'I don't suppose you want to see if your cousin Pramod-*bhai* has replied from Zimbabwe?'

Nirmala had lost all interest in the email. Ajay's supreme betrayal was a crushing blow. She could think of nothing else. Hema patted her shoulder sympathetically. 'You'll be careful, won't you?'

'I will.' With a determined effort and heavy heart, Nirmala picked up her bag and stood up. 'I'll see you tomorrow.'

Chapter 13

The next morning, Nirmala watched Ajay carefully for any signs of furtive behaviour. Now that she knew where he was going for the day, she paid extra attention to his movements. But he was the same as always; grumpy and demanding.

While she was completing her chores, she heard him questioning Varun about going to Hema's flat where there were no children for him to play with. He spoke with a sneer in his voice, mocking the couple's childlessness. He was aware that Hema was having problems becoming pregnant. She wanted to lash out at him, tell him to leave her friends alone and call him out for being deceitful. But she was nervous about how he would react. She needed a definite plan of action before she could tackle him.

Varun was excited about going to Hema and Ashvin's apartment, where he was always made to feel special. When they got there, the couple made a great fuss over him. Ashvin, in particular, immediately began to play with him, teasing him and showing him his electronic gadgets. Varun adored him, looking up to him as some sort of superstar. Nirmala watched their excited interaction and wished he had this kind of relationship with Ajay.

'You had a big shock yesterday,' said Hema, her brow furrowed with worry. 'Did you get any sleep?'

Nirmala grimaced. 'No. But let's talk about it later.' She tilted her head towards Ashvin and smiled. 'He's going to be a wonderful father one day.'

Hema sighed. 'Who knows if that will ever happen. Nothing seems to be working for us; not even IVF. Now I'm trying to persuade Ashvin about surrogacy, but he's not keen at all.'

Nirmala looked over at the jumble of arms and legs on the floor where Ashvin wrestled playfully with her son. She knew how desperately her friends wanted children. Perhaps surrogacy *was* the answer for them, as it was for a number of couples she knew who had been through the process. 'Give him time,' she whispered. 'I'm sure he will come round.'

Hema gave her a resigned look before walking to the kitchen. 'Come. Let's get the food out.'

Before long, they were all enjoying tasty, home-made *pau bhaji*, warm bread with plenty of butter piled with tangy, masala potatoes. Nirmala watched Varun tucking in with relish and felt a rush of love for her two special friends. They made life so much more bearable.

'After this, who wants to watch *Harry Potter*?' asked Ashvin, knowing what the answer would be.

'Me, me, me!' came the reply.

It wasn't long before the iconic soundtrack was ringing out and Varun was sitting wide-eyed with Ashvin in front of the DVD player and television screen.

Hema led Nirmala to her spare room. 'Let's go and find some peace.'

The room was small, but light and airy. The windows facing the back were open, letting in a welcome breeze. The cream-coloured walls contrasted with the vibrant red covers on the two single beds. The curtains matched the covers, as did the mat between the beds.

On a bedside table stood a tall lamp with a chrome metal base and conical glass shade. An ornamental tiger, the size of her hand, stood proudly beside the lamp. Unlike the usual tigers coloured bright orange with black stripes, this one was a crystal figurine which seemed to be glowing from inside in shades of red, blue and gold.

Nirmala picked it up and turned it around in her hand, marvelling at the changing colours created by the prism effect.

'I love this tiger of yours.'

Hema looked thoughtful. 'Do you still have those old elephant figures we used to play with?'

'Yes. Why do you ask?'

Hema looked hard at Nirmala. 'We used to wonder about the large ears, remember? Maybe they came from Africa.'

For a moment, Nirmala frowned. When realisation dawned, she laughed. 'Of course! Elephants with large ears. Someone must have sent them or brought them over from Africa.'

Hema grinned, then stretched out on one of the beds. Nirmala did the same on the other bed. For a while, they lay silently, looking up at the crystal ceiling light and listening to the muffled sounds of music and dialogue flowing through from the front room. Then Hema turned on her side.

'You really had no idea about Ajay, did you? I'm sorry I had to tell you.'

'You don't need to be. I'm glad you told me. He has been getting more and more difficult to live with, so I really should have noticed something was not right.'

'Don't start blaming yourself for his disgusting behaviour!'

Nirmala stared up at the ceiling again. She was quiet for a very long time. Her eyelids felt heavy and her body felt like it was sinking into the bed. She imagined a hand stroking her forehead, gently sweeping back her hair. She heard her mother's soft voice and saw her father gazing down at her, his light eyes shining with love. A feeling of calm swept over her, and she closed her eyes.

When she opened them again, she was alone, and the brightness in the room had diminished. Through the open window, Nirmala could still see daylight. She heard the buzzing and whirring sounds of computer games. Moving slowly, she stood up, tidied her hair, straightened her *salwar kameez*, and went to join the others. Varun was engrossed in playing video games with Ashvin, but Hema was in the dining room on the computer.

'You're up.' She pointed to the chair beside her.

'I must have been tired. What time is it?'

'Just after four o'clock.' She tilted her head towards the screen. 'Have a look at this.'

Nirmala arched her eyebrows in surprise. 'I got a reply?'

'You did! Just now.'

With all the distress caused by the news about Ajay's deceit, Nirmala had not given any thought to the message sent to Zimbabwe. She stared at the screen, not immediately focusing on the words. Then she pulled the laptop towards her and began to read.

> *Dear Nirmala*
> *Thank you for your email. It was a pleasure, and relief, to hear from you. I wasn't sure if I was writing to the right person and I was worried about how it might be received.*
>
> *Sorry to hear that both your parents have passed away. My father died of a heart attack many years ago, and last year, my grandfather died at the grand old age of ninety-six.*
>
> *As you say, it is strange that our grandfathers told no one about their relationship. I am very curious about why that should be. I am sifting through*

my Mohan-dada's papers and hoping that something in those will give me a clue.

From this email address, I'm guessing that Hema is your second name? And apart from Jasu-foi, are there any other family members?

Here in Harare, our extended family is huge. I have five uncles and one aunt, each with their own families. We run different branches of the same business. My wife is Reena and our son Hemel works with me at the firm. We are also blessed with twin granddaughters. Reena sends her love and says you and your family must come to visit us.

As regards Suparna Mansions, please do not worry. I have no intention of rocking the boat. We do have evidence of legal ownership, including title deeds, records of registered plot sale, building contracts, receipts and more. But as we do not live there, we will not be claiming our rights over it. And I wouldn't dream of uprooting Jasu-foi. If you could forward me her contact details, I will let her know personally.

Email is quick and easy but talking on the phone is instant. So please let me have your cell or home phone number and I will call at a time convenient for you. It will be good to talk.

With warm regards

Pramod

Nirmala blew out her cheeks and sat back, staring at the email.

'What do you think?' asked Hema.

'I'm not sure what to think.'

Hema tapped on the table with her fingers. 'Well, I think you should send a response right now, giving him our telephone number so he can phone you straight away.'

Nirmala looked alarmed. 'Are you mad? I can't do that.'

'Why not? He sounds really nice. He's even invited you to his country.'

'Huh! As if that could ever happen.'

'Just talk to him, Nirmala. See what he has to say.'

Talking to the man seemed too direct to Nirmala. He was a stranger, even though he might be a cousin.

'I'd be more comfortable sending an email.'

Hema tapped at the screen. 'Fine. I'll leave you to it.'

Nirmala re-read Pramod's email, then began to type.

Dear Pramod-bhai

I am using my friend Hema's computer as I do not have one of my own. And I don't have a cell or home telephone.

It is nice to hear about your family and thank you for inviting us to Zimbabwe. I'm sorry but that will not be possible. We could never afford it and also, our son has health problems.

My husband and I have one son and we live opposite Suparna Mansions in a house where I grew up. Jasu-foi has two married sons with families of their own. They occupy three of the flats in the building, while the remaining five are rented out.

Jasu-foi is my nearest relation but I'm sorry to say we are not close. I know that she will not take kindly to your news about owning the property. If you would like to contact her, you can write to her at the Suparna Mansions address. But if you really have no intention of changing things, then I would suggest you don't mention this to her at all.

With regards to you and your family,

Nirmala

Nirmala read it through once before pressing the SEND button. Then she sat reading Pramod's email again, digesting the fact that he was of the same generation as her, yet already a grandfather. His family sounded very large: five uncles and one aunt, each with families of their own.

Hema came over to join her. 'I'm glad you told him about your Jasu-*foi*. He needs to know what a *daakan* she is.'

'Stop it, Hema,' chided Nirmala.

'But it's true. She is a witch. And from what you've told me, she had her mother wrapped around her little finger.'

Nirmala sighed. 'She definitely was Kanta-*ba*'s favourite. My father didn't get much of a look in. He . . .'

She was interrupted by a sudden 'ping' from the computer. They both turned their heads to the screen. Pramod had sent an instant reply. Hema gave Nirmala a *I told you so* look, then held both hands out to the message.

Sucking in her breath, Nirmala faced the screen and read out loud.

Dear Nirmala

Thanks for the immediate reply. You must be at your friend's house.

Your email has made me wonder about many things such as how old your son is and how serious his health problems are. I would like to help. If there is anything I can do, please do not hesitate to ask.

About your visit to Zimbabwe, it would be my pleasure to finance your trip. And of course you will stay with us. By the grace of God, we are lucky people; we have financial security due to our prosperous commercial companies. I can send you all the plane tickets, so please come over with your husband and son. We have very good doctors here, and maybe your son would benefit from our private healthcare system.

From what you say about Jasu-foi, I will not contact her until I know more about the possible rift between our grandfathers, Mohanlal and Harilal. Forgive me for asking but was there also a rift between your father Suresh and his father Harilal? I only ask because property is normally inherited by sons, not daughters. Not that your aunt Jasumati could have inherited Suparna Mansions because we now know that Harilal was the caretaker, not the owner.

Please do give serious consideration to coming for a few months. While here, you could even help me look through Mohan-dada's papers. Who knows? Together, we might be able to solve the family mystery.

Let me know what you think.

Regards

Pramod

'Wow, Nirmala! You have a fairy godfather.'

'Don't be silly. There's no such thing.'

'Yes, there is! This man is the answer to all your prayers. Finally, things are beginning to look up for you.'

'Wait a minute. You don't seriously think I should accept what he is offering?'

'Why not? He's your cousin and he can help you. That's what families do. They help one other.'

Nirmala shook her head in disapproval. 'No, Hema. Don't say that. I can't accept his help, even if he is my cousin.'

Hema sat back, looking disappointed. Turning her gaze to Varun, she paused a moment then touched Nirmala's arm. 'Don't let your pride get in the way, Nirmala. At least think about it.'

Letting out a deep breath, Nirmala stood up. 'It's too much to take in. And it doesn't seem right. Anyway, I have other things on my mind right now. I need to deal with Ajay. I . . . I'll be in touch.'

For the second day in a row, Nirmala left her friend's apartment with worrying thoughts weighing on her mind. She had to find a way to confront Ajay and do what she could to lighten her mental load.

Chapter 14

The next morning, Nirmala woke up with a pounding headache. All night, she had lain awake, thinking about how she was going to confront Ajay. Mindful of his violent temper, she knew she'd have to be careful, but also strong to stand her ground. Her body ached with exhaustion, but she rolled away from him and got ready, her plan of action prepared.

The first thing she had to do was ask her friend Chanda to look after Varun for a while. She would catch her at the school gates where she was bound to be dropping off her older children. Taking two paracetamol tablets for her headache, she gave Varun his own dose of medicine. By the time they left the house, she felt a little better, though her head still throbbed when she made any sudden movement.

Weaving through heavy traffic, they soon reached the school gates. As she'd expected, Chanda was chatting to a group of other mothers, her shrill voice floating over to where she stood with Varun. Nirmala called out to her and waved. Chanda came immediately.

'What's the matter? Is something wrong?'

'Yes. I have a little problem at home and I wondered if you could look after Varun for a few hours.'

'Of course. Nothing serious, I hope?'

Shaking her head, Nirmala bent down to speak to Varun.

'You need to go with Chanda-*masi* now and I will pick you up later. You'll be a good boy, won't you?' She kept her tone firm so that Varun would know she was not going to brook any argument or dissent.

Chanda held out her hand and hesitantly, he took it. Nirmala smiled her thanks and watched them walk away. Then she turned and retraced her steps towards home.

Ajay was rolling up the mattress and getting the room ready for sewing. When he saw Nirmala, he straightened up and spoke to her in a gruff voice.

'Customers are coming today, and the sari blouses are not ready. You will have to do the hand stitching now.'

Nirmala nodded, then walked through to the kitchen to psych herself up for what she was about to do. She stood still for a moment, thinking about what he had said. He had just given her an order, expecting her to jump to it, like an obedient dog. To her shame, she realised that that was exactly what she always did. By not standing up to him, she had allowed him to become a bully. The thought made her flush with anger, both at herself and him.

Nirmala lifted her chin. This was the moment for her to put her plan into action. He had given her a way in. With her heart racing, she walked back to the front room, doing her best to hide her nervousness.

He was sitting at his sewing machine, sorting out blouse pieces. When Nirmala walked up, he handed her a pile without even looking up.

'Tell me, Ajay,' she asked, almost casually. 'Why are the blouses not ready? What have you been doing?'

His head snapped back, as if she had punched him in the face. He looked at her in disbelief. She saw his expression change to irritation. He stood up slowly, putting his hands on the sewing table, his eyes fixed on Nirmala. Leaning forward, he opened his mouth to say something, but Nirmala got in first.

'I know what you have been doing. You have been chasing after a widow woman in Indira Gandhi Chowk.'

His eyes widened and his jaw dropped. Whatever he was going to say remained frozen in his mouth. But he recovered quickly and drew his lips into a sneer. Standing up, he folded his arms across his chest and snorted scornfully.

Nirmala narrowed her eyes and returned his stare. Keeping her voice strong and steady, she continued. 'You have been sleeping with her.'

There. She had said it. Feeling surprisingly bold, she waited for him to respond.

His mouth twisted into a contemptuous smile. Walking round the sewing machine, he stood in front of her and brought his face close to hers.

'So what if I have,' he rasped menacingly. 'What are you going to do? Stop me?' A bit of spittle flew from his mouth towards her.

Nirmala felt disgusted. She took a step back but held his gaze. Controlling her emotions, she lowered her tone and spoke with calm dignity. 'No. I'm not going to stop you. You can carry on with her. But you are going to leave this house.'

Ajay drew back. He gave a little laugh, full of contempt, then stood smiling at her, his hands on his hips.

Nirmala's voice rose an octave higher. 'I want you to take your things and get out today!'

Ajay stopped smiling. He brought his hands down to his sides and clenched them into tight fists.

'I am not going anywhere,' he said, emphasising every word, eyes flashing.

Nirmala held his gaze. 'You know this house belongs to me. By law, I can ask you to leave anytime. And for what you are doing, committing adultery, I can get a divorce. And I will. But right now, you are going to take what you need and go and live somewhere else. I don't care where.'

She paused to let her words sink in. Ajay's expression had changed. Gone was his anger and contempt. He looked incredulous. Slowly, he turned away and walked back to sit at his sewing machine.

'I found out two days ago,' continued Nirmala. 'I never expected you to do such a thing. It is very hurtful. But most hurtful is that you could take food away from *our* son to feed your *other* child!'

Behind the sewing machine, Ajay was up on his feet again, his face filled with fury.

'Who told you that?' he roared. 'Who told you I have another child?'

From somewhere deep inside, Nirmala found the strength to answer in a calm voice. 'It doesn't matter who told me.'

In a flash, Ajay picked up his large tailoring scissors and strode over to stand menacingly over Nirmala. Alarmed, she took a step back. Fear shot through her body and she felt a sudden tightening in her chest. Ajay was holding the scissors above his head.

'So what if I have another child?' he hissed. 'So what? You can't give me what I want, can you? You are useless, and so is your son. He's weak, like a girl, and sick in the head. What do you expect me to do?'

It was not the first time Ajay had thrown this at her. And every time he did, it was like a blow in the stomach. It hurt deeply and left her seething with rage. But today, he was holding a weapon in his hand, and she felt a paralysing stab of fear run through her.

Leaning back, Nirmala eyed the scissors. A tremor of panic went through her. But she was determined not to show it. Holding her head up, she spoke with a confidence she did not feel. 'So you admit it. You admit you have another child.'

Ajay opened his eyes wide and swore. Grabbing Nirmala's shoulder with his left hand, he brought the scissors down with his other, and held the sharp point at her throat. His face was inches away from hers, his eyes wild, his breath hot and heavy. The panic inside her was threatening to burst its banks. Holding her breath, Nirmala stood statue still. But she kept her eyes on his. He was a huge monster towering over her.

He stood like that for what felt like an age. Then he seemed to deflate, his body shrinking in front of her. Lowering the scissors, he went back to his sewing machine. Relieved beyond measure, Nirmala breathed out.

'There is something else you should know.' She surprised herself by saying something she had not prepared, something she had not decided until that moment. 'A letter arrived last week from a foreign country. I didn't know I had cousins living abroad. They have invited me to visit them.'

Ajay's eyebrows were knitted together. He looked completely bewildered.

'What are you talking about? What cousins?'

'My father has relatives in Zimbabwe.'

Ajay looked mystified. 'Where?'

'It's a country in Africa. Varun can have good medical treatment there.' She squared her shoulders. 'I'm going to take him to Zimbabwe.'

Ajay stared for a moment, then laughed out loud, derisively, shaking his head, jeering at her.

'And how are you going to pay for all that? Sell the house?'

Nirmala kept her voice steady. 'My cousin has offered to pay for everything.'

Ajay stopped laughing. He screwed up his face as if he had just swallowed a bitter pill. He looked down for a moment, then stared at her again. She recognised the look of stubborn persistence in his face.

'Don't bother telling me I can't go,' she said firmly. 'You have lost all your rights over me.'

Ajay narrowed his eyes. 'You do what you like, but I am NOT leaving this house.'

Nirmala had hoped he would go without too much of a struggle. But knowing how obstinate he was, she was prepared.

'Fine. If you don't leave, I will go to Ashvin today and ask him to help me apply for a divorce. By the time we are back from our trip, we will be divorced, and you will be forced to move out.' Nirmala had no idea if this was possible, but she was guessing he didn't either.

Blind rage took control over him as he slammed his fist down on the sewing machine table. 'You fucking *rand and benchod*! I curse the day I married you,' he roared and began abusing her in earnest, pacing up and down their small living room like a caged lion. Nirmala stood firm, saying nothing, stifling the urge to run away from him. She wanted to cover her ears to block out the vulgar name-calling and shut her eyes to avoid seeing his hate-filled face. But she forced herself to remain composed and in control.

'This is all your Jasu-*foi*'s fault!' he announced suddenly. 'She's the one who arranged the marriage. And you! Why did you agree? Why?'

Nirmala frowned but remained silent.

'Why?' he asked again.

'You know why,' she said quietly.

'No! I don't. Why would someone like you, with your money and education want to marry me? I had nothing. No money, no house, nothing.'

Nirmala looked away.

'Tell me!' Ajay bellowed.

After all these years, he asks me now, thought Nirmala. He never questioned it before. He was only too glad to leave his village and move up the ladder.

'I married you to please my mother. She was dying, and she wanted to see me settled.'

'Liar!' he snarled. 'You think I don't know about your secret boyfriend? The one from the Brahmin family who rejected you? You were too low caste for him, weren't you?'

Nirmala jerked her head up. So, he'd known about Sudhir. She screwed up her eyes and turned away. He had never thrown this in her face before. Clearly it was a matter of shame for him to know that she had wanted to marry someone else. Someone he could never measure up to.

Closing her eyes, she tried to steady her nerves. She could feel the anger boiling up inside her. He was trying to shift the blame away from himself and project it onto her. She had to take back control.

'Ajay!' she screamed. 'Stop it! You are at fault here, not me. You are the one who has been unfaithful.'

Nirmala's heart was pounding in her ears, and her hands were shaking. She thrust them behind her.

'What happened years ago has nothing to do with today.' Her voice trembled with rage. She tried to calm herself before continuing.

'You think about what I have said. I'm going now to fetch Varun. When I return, there must be no more discussion about this. I don't want him upset. You have to go. I don't care where you go, but you are definitely going.' With that, she swept past him out of the house.

Chapter 15

Frightened beyond measure, Nirmala almost ran up the road. From the corner of her eye, she could see her neighbours watching from their doorsteps. They had obviously heard all the shouting. Some of them called out to her. But she was in no mood to talk to anyone. She quickened her pace, her mind racing over her confrontation with Ajay.

So wrapped up in thought was she that, without intending to, she found herself heading out towards Dudhiya Talav, the lake near the fruit and vegetable market. This was a place she sometimes came to for some solitude. She found a spot where she could sit on a shady bench and look out at the water. It was an oasis of calm. Taking deep breaths, Nirmala managed to calm her jangling nerves. Her heart rate began to slow, and she felt herself start to relax.

Then she remembered the scissors held at her throat, and her fear returned. Ajay had never done anything like that before. She'd thought him incapable of physical violence. Today, he had shown his true colours.

With some effort, Nirmala pushed her fear aside and looked around at her surroundings. She liked being by the lake, even though it was a place her father had always avoided. His sister

Pushpa had drowned in these waters, so it had been forbidden territory for the whole family. He would have been disappointed to see her here. But Dudhiya Talav was like a sanctuary for Nirmala. She came to walk or sit by the lake whenever she wanted to be alone, to clear her thoughts.

Nirmala wished there were more trees and fewer tower blocks surrounding the lake. There were always people gazing down, idly watching others enjoying the tranquil ambience. Even now she could see several flat dwellers sitting in their balconies looking at her. There must have been more privacy years ago when the lake was bigger. Understandably, part of it had been reclaimed for much-needed land for housing the ever-growing population.

A little bird twittered in the tree above her head. Nirmala looked up and saw that it was a sparrow with its typical round head and stout beak. Its wings were striped in buff black and brown. It chirped and cheeped for several seconds before it was joined by another sparrow. Together, they began to sing in loud, lively chirrups.

Nirmala's thoughts turned to Hema. What would she say when she heard about Ajay's threatening behaviour? She would be furious. She would insist that Nirmala take Varun and leave the house immediately. But that would be giving Ajay exactly what he wanted. There was no prospect of him buying a home so he would not want to leave the house. How was she going to get him out?

Nirmala resolved to ask Ashvin for legal advice. And she was desperate to tell Hema about her morning with Ajay. She decided to pay them a visit that evening.

A loud chirrup overhead drew Nirmala's attention back to the birds. She began to muse about these feathered creatures. The humble sparrows were found everywhere: on trees, electric wires, inside crevices and on rooftops. Rats on wings, some people said. But not Nirmala. She liked them, especially their joyful music.

These two seemed to be courting. Or perhaps they were an old couple, relaxed and comfortable together. They were like her parents, Suresh and Tara, happy in one another's company. Theirs had been a love marriage; that much she knew. Very different from her own.

If only she had been able to marry Sudhir. She wondered how he would react if she told him about Ajay's violent behaviour. Without doubt, he would be horrified. Nirmala had a sudden and strong urge to see Sudhir, to confide in him, ask him to help her out of the mess she was in. She pictured his face, warm and generous, ready to defend and protect her.

Nirmala felt hot tears rising to her eyes. She was sinking into deep self-pity, and knew she had to snap out of it. It was not Sudhir's responsibility to look after her and it was not fair on him to see how deeply she still cared for him. Nevertheless, Nirmala felt an ache in her heart, an intense yearning to see him and hear his voice. It took all her strength to turn her thoughts away from him.

Without planning to, she had told Ajay that she was going to Zimbabwe. Could she really do that? The invitation from Pramod Dayal was undoubtedly genuine and sincere. If everything was paid for, perhaps she should take up his offer. Varun needed medical attention and this opportunity was too important to forego. His good health should be her priority.

The trip to Zimbabwe was also an opportunity to find answers to the questions that had plagued her for so long. Such as why was her aunt Jasumati so dismissive of her? Why did she dislike her brother Suresh so much? What happened between them all those years ago? And why did her father Suresh walk away from a life of luxury?

Accepting the offer of a trip to Zimbabwe would be the right thing to do. She would find the strength and confidence to go there with Varun. But would she have the strength to force Ajay out of her home and out of her life? Nirmala wasn't so sure.

PART 2

May 2016 Harare, Zimbabwe

Chapter 16

Nirmala emerged from the aeroplane and stood for a moment at the top of the steps leading down to the tarmac. A wave of warm afternoon sunshine washed over her. Looking up, she saw a sapphire-blue sky with a few fleecy white clouds drifting lazily across. The air felt fresh and cool, unlike the hot, humid air in Mumbai. She took a deep breath, filling her lungs, relieved to finally arrive in Harare.

Descending slowly, she held a cabin bag in one hand and Varun's wrist in the other. He was unsteady on his feet, having just woken up. He'd had a good sleep during the fourteen-hour journey, especially during their connecting flight from Addis Ababa.

It was the first time Nirmala had travelled by plane and she was nervous about the customs and passport controls. Navigating the checks at Mumbai airport had been challenging with Varun and the luggage to keep hold of. She was not looking forward to repeating the process inside the Harare airport terminal.

She needn't have worried, however, because the arrivals procedure in Harare was straightforward. The airport was significantly smaller than Mumbai's and their plane was the only one that had landed in the last hour. The queue of passengers moved along at a steady pace, first at the visa counter, then at passport control. With quiet efficiency, the immigration officers stamped their brand-new Indian passports and waved them through.

At the luggage area, after each bag was scanned, Nirmala retrieved two cases, borrowed from Hema, and tried with difficulty to pile them onto a trolley. Seeing her struggle, an airport worker came over to help. Effortlessly, he placed the bags one on top of the other. Looking down at Varun's tired face, he grinned and lifted him up to sit on top of the pile.

'Nirmala! Over here.' The cry came from the midst of a crowd waiting for the new arrivals. She made her way towards a couple waving at her.

'Welcome to Zimbabwe,' said the man, smiling broadly. 'I am Pramod, and this is my wife, Reena. Good to see you in the flesh after so many emails and video calls.'

Of medium build, average height and thinning grey hair, he was dressed in casual black trousers with a blue short-sleeved shirt, open at the neck. His wife was a beautiful middle-aged woman, elegant in tailored navy trousers and a pink silk blouse. Her straight brown hair was shoulder-length with a side fringe that framed her smiling face. Her eyes were bright and sparkly. Nirmala saw genuine welcome in her demeanour and felt instantly drawn to her.

'*Namaste*, Reena-*bhabhi*.'

Reena put her arms around her and squeezed her tightly. '*Namaste*. I'm so happy you have come to visit us.' Turning to Varun, she said, 'And this must be your son.'

With a serious face, Varun bowed his head over folded palms.

'*Namaste*, Varun,' said Pramod. 'Now, let's get you off the mountain, shall we?'

As soon as he was set down, Varun moved to touch their feet to receive their blessings. The couple patted him on the back. 'It's nice to see children following our traditions,' said Reena. 'I'm afraid no one does that anymore in this country.'

'Now come' – Pramod took hold of the trolley – 'we're going straight home where you can have a rest after the long flight.'

They all trooped out into the sunshine. Nirmala was struck by the brightness of the light around her. As they walked away from the airport terminal, she experienced a feeling of space and wide open sky; something she was not used to. Looking back at the impressive facade of the terminal, she was dazzled by the glare of the sun's reflection on the glass.

They soon reached an open-air car park, where a formal-looking African man in a grey uniform approached them. His light-weight jacket and trousers reminded Nirmala of the pictures she'd seen of people going on safaris. Pramod handed over the trolley to him.

'This is Abbot, our driver.'

'Good afternoon, Madam. Welcome to Zimbabwe.' His smile revealed a row of perfect white even teeth.

Nirmala noted his strong Zimbabwean accent. His *madam* was more like *meddem* and *welcome* more like *werrcome*. He sounded very different from Pramod and Reena, who spoke English with a strange twang. She wondered why that was and what they would make of the way she spoke English.

The engine started with a soft growl, then purred as the minivan moved smoothly away from the airport and onto a modern dual carriageway. She noticed billboard advertisements on the side of the road and posters of the country's president. Streetlights spaced at regular intervals stood on tall gleaming poles, looking clean and new.

Everything seemed surprisingly grand. Nirmala's online research had led her to believe she was going to a struggling third-world country. So far, there were no signs of poverty. The road was impressive, but there didn't seem to be many cars using it.

'It's your first time out of India, isn't it?' Reena was looking at her with interest.

'Yes.'

'It must seem very strange.'

'Yes. I was wondering where all the people are.'

'You'll see them when we get closer to town.'

Pramod turned around. 'You must have heard about our financial crisis. We had sky-high inflation, and most of the indigenous population lost everything. Thankfully, things have improved a little.'

'Look ahead, everyone.' Reena pointed to a stone structure arched over the dual carriageway. It looked like a bird stretching its long neck across the road and burying its face in the ground on the other side. The words 'Zimbabwe 1980 Independence' were etched across the arch.

'The old name for this country was Rhodesia,' said Pramod.

Nirmala smiled. 'I know. An old man who lives in Suparna Mansions told me my Harilal-*dada* used to receive letters from Rhodesia.'

Pramod became serious. 'My grandfather Mohanlal must have sent those. I still can't get over how they were real brothers and never told anyone.'

Reena changed the subject. 'You've come at the right time. The weather is very nice in May: dry and sunny every day. The hot, rainy season has just ended, and you can see how lush the land is. Soon the ground will start to get dry. But we'll still have beautiful flowers and shrubs for some time yet.'

Nirmala looked out of the window at the green landscape. There were leafy trees and bushes all along the route, some with beautiful blooms. Through the trees, she saw field upon field covered with emerald-green grass. Every so often, a pretty bungalow enclosed within low whitewashed walls came into view. Through their gates she could see gardens filled with colourful flowers.

Pramod called out from the front. 'If you look ahead, you can see the Harare skyline. The traffic is always bad around there, so we'll take a left soon to avoid that.'

The trees and fields gave way to more bungalows, apartment blocks and little roadside shops. At last, Nirmala could see people walking, cycling or sitting by the roadside selling fruit and vegetables. The women were dressed in long, drab skirts or dresses, their heads covered in scarves, and the men wore clothes that looked grey and old. Little children sat or played near them – not very energetically, Nirmala thought. They all wore sombre expressions on their faces, looking up languidly as their car drove past. It was clear to Nirmala that this was the poverty in Zimbabwe she had read about.

Reena spoke to Varun. 'I hope you like swimming. We have our own pool in the back garden. And there are parks and playgrounds all around, so you will have lots of fun things to do.'

Nirmala looked down at Varun. He was staring silently out of the window. He sat so still that she worried he was having one of his turns. Anxiously, she reached out to stroke his face. He turned around immediately. Nirmala sighed with relief.

It wasn't long before the minivan slowed down and turned into a tree-lined avenue, then immediately left onto a short side road. It stopped in front of imposing wrought-iron gates. Through the vertical bars, Nirmala could see an impressive two-storey mansion. She watched in fascination as the gates opened automatically, and they moved smoothly onto a sweeping asphalt driveway. It curved majestically towards another gate at the other end.

The minivan stopped in front of open French doors made of thick glass panels. Floor-to-ceiling windows on either side of the doors had open louvre shutters. Emerging from the minivan, Nirmala tried to look inside, but the reflection of the sun on the glass wall made it impossible to make anything out. Squinting in the bright sunlight, they stood beside a beaming Pramod. He was about to say something when two little girls of around three years of age came bounding out through the door.

'*Dada!*' they cried, jumping up and down excitedly. Pramod introduced them as Sonia and Suraya, his twin granddaughters.

Two women followed the girls out. One was elderly, wearing a white sari, and the other was young, dressed in jeans and a bright flowery top.

'This is my mother, and this is our daughter-in-law, Kavita.'

When everyone had exchanged greetings, Kavita led the way inside. They entered a long rectangular room with maroon-coloured sofas and armchairs around an oval coffee table. At the far end, there was an enormous cabinet with books and artefacts placed in a neat order on the shelves. A large flat-screen television sat in the centre of the cabinet.

Reena invited them all to take a seat, then turned to give instructions to their domestic servant to take their cases up to the spare room.

'Now tell me, Varun, are you hungry?' Reena was looking at Varun. 'The twins have helped bake gingerbread men for you.'

Varun stared at the little brown men with buttons down the front of their coats. He was reluctant to bite into them. Nirmala took one to show him what to do. She knew this was the first of many new experiences they were going to enjoy.

After they'd had some tea, Reena showed them to their room. 'Make yourselves at home. We normally have supper at around seven o'clock. But today we will eat earlier because some of the extended family are coming round to meet you.'

They walked through a corridor, passing a bathroom and tall under-stairs cupboards, and entered a large reception area with polished parquet flooring.

A beautiful vase with fresh cut flowers was placed on a stand beneath a little alcove shelf housing a green landline telephone. This was clearly the main entrance area. Nirmala wondered how many other entrances there were in the house.

They trooped up a long wooden staircase, a wide strip of ruby-red carpet was fitted down the middle of the wooden steps. On the walls there were framed prints of Moghul miniatures.

At the top of the first flight, Reena opened a door and stepped inside a large room. It held a double and two single beds, with bedside tables in between. A large wardrobe, dressing table and two armchairs were placed against the wall at the far end. Three sides of the room had large windows through which the strong sunshine streamed in. Beautiful green curtains were held in place by elegant rope tiebacks.

'The bathroom is just at the top of the second landing,' said Reena. 'Have a shower if you like. There should be plenty of towels in there.'

The twins had followed her up and were staring openly at their guests. Reena shooed them out of the room. 'Downstairs, girls. We must leave them to rest. You'll have plenty of time to make friends later.' Turning to Nirmala, she smiled. 'Join us whenever you're ready. There's no rush.' Before leaving, she gave Varun a motherly pat on the cheek. 'We'll see you later.'

For a moment, Nirmala and Varun stared at each other speechlessly. Then Varun gave a loud whoop. He climbed onto the double bed and started bouncing with joy. 'It's nice and soft, Mumma! Not like our beds.'

'I know! I think there's going to be lots of things nicer than ours here.' Lifting him off the bed, she gave him a tight hug. 'Now, come on. Let's find the bathroom so we can wash. And then we should both have a lie down.'

It wasn't long before they were both under the covers. Varun shut his eyes and very quickly drifted off to sleep.

Sleep wasn't so easy for Nirmala. Being in a new place and meeting new people was a welcome distraction from her problems at home, but at the back of her mind, she kept thinking about Ajay and worrying about what lay ahead for the two of them.

She thought about her last day in Navsari. Hema and Ashvin had waved them goodbye at the train station. She would be forever grateful for the help they'd given her with all the preparations. There had been a lot to do, especially with passport applications, collecting the money transfers that Pramod had sent and booking the travel tickets. She would never have managed it all by herself. Picturing their receding faces as the train pulled away, she felt a warm glow of love and gratitude.

But even as she thought of them, her gut twisted into a knot as Ajay crashed into her mind again. She had a mental image of him snarling at her. *So what if I have another woman? So what if I have another child? You can't give me what I want. You are useless and so is your son.* Nirmala tried to block out those vicious and painful words from her mind.

On the night of their fight, Ashvin had come home with Nirmala to speak to Ajay, warning him to stay away. Ajay had slunk away like the coward that he was. He had disappeared for a few days, only to return for some of his things. He told her that within a month, before they returned from Zimbabwe, he would have moved out completely. The problem was, she didn't believe him. She knew he would not go without a fight, and that knowledge almost paralysed her with anxiety.

Chapter 17

Just after six o'clock, Nirmala and Varun joined the family in the lounge, where they were watching television, with drinks and nibbles. The room was sumptuously decorated with a blue sofa set, and carpet and curtains in harmonious shades. A warm glow was created by soft lighting. A crystal chandelier was hanging from the high ceiling.

Commanding immediate attention was an impressive art piece housed in front of an elegant fireplace at the far end. It was an enormous copper panel on which was carved a mother elephant with her two calves standing under a tree. They seemed to be posing, staring right at them, as if a cameraman had been standing in front of the trio taking their picture.

Nirmala was mesmerised by the elephants. There was just something about this beautiful giant of an animal that brought out a sense of wonder in her. She loved elephants, but right now everyone was looking at her expectantly. A young man walked over to her with a smile. She knew instantly that he was Pramod's son. The resemblance was very strong.

'Namaste, *Foi*. I'm Hemel.' His voice was surprisingly rich and deep. 'And this must be Varun. *Howzit*, little man?'

Varun was looking at the twins sitting on the carpet, absorbed in assembling a jigsaw puzzle. Nirmala nudged him forward to sit with them, but he chose to stay with her as she joined Reena on the sofa.

'We usually have drinks and snacks before supper every evening. I made vegetable samosas today. Do you want to try one, Varun?' Reena tempted him by holding out a plateful.

He took one without hesitation and ate it up in no time. He reached for another when offered again.

Pramod beamed. 'So now we know Varun likes samosas. You must tell us what he doesn't like, Nirmala, so we can avoid that.'

The question took Nirmala by surprise. Her hosts clearly had no idea how difficult things were for them in India. *Daal* and rice was all they ate most days. Anything else was a treat. She fiddled with the ring on her finger as she thought of how to respond.

'Is anything wrong?' Reena touched Nirmala's hand.

'No. Nothing's wrong. Varun never fusses about food. He eats everything.' She smiled faintly as she looked at Pramod. 'It's so kind of you to do this for us. Making all the arrangements, sending money and . . . and everything. It is too generous.'

'Nonsense. We are family, aren't we?' replied Pramod.

Reena patted her hand. 'We are just happy we found you, and glad you agreed to come.'

'The extended family can't wait to meet you,' added Pramod. 'Suparna-*foi* will be here around eight o'clock.'

Nirmala looked puzzled. Pramod laughed out loud. 'Yah, I did say Suparna-*foi*. Our aunt was named after Suparna Mansions. Or maybe the mansion was named after her.'

Nirmala was even more puzzled.

Pramod continued. 'Suparna-*foi* is my grandparents' youngest child. That's Mohanlal's and Bhanu's daughter. That makes her your father's first cousin. Suparna-*foi* is the youngest of six siblings and the only female. My grandparents were thrilled to have a daughter after five boys. The happiness must have been so great that we believe when the mansion was completed in Navsari, they named it after her.'

Nirmala was speechless. Pramod laughed again.

'We think we've worked it out. Suparna Mansions was completed just after Suparna-*foi* was born in 1952. The timing seems to fit, don't you think?'

'Yes. I suppose so. That is so . . .'

Nirmala was at a loss for words. All her life, she had looked up at the four-storey mansion and wondered about the name. The property belonged to Mohanlal, whose daughter was called Suparna, so the explanation was plausible.

Reena patted her hand again. 'Because of this connection, Suparna-*foi* is very keen to talk to you. She's going to have lots of questions for you about the mansion.'

Pramod looked irritated. 'She can be quite forceful sometimes. But don't worry. I won't let her overwhelm you. She is my father's sister, but because she's not that much older than me, I can speak freely with her.'

Nirmala wondered how it was that Pramod was a similar age to his aunt. 'Was your father much older that Suparna-*foi*?' she asked.

'Yes. He was the oldest sibling, and she was the youngest.' He looked at Varun sitting quietly. 'The first thing we must do is get Varun seen by the specialist. I'll try to book an appointment for tomorrow. After you told me what your doctor said, I made some enquiries and found out we have a leading neurologist running private clinics right here in Harare.'

Nirmala felt her throat constrict. She was so grateful to this kind and generous man. If he could make it possible for Varun to get better, she would be forever in his debt.

Reena squeezed her hand then stood up, looking at her daughter-in-law. 'Come, Kavita. Let's get the table ready.' Nirmala started to get up. 'No, no. You are our guest. We will call everyone when it's ready.'

The meal was a splendid affair, with several mouth-watering curries, side dishes, paapad and pickles. They all sat together round a large table set with a white linen tablecloth laid with fine china plates and crystal water tumblers. Silver cutlery was placed beside each plate, but Nirmala noticed that most of them remained untouched because they ate with their hands in true Indian fashion.

An elegant enamel sink sat in one corner of the dining room with a double door unit beneath it. Soap and towels were placed at the side for everyone to wash their hands before and after meals. One by one, they all washed up then followed Pramod back to the sitting room to wait for his aunt.

His mother began to prepare little triangular *paan* parcels: stuffed betel leaves. She had a special rectangular box to store the ingredients. Nirmala had seen many *paan* boxes, but this one was exquisite: solid silver with ornate patterns of peacocks in a garden of flowers.

She held out the first parcel to Nirmala. '*Paan bhave che?*'

Nirmala confirmed that she did like *paan* and placed the whole offering in her mouth. She savoured the sweet and nutty flavours, taking care not to open her mouth as she chewed, lest the red juice dribbled down her chin.

'It's not good for you, you know,' Hemel teased her.

'Ach, there's nothing wrong with it,' his father said. 'People chew it for digestion all the time in India. Isn't that so, Nirmala?'

She nodded but kept her lips firmly sealed.

'My grandfather, Mohan-*dada,* used to have two every day of his life and suffered no ill effects. That silver *paan-no daabro* was his, and we think of him every time we use it.'

Just then, the doorbell rang. Hemel stood up and walked swiftly to the front door. Nirmala heard a loud metallic click as he turned the lock, followed by noisy greetings from what sounded like a crowd of people.

'Hi, howzit, Hemel. *Mehmaan avi gya?* Are they here?'

Hemel's rich voice rang out. 'One at a time, please! Come and see for yourselves.'

Two little boys came running in. They looked around quickly and made a beeline for the twins, who were back on the carpet with the jigsaw puzzle.

Pramod and Reena stood up, so Nirmala followed suit. A group of people walked in, headed by a middle-aged woman, whose eyes scanned the room before settling on Nirmala. They were sparkling with eager anticipation.

Nirmala took one look at her and gasped. The woman was the spitting image of her aunt Jasumati in Navsari. Tall and slim with the same high cheekbones, slightly upturned nose, full lips and pointy chin. The hair was straight and long, held back with a grip at the nape of her neck. Her skin colour was much darker than Jasu-*foi*'s, but in height and build, she was the same. Even the way she held herself with back straight and chin up reminded her of her aunt, Jasu.

The woman hurried forward with a smile so wide that her eyes crinkled up at the corners. But the smile wavered when she saw the shock on Nirmala's face. She glanced at Pramod, who turned to Nirmala in surprise.

'This is my aunt Suparna. You know? We said she was coming to meet you?'

Nirmala collected herself and moved forward. 'Oh yes. *Namaste, Foi.*'

'*Namaste.*' Suparna gave her a hug, then held her at arm's length to study her face. 'You look like you've seen a ghost.'

'I thought . . . No. I mean . . . You look just like someone else.'

'Who?'

'My father's sister, Jasu-*foi*.'

'Oh.'

'That's not surprising,' said Pramod. 'They are first cousins after all. Now, come on, sit down, everyone. And Nirmala, meet the rest of the family. Suparna-*foi* has forgotten her manners.'

When all the greetings were over, Suparna sat beside Nirmala and took her hand in both of hers. 'When I heard you were coming, I was thrilled. I want to know all about you, your family and the house that has my name. But first, tell me: do I really look so much like Jasumati?'

'Yes. Very much. But you don't *sound* like her.'

'Oh. How does she sound?'

'She doesn't talk very much.'

'Whereas I can talk for Africa! And I make so much noise that even President Mugabe can hear me in his palace!'

Hemel was curious about the family connection. 'How exactly are you related to this auntie in India?'

'Jasumati and I are first cousins because our fathers, Mohanlal and Harilal, were brothers. Their mother was Godavari-*ba*, who is grandmother to both me and Jasumati.'

Hemel looked thoughtful. 'And Nirmala-*foi*'s father Suresh?'

'Suresh and Jasumati are brother and sister. So Suresh is also my first cousin.'

'Amazing,' said Hemel.

Suparna's husband spoke for the first time. 'What do you think of our country so far, Nirmala?'

Pramod jumped in before she could respond. 'We haven't taken them anywhere yet. We'll start tomorrow.'

Suparna twisted round to Pramod. 'We should start making plans right now. They must see all the sights like Lake Kariba and Hwange National Park and Chinhoyi Caves and the Zambezi River and Victoria Falls and . . .'

'Stop, please.' Pramod held up one hand. 'They've only just arrived.'

For a second Suparna stared, then she threw back her head and laughed again: loud, hearty laughter that made everyone smile and the children look up from their game. She squeezed Nirmala's hand.

Sitting back, Nirmala listened to them discussing and debating the plans. They were a loud, noisy family, often all talking at the same time. They fell into generational groups, with the younger couples chatting to one another, the little ones making friends on the carpet, and her hosts quibbling with Suparna about who should take the visitors where.

These were people she had never met before. And yet their welcome was filled with such warmth. And they were incredibly wealthy! Nirmala felt a wriggling sensation inside her. It was the worm of envy that sometimes invaded her senses when she compared her life with that of the rich. Closing her eyes, she tried to expel those thoughts from her mind.

Tiredness crept over her. The rise and fall of the voices around her sounded muffled, as if coming from far away. She saw Reena watching her.

'Time for bed, I think,' she said.

Suparna stopped mid-flow and turned to Nirmala. 'Ach, shame. You must be so tired. You go to bed and we can talk some more tomorrow. I'll come to see you every day if you can stomach that!'

Nirmala called Varun over to bid everyone goodnight. Her gaze swept around the room, coming to rest on Pramod.

'This feels like a dream. I can't believe we are here.'

Pramod nodded, looking thoughtful. 'It's a mystery why no one told us about our family connection. We need to find out why it was kept secret for so long. Now that you're here, we can try and solve this mystery together. But not tonight. Have a good sleep, Nirmala. See you in the morning.'

Chapter 18

When Nirmala woke up, the room was in semi-darkness. For a few moments, she could not work out where she was. As her eyes adjusted to the gloom, the events of the past few days rushed over her and her heartbeat quickened. The coming weeks were going to be full of new and exciting experiences.

A small digital clock by her bed gave off a soft red glow in the gloom. The time was 5.45 a.m. Nirmala was wide awake, but it was too early to get out of bed. Her body clock was still on India time. Surrounded by complete silence, Nirmala welcomed the quiet calm, so unlike that in her home city.

After a while, her ears picked up a small sound coming from outside. She recognised it as the gentle warble of a bird. The sound became louder with more birds joining in. Soon there were more twitters, followed by tweets, cheeps and chirrups. Full-blown chattering ensued. It was a dawn chorus unlike any she'd heard before. The music was loud, and the tunes were sung by a much bigger choir. The songs were being belted out with gusto.

She got out of bed and drew back the curtain closest to her. Trees with thick trunks and leafy branches stood tall only a few feet away from the window. Perched on the branches were the noisy birds that were chanting their loud morning mantras. Nirmala looked beyond the trees and saw the dawn breaking. The dark sky was boasting beautiful colours near the horizon: pink, purple and gold.

As she watched, the sky grew brighter and light began to creep into the room. Reaching up, she pushed the lock button on the window handle and gently turned it, pushing the window outwards.

A cool breeze floated in, bringing with it the sweet scent of flowers. She breathed in deeply and tried to identify the different smells. The distinct perfume of roses was instantly recognisable. The other fragrances were new to her. She thought about the flower gardens in Navsari, so often ablaze with pungent marigolds, honey-scented jasmines and fruity frangipani. The gardens in Africa were bound to be very different, and she relished the thought of seeing new and unusual blooms.

It was too early to get ready for the day, so Nirmala got back into her bed and lay still, resting her eyes. Eventually, she heard footsteps on the stairs, then the distant sound of a door being unlocked. The clock told her the time was 6.35 a.m.

'Rosemary! Come!' It was Reena, calling for the maid.

Nirmala gave Varun a gentle shake. 'Wake up, *dikra*. Let's get ready and see what's going on.'

After showering and getting dressed, they found their way to the kitchen. From the aromas wafting through the house, Nirmala knew breakfast was being prepared.

'Goodness! You are up early.' Reena beamed as she wiped her hands on her apron. 'Take a seat and I'll make you some tea.'

Nirmala sat with Varun at the kitchen table, already laid out with cups, saucers, plates and spoons. It was a large, square kitchen with a side room leading out to the back garden. Rosemary was busy at the sink, but she turned around to greet her. She was wearing a light-blue uniform with an apron tied around her waist.

Daylight was flooding in through the windows. They were too high up for Nirmala to see anything, but from the open back door, she saw lawn and a path leading to what looked like a vegetable patch. She was about to ask if she could wander outside when she heard raised voices coming from the front lounge. It sounded like an argument. *Why must you be so stubborn!* That was definitely Hemel's deep voice, and he was shouting at his father.

Reena stopped what she was doing and hurried to the lounge. Nirmala heard her telling them off, reminding them that they had guests. When she returned, she apologised, making light of the argument. 'The men in our family have very short fuses. They forget their manners sometimes.'

Pramod and Hemel came in together and sat down at the table. Both looked annoyed.

Pramod gave them a tight smile. 'Don't mind us, Nirmala. We have a problem with one of my uncles and he sometimes causes trouble for us.'

'Sorry, *Foi*.' Hemel looked sheepish.

Pramod spoke to Nirmala. 'You're up early.'

'It's nearly 10.30 a.m. in India.' Nirmala put a bounce in her response to lighten the mood. Whatever disagreement there was between father and son, it was none of her business.

'In that case, you had a very good sleep!' said Pramod with a little chuckle.

Reena placed a pot of tea in the middle of the table, then cereal, toast, butter, cheese and jam. Finally, she set down a dish with steaming hot *dhokra* with coriander chutney on the side. The men began to help themselves and within ten minutes, they were finished. They walked out together, their quarrel either forgotten or put on hold. Their places were taken by Kavita and her twin daughters, who also left as soon as they had eaten.

'They go to a nursery school in the mornings,' explained Reena.

With breakfast over, they went out to the back garden. Immediately Nirmala felt the warmth of the sun on her face, but the air was still cool enough for her to keep her *odhani* wrapped around her. The garden path forked in two directions: one leading to the vegetable patch and the other to a swimming pool.

Varun was already skipping towards the pool, which was surrounded by a wooden fence and gate. Reena lifted the latch to let him in.

Nirmala watched him run towards the water. All at once, she felt a cold chill wash over her. Her stomach tightened and she stopped dead in her tracks. The image of a drowning child flashed through her mind.

'Stop! Not too close,' Nirmala called out in alarm, her legs feeling weak.

She watched Reena draw him away from the water's edge. 'It's okay. He's safe.'

Shakily, Nirmala walked over to join them. Reena touched her arm.

'I wouldn't let anything happen to him, Nirmala. You mustn't worry. This gate is always closed, and children aren't allowed in without an adult. Our gardener knows to keep an eye.'

Looking behind her, she saw that the gardener was indeed watching from the gate. Nevertheless, she kept a beady eye on Varun herself.

Reena put her arm around Nirmala. 'I know about your father's sister who drowned. Pramod told me her name was Pushpa and she was only nine years old. That must have been terrible for your family.'

Nirmala nodded. She and Pramod had spoken about their family histories in the months leading up to their departure date.

'I don't think my father ever got over that. He always felt he was to blame for her death. She drowned whilst trying to save him.'

Reena gave her a sympathetic squeeze. 'Pramod believes that your aunt Pushpa's drowning might be linked to the family secret.'

'Yes. I believe that too. I'm hoping we find something in Mohanlal-*dada*'s papers to shed some light on the whole thing.'

Varun was standing at the shallow end of the pool, watching the sun's rays reflecting on the water, making it shine with a dazzling silver light. The water seemed to sparkle like diamonds bouncing on a shimmering blue sari.

From somewhere close by, they heard dogs barking loudly, making the boy jump.

Reena smiled. 'It's okay. They're just our guard dogs, letting us know that someone is at the front gate.'

She led them through a side gate which opened out onto the driveway. They watched Kavita park her car and emerge. She told them that a medical appointment had been booked for Varun at 2 p.m.

'I will take you into town after lunch,' she said to Nirmala before making her way inside the house.

Reena continued to the front garden. As they followed, Nirmala recognised the leafy trees from early morning. The trunks were outside the property, but the branches were hanging over part of the driveway, like an umbrella over their heads. The rustling leaves sounded just like whooshing waves on a beach.

'How far are you from the sea?' she asked.

'Very far. If we want a beach holiday, we go to Mozambique or South Africa. What we have in our country are the beautiful rivers and lakes which we can't wait to show you.'

They stepped off the driveway onto a wide sweep of lawn. It was laid out in two terraces and encircled by neatly trimmed hedges. Three rows of flowery plants were laid out near the front of the house. Nirmala realised this was where the early-morning scents originated. An abundance of pink roses grew tall in the rows, together with other colourful blooms which Nirmala had never seen before. She enjoyed the heady bouquet for the second time that day.

She was aware of being close to a busy road. There was no hooting and honking of horns, but the rumble of engines was unmistakable in the background.

'We're just a street away from one of the main roads into town.' Reena looked in the direction of the bougainvillea and hibiscus hedges at the side of the house. Then she pointed at three trees in the middle of their garden. 'Those are lychee trees. Every December, they bear so much fruit that we fill up buckets and give them away to friends and family.'

Reena led them towards the main front door. They followed her up five or six wide concrete steps to a large porch area. The floor was painted and polished in deep red. A low wall seat enclosed part of the porch within which sat a three-seater garden swing.

Nirmala looked at Varun. 'It's like our *jhula* at home, isn't it?'

Grinning, he hopped on and immediately began to swing back and forth. Nirmala and Reena sat on the wall seat with their backs to the garden.

'You know what, Varun? We have something very special in this house. If you walk round the front garden, you will soon come to it. Why don't you go exploring?'

Varun immediately rushed away looking excited.

'We have a small conservatory area filled with toys and games. You can enter through the house or the garden. It's a little playhouse for the twins and their safe space. They can spend hours in there, especially if they have playmates.'

Nirmala sat back and sighed. It gladdened her heart to see her son having fun. He was being pampered, and he deserved every minute of it, especially after what had happened back home.

She cast her mind back to Ajay's sulky face in the weeks before they left. He had come home several times on some pretext or other, breaking his promise to stay away. It hadn't been easy making the travel arrangements with him skulking around. Although he didn't cause any major problems, he had watched her and Varun with resentful, accusing eyes, as if *he* was the one being betrayed.

She'd spoken to Varun about Ajay going away, explaining that he would still come to see him if he wished. Unsurprisingly, Varun had accepted the situation without too many questions. When he did come round, Ajay had been less grouchy than usual, but he hadn't made much effort to endear himself to his son. Nirmala worried about the mental scars Varun was bound to have and she hoped this holiday would go some way towards healing them.

Reena was pressing her arm. 'Are you okay?'

Nirmala nodded, sucking air through her teeth.

'Life is hard for you in India, isn't it?'

Nirmala dropped her gaze. Reena moved back, saying nothing more. Eventually, Nirmala looked up and smiled ruefully. 'Pramod-*bhai* must have told you about my husband. We are . . .'

'I know,' said Reena, patting her hand. 'Don't upset yourself. You must try to forget about it while you are here and enjoy yourself.'

Just then, they heard the telephone ring inside the house and a few moments later Kavita opened the front door. She looked concerned.

'That's Ramu-*dada* on the phone. He wants to speak to you.'

'For God's sake!' Reena's annoyance took Nirmala by surprise. 'Why can't he leave us alone?'

Nirmala looked at her irritated face, brows drawn together. Whoever was on the phone was clearly persona non grata. 'Tell him I'm busy with our visitors and Daddy will call him later.'

Kavita retreated, shutting the door behind her. Nirmala stayed quiet, twisting her body to look out at the beautiful garden.

Reena clicked her tongue in annoyance. 'That was Pramod's uncle. The one that Pramod and Hemel were arguing about this morning. Ever since Mohan-*dada* died last year, Ramu-*kaka* has been throwing his weight around. He is the head of the extended family now and tries to bully everyone, especially Pramod. There's always one in the family, isn't there?' Shrugging her shoulders, she stood up. 'Let's go inside and relax until lunch. After that, you have Varun's medical appointment.'

Chapter 19

Dr Christopher Kwaramba was sitting at his desk facing a computer screen when they entered his office. He stood up immediately and came forward to greet them. Short and stocky, he had a shock of white hair flared like a flame around his dark, bespectacled face. Nirmala guessed his age at around sixty years.

Smiling broadly, he revealed a neat row of dazzling white teeth. He chuckled as he shook hands with Pramod and Nirmala, then leaned forward to say hello to Varun. Wearing a dark suit and tie, he looked very professional. Tan-coloured leather brogues added a touch of elegance to his appearance.

'Please sit down. You too, my boy.' He patted Varun's head and returned to his desk to check his screen. 'Vaaroon, isn't it?'

His pronunciation made Nirmala smile. She glanced at her son seated next to her, looking small in the high-backed chair, his feet not reaching the floor. He looked nervous, clearly feeling intimidated by the specialist who was going to examine him. She reached for his hand and squeezed.

'So, tell me' – the doctor spoke to Nirmala – 'what exactly happens when Vaaroon has one of his episodes? Mr Dayal has told me something about it. But in your own words, please describe it for me.'

Nirmala began to explain the problem: the symptoms, when they had started, the diagnosis, treatment and her concerns for the future. Dr Kwaramba listened intently, asking a few questions when he needed more detail. His face remained warm and friendly throughout, encouraging Nirmala to speak openly and without hesitation. From time to time, he glanced at Varun, and when Nirmala finished, he tapped out some notes on his computer.

Then he turned to Varun with a smile. 'Okaaay.' He dragged the word out in a sing-song way. 'I need to hear from you now. Do you know what is happening to you when you go very quiet?'

Varun's face clouded over and he threw Nirmala a quick look.

'It's okay, *dikra*. Tell the doctor what happens to you.'

Hesitantly, Varun answered. 'I know afterwards.'

'So afterwards, you know something has happened to you, yes?'

Varun nodded.

'Do you always know something has happened?'

Varun considered before answering. 'Not always.'

'So, sometimes you don't know. Hmmm. And how do you *feel* afterwards?'

'Like falling down.'

'Because you are dizzy?'

'Yes.'

'And before you go quiet, do you have a feeling it's going to happen?'

'Sometimes.'

'Do you feel hot or cold?'

'Hot. And a little scared.'

'Does it happen a lot?'

Varun frowned.

'I mean, does it happen every day?'

'No.'

'Maybe once every week?'

Varun thought for a moment. 'Not every week.'

The doctor looked thoughtful. 'Good. Good. That tells me a lot.' He tapped out more notes. Then he came round to pull up a chair beside Varun. He turned both chairs so they could face each other.

'Now I want you to do something for me. Shut your eyes and breathe in and out very quickly. You know when you get out of breath after running up the stairs? You breathe very fast, don't you? That's what you need to do now. And at the same time, I want you to count from one to ten again and again.'

Varun looked confused and slightly alarmed. The doctor chuckled.

'It's not hard. Let me show you.'

He began to demonstrate, puffing up his chest and breathing fast and loud. When he started counting, his voice took on a strange musical sound, and he looked so comical that Nirmala felt an overwhelming desire to giggle. Varun shot her a look and she saw that he was also trying hard not to laugh.

The doctor stopped, and seeing the grin on Varun's face, he laughed out loud. 'I look silly, don't I? I know. But it's fun too. Try it.'

Slowly, Varun began. After a few failed attempts, he finally got it. Dr Kwaramba made a circular motion with his hand to keep Varun hyperventilating for what seemed like a long time. Nirmala worried that Varun was going to pass out. Surprisingly, he kept going for almost three minutes. Then, without warning, he stopped and stared straight ahead, eyes wide open. Nirmala pressed her lips together in concern.

The doctor watched Varun closely. He waved his hand in front of him, then snapped his fingers. No response. He stood up, sat down again, and called his name. Still no response. Varun was statue still, looking vacantly ahead, completely zoned out.

Then, without warning, he blinked and breathed out noisily. He slumped in his chair, drained of energy. Nirmala reached out and drew him close. He dropped his head onto her lap. Pramod leaned over, tutting with concern, and rubbed the boy's back.

Nirmala stroked her son's hair, but her eyes were searching the doctor's for answers. He sat back, observed Varun's face, then reached forward to feel the boy's forehead.

'Hmmm. He does feel hot.'

Returning to his seat, he tapped out further notes, and when he was ready, addressed both Nirmala and Pramod.

'I would like to run an EEG to confirm the diagnosis. The electroencephalogram will trace the electrical activity of the brain. But the test I have just carried out and the medical history both suggest that Vaaroon has Childhood Absence Epilepsy.'

Nirmala puckered her brows and sucked in a quick breath, unable to hide her frustration. 'But we already know that, Doctor. I was hoping you could tell me how it can be cured.'

Dr Kwaramba screwed up his eyes and sat back in his chair. He tapped his fingers on the desk, focusing his attention on Varun. Nirmala looked fixedly at him, waiting for him to answer her. Eventually he did.

'Your doctor in India must have told you what to expect, and I am sure you have checked on the internet as well. The prognosis is good. Ninety per cent of children with CAE grow out of the condition when they reach puberty.'

Nirmala shook her head. 'But will *my* son be in that ninety per cent.'

The doctor turned down the corners of his mouth. 'I can't give you any guarantees.'

Nirmala looked away, feeling deflated.

'But I *can* tell you how you can help him get there.' He chuckled at her quick turn of head. 'You see, after I qualified as a neurologist, I went to England to specialise in paediatric neurology. CAE is not that uncommon, and I have treated many children like Vaaroon. And the majority of them have grown up to be completely free of seizures.'

Nirmala found she could not speak but her eyes shone with hope. Pramod took over.

'That is good news, Doctor. What should we do next?'

'Okaaay. The first thing is for us to book EEG and MRI tests. This will give us detailed images of the brain so we can rule out other possible conditions. We'll also do some blood tests. After that, I might change his prescribed medicine from sodium valproate to ethosuximide. It's more costly, but in my experience, it has a better efficacy and safety profile. Are you okay with that?'

Nirmala found her voice. 'The cost. I don't think . . .'

'Yes. That's fine.' Pramod cut in, waving away her objection.

'Good. Then leave it to me. You will hear from us tomorrow or the day after.' Standing up he looked directly at Nirmala. His voice took on a gentle tone.

'There is every chance your son will grow out of it, so please do not worry. I am hopeful because the frequency of episodes is low, and you have come to us at an early stage. We will treat the condition with medication that will reduce the frequency or even stop the episodes completely. Don't let this prevent you from enjoying your holiday in our beautiful Zimbabwe.'

Pramod stood up to shake his hand. 'I will make sure of that. Thank you for seeing us today.'

'You are welcome.' Dr Kwaramba was chuckling again as he ushered them out of the office. 'Take care, Vaaroon. Bye-bye. Bye-bye.'

Nirmala walked out feeling more hopeful than she'd been for a long time. Her feet felt lighter as she stepped out onto the pavement. She gave her son a tight hug and looked over his head to thank Pramod again.

'You have to stop thanking me. We are family.' He patted Varun's head. 'Come on now. I'll take you to our showroom.'

They made their way to the back of the building where Pramod had parked his car. On the way, they walked past several vendors sitting on the wide pavements selling all manner of things, from socks and shoes to pots and pans. Many of the goods looked old and used, and there seemed to be more sellers than buyers.

'They are not supposed to set up their stalls like this,' Pramod explained. 'But life is hard for so many people here. We have a corrupt, self-serving Government which does nothing to help those in need. They come to the city from far afield just to make a few dollars.'

Nirmala was reminded of the poverty in India. A lot of vendors had the same sad and defeated expressions on their faces. The difference here was the absence of crowds.

'It seems very quiet. Is the whole city like this?'

Pramod laughed. 'No. Some parts are very busy. This is the office area, so the workers will only come out after 5 p.m. The main traders and shoppers are around Harare Train Station. And further south, there are townships like Mbare, where it is so crowded you will feel like you are in India. That's the real city. But we don't go there to do our shopping. Only to show visitors what it looks like.'

'Where do *you* go to buy things?'

'We generally go out of the city area to big supermarkets and retail outlets. Things are more expensive so only those who are reasonably well-off can shop there. Fortunately, most Indian families have businesses which are still financially viable, even in this economic climate.'

'Are there many Indian people here?'

'No. In the whole of Zimbabwe, there are only about 9,000 people of Indian origin. That's out of a total population of around 16 million.'

It was a short, ten-minute drive west to Pramod's workplace. Their building looked new and modern, all glass and steel on the outside. When they stepped through the entrance, Nirmala was amazed at how bright it was. Light poured in from all sides and the high ceilings made the enormous room feel airy and spacious. Rows of shelves and counters were stacked with a variety of domestic appliances such as microwaves, electric kettles and blenders. Although not packed with customers, Nirmala saw several potential buyers wandering around the aisles looking at the displayed items.

'This is our showroom. Let's go straight to the playroom at the back. You can look around later.' They walked past a small reception desk, staffed by a young African girl wearing a smart grey business suit, then along rows and rows of light fixtures and fittings. At the centre of the building was a circular counter with two cash registers behind which sat at least four employees. They stood to attention when they saw their boss go past. Pramod nodded to them then led Nirmala and Varun past the final section with free-standing fridges, freezers and cookers. At the end of that, Pramod opened a glass-panelled door and took them inside.

The room was filled with bookshelves, small chairs, a table and cushions on a carpeted floor. A young woman with a lanyard round her neck sat near the door. Nirmala counted ten children of all ages seated around the space, some with books and others with toys or games. A few looked up, then carried on with their activities.

Varun was gazing at some Lego bricks on the small table. Pramod smiled and told him he could go and play with them while he took his mother away for a while. Then he spoke to the girl at the door.

'Blessing. This madam is our visitor from India. We're going upstairs, so keep an eye on her son, okay?'

'Yes, *Baas.*'

Nirmala walked over to Varun to say she would be back soon.

'Blessing? Is that her name?' she asked as they walked up a flight of stairs.

'Yah. The Shona people often choose names which show their gratitude to God. Blessing is the English translation of her Shona name.'

'Do you all speak the Shona language?'

'I'm afraid not. We were never given that option at school. Everything is in English. We did go to Gujarati school, so we can read and write in our own language. Just about. But we converse in English all the time.'

They had reached the main office where they found Pramod's son Hemel on the telephone and his wife Kavita on the computer. Hemel ended the call and pulled out a chair for Nirmala. He gave her a smile, but she noticed that it faded when he looked at his father.

'What's wrong?' Pramod asked. 'Who was that on the phone?'

'Ramu-*dada.*'

There was a moment's silence. Nirmala recalled that this was Pramod's troublesome uncle.

'What did he want?'

Hemel hesitated, shooting a glance at Kavita.

'Has he been interfering again?' Pramod looked annoyed.

'No. He just wants to talk to you.'

'Well, I don't want to talk to him.'

Kavita stepped in. 'Ramu-*dada* phoned home too. Mummy said you would call him back.'

'What? He had the cheek to phone home?'

'Calm down, Daddy.' Hemel spoke in a quiet voice. Looking incensed, Pramod was about to speak, but Kavita cut in quickly.

'Shall I show Nirmala-*foi* the rest of the offices?'

Pramod paused for a moment, then shook his head in resignation.

'No. I think Nirmala should know what's going on. It's better she hears it from us, and not from the gossipmongers in the family.' Arms folded, he leaned back against his desk. 'Ramu-*kaka* is my father's brother, second in line after *my* father who was the eldest. He's seventy-four years old, but strong and very stubborn. Since my grandfather passed away, he has become a pain the neck.'

Nirmala wondered why she needed to know this.

'Ramu-*kaka* is not happy that I have inherited Suparna Mansions.'

Nirmala raised her eyebrows.

'He thinks it should have gone to him. Buying and selling properties is his line of business, so when he heard there was a family mansion in India, he immediately thought it would be his.'

Nirmala remained silent.

'My grandfather was a very shrewd man. I believe he left it to me for a reason. Exactly what he had in mind I don't know. But I'm determined to find out.'

Nirmala knitted her eyebrows together. 'Is my coming here going to be a problem?'

'Not at all. Everyone is pleased you are here.'

'Even your uncle Ramu?'

Pramod blew out his cheeks. 'Ramu-*kaka* is never happy. He wants me to sell the mansion and is furious that I won't listen to him.'

He turned to gaze out of the window, looking thoughtful. 'The problem is, Ramu-*kaka* is contesting my grandfather's will. He's going to court to try to take Suparna Mansions away from me.'

Nirmala watched his troubled face. 'Why is your uncle so keen to sell?'

'Because he's money-mad. He thinks the sale will bring in a lot of cash. He's also convinced he will win the court case and the money released from the sale will be all his.'

'So . . . why won't *you* sell?'

'Because I don't believe my grandfather wanted it sold. Suparna Mansions was special to him, I'm sure of that. And I'm going to find out why.'

Hemel shook his head. 'I keep telling you to talk to him. Please talk to Ramu-*dada*.'

'Why do you keep saying that, Hemel?'

'Because he is threatening to send his team to India to turf out all the occupants and find a buyer.'

'That's ridiculous. He can't do that. It's not his property.'

'Yah, but you know what he's like. He'll cause problems.'

Alarm bells were beginning to chime in Nirmala's head. 'If he does that, Jasu-*foi* will also cause trouble for you.'

Pramod tutted. 'Nothing is going to happen. My uncle is all talk and no action. You have nothing to worry about.' He flashed her a smile. 'Now, let Kavita show you around then take you all home. Go and have some fun.'

Nirmala wished she could believe him. If Jasu-*foi* was going to be harassed, she would cause untold problems for everyone. Nirmala tried to push these thoughts out of her head, but a seed of doubt had settled in her stomach. She couldn't help feeling worried as she walked away with Kavita.

Chapter 20

Kavita drove with care up a steep hill. The narrow, winding road took them past thick, overgrown foliage which cast a shadow around them as they made their way to the top. When they arrived at a small clearing, Kavita parked and switched off the engine.

Nirmala stepped out and surveyed the shrubs and bushes surrounding them. She did a slow 360-degree turn, noting the long reedy grass which looked in need of a good trim. Looking up, she saw tall leafy trees forming a dense canopy above them, hiding the sun and making the area feel dark and gloomy. The place had a wild and neglected look about it.

'This is our *kopje.*' Kavita indicated the surroundings with a sweep of her arm. 'I know what you're thinking, *Foi*. It looks a bit rough. But follow me up these steps to the very top and you'll see amazing views. I promise.'

'Okay. Let's go.'

They followed Kavita up a gradual slope with about fifty wide steps to climb. All around them, the grass grew untamed and the umbrella of trees barely allowed the sun's rays to filter through. A few eye-catching flowers growing on either side of the stone steps brought a bit of colour to the surroundings. But there was an unpleasant odour in the air.

Within minutes, they were at the top. The trees made way for a large, flat paved area with a three-foot circular walled section which looked as if it had seen better days. A terraced garden of sorts fell outwards, with evergreen trees, ferns and cactus-like plants laid out across and over the hilltop. Nirmala was glad to be under blue sky and sunshine once again. But there was a nasty smell emanating from the bushes on their right. Turning to look, Nirmala noticed a pile of litter pushed to one side and a dog rummaging inside it.

'Don't look there, *Foi*!' Kavita spread her arms wide and ushered them to the other side. 'Come this way to see the views.'

Sure enough, the views were impressive. Nirmala could see a panoramic vista of Harare city centre surrounded by residential houses, a big football arena and a well-planned road network across the capital. The infrastructure seemed solid and modern.

'We used to come here a lot when we were children. There were gardens here with beautiful flowers and plants.' Kavita scanned the area with a sad, resigned look. 'The place is in ruins now. The country has no money to maintain anything.'

Nirmala patted Kavita's back. 'It may be neglected, but it hasn't taken away the spectacular views. Wish we had something like this in Navsari.'

Kavita gave her a rueful smile. 'We are told this is where the first European settlers came to see the vast green buffalo plains. They set up camp around this *kopje* and built their town called Fort Salisbury.'

'Why is this called a *kopje*?'

'It's the Afrikaans word for a hill. That was the language of the Dutch who settled in South Africa.'

'What happened to the African people who were here before the Europeans?'

'They had to move aside because King Lobengula signed their land away to Cecil John Rhodes. People say he was tricked. Soon after, the land was officially declared a British colony. The white settlers liked it here so much that when Britain wanted to give it back to the indigenous people, they refused. They formed a minority government and forced everyone to live segregated lives. I'm told it made life very difficult for everyone except the whites. Thank goodness we don't have that system anymore.'

Nirmala reflected on the time that Pramod's grandfather had come to settle. 'Do you know when Mohan-*dada* first came here? Which year?'

'I don't know exactly, but it was around the time when Rhodesia was still quite a new country. Probably in the 1930s. There were very few families from India settled here at that time. At some point, the single men went back to the home country to get married. But they returned with their wives to start their families here. That's how the Indian community grew over the decades. Many went on to become successful businessmen, like Mohan-*dada*.'

Nirmala looked at the view of the city and imagined herself growing up with all her cousins in this land. If her grandfather Harilal had followed in Mohan-*dada*'s footsteps, she might have been part of a wealthy family. Would she have liked that? She would definitely have enjoyed being rich.

A sudden shout from Varun jerked their attention away from the views. 'Mumma! Come and look.'

He was sitting on a flat rock, pointing excitedly at something on the ground. They walked over quickly. Something worm-like was moving on the stony ground. About six inches long and half an inch wide, it seemed to have hundreds of tiny paired feet under its shiny black body.

'What is that?' Nirmala asked.

'It's a chongololo.'

Varun repeated the word over and over again, laughing hysterically at each pronunciation.

Kavita laughed with him. 'It's the king of creepy-crawlies but harmless. Even though it has hundreds of little legs, it moves very slowly. See what it does when I touch it.'

She picked up a twig and used it to gently touch the creature's back. Immediately it curled up into a tight spiral. Varun gasped.

Nirmala shook her head in wonder. 'I've never seen anything like it!'

'It's weird,' said Varun.

Kavita laughed. 'You're in Africa now. You will see lots of weird creatures.'

Varun looked around nervously. 'Even snakes?'

'Even snakes. But don't worry. They won't come near us here.'

It was soon time to head for home. 'A few more families are coming to meet you tonight,' said Kavita. 'I should warn you: some of them are not very nice. They are jealous of Daddy because they think he was Mohan-*dada*'s favourite grandson. They also believe that Ramu-*dada* should have inherited Suparna Mansions.'

Nirmala rolled her eyes to the heavens, making Kavita laugh. Back in the car, Kavita drove them slowly down the hill.

'It's a one-way road up and then down, so there's no fear of oncoming traffic.'

Just as well, thought Nirmala. The road was far too narrow for comfort.

There was a surprise waiting for them when they reached home. Pramod's aunt Suparna was waiting there to greet them.

'Hello you two. I couldn't wait to see you again.' She gave Varun a hug, then enveloped Nirmala in her arms.

'I'll take Varun to play with the twins,' said Kavita. 'You two can chat in the blue lounge.'

When they were sitting comfortably, Nirmala described the events of the day. When she explained what had happened at the clinic with the neurologist, Suparna nodded sympathetically.

'It sounds like positive news to me. The prognosis looks good. Why don't we go to our Omkar temple tomorrow to say a special prayer for Varun?'

'I'd like that.'

'Good. Now, tell me all about yourself. What's it like in Navsari, what do you do every day, what does your husband do, what's my cousin Jasumati like, and so on and so on. I want to know everything.'

Nirmala looked away, feeling a little unsettled by the barrage of questions. But when she glanced up, she saw that Suparna's lips were twitching.

'I am very nosey, aren't I?' she chuckled. 'You mustn't mind me. Just tell me to mind my own business. I won't be offended.'

Nirmala couldn't help laughing with her. 'I don't mind, really.'

'You're a very sweet child. How old are you, Nirmala?'

'Twenty-nine.'

'Were you very young when your parents passed away?'

Nirmala became serious. She paused for a moment, then sucked in air between her teeth. 'When Pappa died, I was fifteen. It was a big shock because it happened so suddenly. Heart attack. And Mummy was already bed-bound after a stroke. Pappa had sold his business to stay home with her. But when he died, I left school to look after her. She died in my arms; three months after my wedding.' Nirmala looked down at her hands, feeling the sadness that always enveloped her like a dark cloak whenever she thought of that terrible day.

Suparna reached out and stroked Nirmala's hair. 'That must have been very difficult for you. I hope Jasumati looked after you.'

Nirmala said nothing. There was a long stretch of silence before Suparna spoke again.

'What about your husband?'

Keeping her head down, Nirmala shook her head slowly. She heard Suparna make a soft tutting sound. 'You poor thing. Life has been very hard for you, hasn't it?'

Nirmala looked up at last. 'It *was* hard at the time, but I got through it. After I had Varun, life became very busy.'

'I am sure it did.' Nirmala inclined her head. 'You're a brave girl, Nirmala. Flying out for the first time to a strange place to be with people you've never met before, shows just how brave.'

Nirmala had not thought of it that way. It *was* a brave decision to leave everything the way it was back home and travel so far with Varun. Her problems with Ajay had not been resolved and she would need all her strength to deal with the difficulties ahead.

'I used to be much braver when I was little,' she said. 'My father used to call me a *vagh* because he said I was fearless, like a tiger.'

'Your father's little *vagh*. What was he like, my cousin Suresh?'

Nirmala pictured her father's kind face. 'He was a quiet man, mild-mannered and soft-spoken. Easy-going and cheerful most of the time. People said he had the same personality as his father, Harilal.'

'Easy-going and cheerful. If that was Harilal, he was very different from his brother Mohanlal, who was usually stern and loud. Most people were afraid of him.' Her eyes twinkled. 'But not me. I suppose it's because I was his only daughter.' She twisted her body to look up at a photograph hung on the wall above the window. 'That's him in the picture with my mother.'

Nirmala walked over to stand below the beautifully framed black-and-white photograph. A couple in their sixties sat on either side of a small table with a flower vase placed in the middle. Without the distraction of colour, the clever use of light and shade in the photo gave the images greater focus. The man looked distinguished in his double-breasted suit, dark tie and black brogues. He looked straight into the camera with a severe expression on his face. Nirmala could imagine him laying down the law and instructing people to do as he said.

His wife, on the other hand, looked warm and good-humoured. Wearing a sari with a flowery border, she rested one elbow on the table and gazed into the camera with the hint of a smile. There was something about her face that looked familiar to Nirmala, but she wasn't sure what it was. Her eyes seemed to be sparkling. Going on tiptoe, she tried to take a closer look. But the photo frame was too high up.

'I've forgotten your mother's name,' said Nirmala apologetically.

'Bhanu. Her name was Bhanu. Pramod told me your grandmother's name was Kanta. They must have known one another at some point. Or at least, known about one another.' Suparna gazed at her mother's face. 'I wish I looked like her. But I take after my father's mother, Godavari-*ba*. Sounds like Jasumati has too, if she looks like me. Godavari-*ba* is her grandmother too. Who do you look like?'

'My mother. Her name was Tara.'

'I'd love to see a photo of Tara and Suresh.'

'I have a small photo in my purse. Let me show you.'

Suparna held the little picture in her hand, took off her glasses, and brought it close to her eyes. 'I'm short-sighted,' she explained as she scrutinised the photo for a long time. 'They look very happy together.'

'They *were* happy.'

'I don't suppose you have a photo of Jasumati?'

'No, I don't. Sorry.'

Reena walked in at that moment. 'You'll stay for supper, won't you, *Foi*?'

'Oh no, I can't! I must fly. They'll be waiting for me at home. I'll come again tomorrow.' She was out of the door before they could say a proper goodbye.

Reena shook her head. 'That's Suparna-*foi* for you. Always in a rush.'

~

That evening, after supper, they were visited by more members of Pramod's extended family. When the room became full, the children were led away to play in another room. Nirmala wondered which family members thought Ramu-*kaka* should have inherited Suparna Mansions. On the face of it, they all looked warm and welcoming. Once again, there were discussions about the different attractions around the country and friendly banter about who should be given the chance to take them there. Pramod was holding them off, saying he would let them know when he had drawn up a plan.

The noise level was so high in the room that Nirmala did not hear the doorbell ring. It was only when a sudden hush descended over everyone that she noticed two men standing in the doorway. The older of the two was looking directly at her.

Hemel, who had let them in, ushered the older man to the chair he had vacated. Once he was seated, Hemel turned to Nirmala.

'This is Ramu-*dada*, the oldest member of our family.'

So that was the uncle causing all the trouble. Nirmala stood up and went to touch the older man's feet for his blessings, as was customary in India. 'Namaste, *Kaka.*'

The man peered at her over the rim of his glasses. She looked back at him openly while he scrutinised her with sharp, alert eyes. He had a thin, bony face on a slim, slightly hunched body. At seventy-four, he was smartly dressed in trousers, shirt and a grey cardigan. When he spoke, it was with a gritty, gravelly voice.

'So. It was *you* my father hid from us all these years.'

His face was devoid of expression, but there was a hard edge to his voice. Nirmala sensed he was trying to intimidate her. She gave him a smile but lifted her chin up in a small gesture of defiance.

'*Ji, Kaka*. We also didn't know anything about this branch of the family.'

She saw his eyes narrow, as if he was trying to focus. His thin lips were pinched together.

'And your family still live in my father's property.'

It wasn't a question, so Nirmala said nothing. There was a heavy silence in the room. She was aware of everyone listening as she continued to look politely at the uncle.

His expression had begun to change. An arrogance crept over his face. He grunted at Nirmala, then shocked her by challenging her in a low, aggressive voice.

'Do you think you can live free of charge in someone else's property *all* your life?'

Before Nirmala could respond, Pramod came striding over to them.

'Stop it, *Kaka*! That is rude.' He looked angry and embarrassed. Reena came forward to lead Nirmala back to her seat.

The older man looked up calmly at Pramod. 'You are a fool. This girl and her family are freeloaders. Can't you see that?'

'Ramu-*kaka*! That is out of order.'

Nirmala watched the two men glowering at one another. She wanted to explain that it wasn't she who lived in Suparna Mansions. But Reena had placed a hand on her arm, as if to say don't move and don't say anything.

The uncle scowled. 'I came here to give you good advice. But I can see I'm wasting my time.' He raised his voice. 'This girl,' he spat, pointing at Nirmala, 'this parasite, is here to fleece you, and you are too stupid to see that!'

By now he was shouting, gesturing dramatically, pointing his finger at Pramod. 'My father should *never* have left you that mansion because you know *nothing* about property. Why he thought you could handle this, I will never understand!'

Still glowering, he turned his attention to his two brothers in the room, sitting in silence, looking uncomfortable. 'None of us can understand it!' he announced.

His brothers suddenly seemed very interested in their hands or the carpet. They reminded Nirmala of nervous schoolchildren being reprimanded by their angry teacher. They seemed afraid or in awe of their older brother, but also uneasy at his explosive behaviour in front of guests.

Ramu's eyes were back on Pramod, who stood only a few feet away from him. 'You should take advice from your elders!' he yelled. 'We know what's the best way to deal with this, but you are too stubborn to listen.' He paused for a moment, glaring up with murderous eyes. He gave a phlegmy cough then cleared his throat noisily. Patting his chest, he seemed to calm down a little.

Slowly he got up from his chair and stood in front of Pramod. With narrowed eyes, he spoke in a low threatening voice. 'You always were a softie. Just like your father. I never knew why my father could not see that. He can't have been in his right mind when he decided to give you the mansion. He didn't know what he was doing, and I am going to prove that. Be warned, Pramod. I am taking you to court and I am going to win!'

Shooting a venomous glance at Nirmala, he called his son to take him home. He walked out holding his head up imperiously.

As soon as the front door closed behind them, people started shaking their heads and muttering. Pramod gave Nirmala an embarrassed look.

Nirmala was speechless; too shocked to find the words to put him at ease. The uncle's behaviour had put a dampener on the mood in the room and it wasn't long before everyone began to leave, some of the women apologising to Nirmala on their way out.

When they had all gone, Pramod sat down heavily, shaking his head in disgust.

'Ramu-*kaka* is just too much!'

Hemel stood with his hands on his hips, angry with his father. 'I tried to tell you he was going to explode. You should have talked to him. You could have stopped him from coming here.'

'There's no stopping him, Hemel. He always does as he pleases. And because he's my uncle, I can't be too rude to him.'

Nirmala found her voice. 'Do you think he will try to contact Jasu-*foi*?'

'Very unlikely. But even if he does, there's not much he can do.'

Reena stood up abruptly. 'I think we should forget him now. Nirmala is only here for a month and we haven't even planned the sightseeing trips.'

'I can't make any plans tonight.' Pramod was still smarting. He exhaled heavily then nodded. 'We'll do the planning tomorrow.' Turning to Nirmala, he added, 'We must also make a start on Mohan-*dada*'s papers. There is a lot to trawl through. If we want to solve the mystery of why we knew nothing about our family connection, we'll have to go through everything with a fine-tooth comb.'

'It will all seem easier tomorrow,' said Reena. 'Come on, Nirmala. Varun will be tired out by now. It's time everyone went to bed.'

Chapter 21

When Nirmala joined Pramod and Hemel at their office the next morning, they were busy at their individual desktops. Pramod pulled up a chair for her to sit beside him.

'Where's Varun?' he asked.

'At home. He's very happy to be with Kavita and wants to play with the twins.'

'Good. Now let me show you something. But first, I must apologise again for my uncle's appalling behaviour last night. I've asked Suparna-*foi* to have strong words with him.'

Nirmala frowned. 'I hope there is no falling out because of me?'

'Don't worry. She knows how to handle him. He might be her older brother, but if anyone can put him in his place, she can. Now, let's forget about him. Look at this.' He turned his screen towards her.

Nirmala smiled. It was an image of Victoria Falls with its magnificent curtain of water cascading down a sheer drop of hundreds of feet. She had done her research on Zimbabwe before the trip.

'You'll be seeing it for real soon. I've organised a week-long trip for us, starting next Monday. We'll be joined by Suparna-*foi* and her husband.'

Pramod then showed her pictures of lakes, mountains, wild animal parks, and the spectacular rock structures of the great Zimbabwe Ruins.

'In the four weeks that you are here, we will take you to see all these places. There won't be any crowds because tourists are thin on the ground. They think this is a dangerous country, which it isn't of course. You'll see.'

Pramod shut down the computer and pushed back his chair. 'We should go and look at *Dada*'s papers. But before we do, I want to give you something.'

Sliding open the top drawer on his right, he lifted out a white envelope and handed it to Nirmala. 'There is some spending money in here. You'll need our local currency to buy things when you're out and about. Keep that with you.'

'Oh no. I can't take that.' Nirmala was embarrassed.

'You can and you must.' Pramod was firm. 'Think of it as a loan. You can pay it back whenever.'

Nirmala remembered what Hema had said about not being too proud to accept help. She decided to accept graciously and pay back when she was able to, even if it took years.

Pramod stood up. 'Now come. Let's go to the folders.'

'Folders? I thought you said papers.'

'Papers, documents, letters, photographs and a whole lot more. All of them in a stack of bulging folders. *Dada* was a stickler for keeping things tidy and organised. But when I found all these folders in his safe, I realised that he was also a hoarder. He stuffed all sorts of things into dozens of files. Come and see what we found.'

He led the way out of the office and up the stairs to the top floor. 'This used to be Mohan-*dada*'s domain. He was here in his office almost every day, working on whatever projects or personal things he had on the go. As he got older, he came less often.'

'The stairs must have been difficult for him.'

'Oh no. He had no such problems even when he was in his nineties. He was strong like that right up to the end. If anyone asked, he always used to say he was fit and fine. Never complained about his health. Then one day, he just couldn't get out of bed. He'd suffered a massive stroke in the night. He died the next day in hospital.'

He moved towards a closed door at the end of the corridor. She watched him take a set of keys out of his pocket and unlock the door. Opening it, he stepped inside and flicked a switch on the wall. Nirmala followed him into a small rectangular office with no windows.

The only furniture was a desk pushed up against one corner, a chair with castors under it and a waist-high shelving unit along one wall. Dominating the room was a large capacity security safe standing tall in the far corner. Made of solid steel, it was about five feet high. It looked like an old-fashioned fridge with a black disc in the centre housing a handle and keyhole. It was clearly very old. Nirmala had never seen anything like it.

'This safe has been in the family for donkey's years. *Dada* was the only one who came into this room, and he kept the key locked in his own office.'

'He didn't allow anyone in?'

'He didn't invite anyone, so nobody came in.'

'Not even your father?'

Pramod shook his head, looking amused.

'Didn't you wonder what he kept here?'

'Not really. We knew there was a safe in here where he kept some jewellery and cash. But we didn't give it too much thought. He was always in complete control of everything, so we never questioned it. Does that sound strange to you?'

'It does. You must have wanted to ask him.'

Pramod laughed. 'If you had known *Dada*, you would have understood. He was a law unto himself.'

Nirmala looked at the safe. 'When you finally opened it, what did you find?'

'A small amount of gold and diamond jewellery, some expensive wrist watches, cash and dozens of folders. Apart from the folders, everything else was handed over to be included in *Dada*'s total estate.'

Using one of the keys in his hand, he unlocked the safe and pulled open the door. Nirmala gasped at the piles of brown document folders. She counted five shelves, each holding numerous folders stacked one on top of the other. 'How many are there?'

'A total of sixty-six. And I have only managed to go through seven so far.'

Nirmala pressed her lips together and cast her eyes round the room. The desk and shelves were laden with papers. Pramod followed her gaze.

'That mess is down to me. I've been looking through the contents and trying to make sense of it. Nothing is saved in date order or in any other kind of order. Everything is jumbled up. There are all sorts of things filed going back over a hundred years.'

Pramod stood with his hands on his hips, looking from the desk to the shelves. 'I tried to devise some sort of system.'

Nirmala blew out her cheeks slowly, thinking about the time-consuming task ahead. She began to consider how they could become more organised.

'Have you thought about computer systems for recording and listing all this?'

'No. I'm a bit of a Luddite when it comes to modern technology. I did ask Hemel to help me, but he took one look at all this and walked out. He has no interest in what he calls ancient history.'

Nirmala looked at the piles of folders and wondered how Pramod had managed to find any information about her family.

'How did you find out about my father?'

'That part was in Mohan-*dada*'s will. When the lawyer read it out, he dropped two bombshells: one, that *Dada* owned Suparna Mansions, and two, that he had a younger brother called Harilal. In addition to the property deeds and other legal documents, there was a declaration from *Dada* that in lieu of any rent payments, his brother had agreed to live in the property with his family and manage all the finances. There was an additional more recent note that as Harilal was deceased, the arrangement now lay with his son Suresh. I realised that Suresh was my uncle. That's why I wrote to your father.'

'But my father didn't know anything about this. And he died fourteen years ago.'

'Well, *Dada* must have lost contact with your family before that. He died last year thinking your father Suresh was still alive.'

'Maybe all contact was lost when my grandfather Harilal died.'

'Could be. I did wonder how Mohan-*dada* found out about Harilal's death.'

Nirmala gave this some thought. 'My grandmother Kanta lived for many years after Harilal-*dada* died, so *she* must have notified your grandfather. I've been thinking about our grandmothers, Kanta-*ba* and Bhanu-*ba*. How did they feel about all the secrecy?'

'Who knows.' Pramod shrugged his shoulders.

'In those days, women had no say whatsoever. Men made all the decisions and wives had to go along with their husbands' wishes. The secrecy was probably easier for them because the two families lived so far apart.'

Pramod nodded, looking at all the paperwork around them. 'The answers to our questions are somewhere in these papers. I'm sure of it.'

'I hope you are right.' Nirmala's desire to find answers felt more urgent than ever. Why did the brothers keep their relationship secret? If these papers held the answer to that question, perhaps it would lead to other answers such as why her grandmother Kanta had favoured Jasumati over Suresh. And why Suresh had walked away from a life of luxury. Nirmala hoped with all her heart that some of the answers would help to improve her own life and that of her son.

Pramod shook the keys in his hand. 'After Mohan-*dada* passed away, I opened the safe and gave all the material contents to the lawyer. He confirmed that the folders could stay here because they were just personal papers of no financial worth. I was left to do whatever I wanted with them.'

'What did the rest of the family think?'

'They told me that unless there was anything legal among the papers, I was welcome to keep them. Ramu-*kaka* took one look at these and told me to throw it all away.'

Nirmala gasped. 'That's shocking.'

'That's what he's like. I believe he was jealous of my father because as the eldest son, he had my grandfather's ear. Ramu-*kaka* was always trying to pick a fight with him.'

'Did the other brothers respect your father?'

'Yes. But a couple of them also wanted me to get rid of these folders. They claimed it was wrong to go through this because we didn't have their father's permission.'

Nirmala could see why someone would feel that way.

'But I don't believe that,' Pramod continued with feeling. 'I knew *Dada* better than most, and I think he left these here deliberately. He was a very private man. I think he put his thoughts in these folders and there's something in here that he wants the family to read.'

Nirmala wondered why, out of all his grandchildren, Mohanlal had trusted Pramod with the key to his safe. Perhaps he *was* the favourite, as some family members suspected.

'How come you knew Mohan-*dada* better than others did?' she asked.

'*Dada* lived with *our* family because my father was his oldest son. He was always there for us, especially when my father passed away over thirty years ago. I was only twenty-two years old then. Mohan-*dada* was my hero. In many ways, he moulded me and taught me a lot about life, and how to work hard and be successful. Not just in business but in the way we live with the people around us.'

Nirmala was moved by the love she could feel in Pramod's words. 'I can see you still miss him.'

Pramod sighed. 'I do. But I count myself lucky to have had his guidance for so many years. Now I'm keen to discover what it is he wants me to find in these papers.'

Nirmala cast her eyes over the stacks of files. She moved to the desk and looked into a box holding photographs and pictures. She picked up a postcard-sized black-and-white photo. It was a portrait of a glamorous woman from the 1950s or '60s, with pouty lips and long wavy hair flowing down one side of her face. She looked strangely familiar. Turning the picture over, Nirmala read the name and smiled. 'Madhubala 1969.' Mohan-*dada* was obviously keen on this beautiful movie star of yesteryear.

'She was the Aishwarya Rai of her time, wasn't she?'

Nirmala picked up another photo. This she recognised immediately. It was Suparna Mansions, looking majestic, grand, beautiful. The date on the back was 1952, the year construction was completed. So this is what it looked like when it was new. Nirmala pictured its present condition with walls crumbling, paint peeling and stonework damaged.

'This was my father's beautiful childhood home,' she said with sadness. 'It looks terrible now. I live across the road, and every day, I watch it falling apart.'

Pramod was silent for a moment. Then he asked, 'Jasu-*foi* is not looking after it?'

Nirmala sighed, shaking her head. 'She doesn't seem to care about it. The family apartments on the top floors are nicely done up with expensive things inside, but the outside doesn't matter to her. I'm afraid she's a bit tight with her money.'

'Look. We'll deal with that another time. Right now, we have to sort all this out.' He waved his hand across the room. 'If you're up to it, we can begin tomorrow?'

'Yes. Tomorrow.' As always, Nirmala needed time to think about this and was glad Pramod was not expecting her to begin right away. She took one last look at the photo then followed her cousin out of the room.

Chapter 22

Their plan to work through the folders was scuppered by Suparna, who insisted on taking Nirmala and Varun out for the day. She telephoned Pramod in the evening to say that he would have to arrange another time for trawling through the old papers. Nirmala could tell Pramod was not pleased.

'I would rather get started on Mohan-*dada*'s folders. But you'd better do as she says, or we'll never hear the end of it.'

Nirmala's thoughts were also on the folders, but she made sure she and Varun were ready to be picked up by 9 a.m. As usual, Suparna came in like a whirlwind, loud and cheery as ever. She put Nirmala at ease straight away.

'I heard what happened the other night. My brother Ramu was talking from his backside again. He's crazy, you know, and the older he gets, the crazier he gets.'

Nirmala smiled a little uncertainly.

'It's true. I think he's losing his marbles. If I had been there when he spoke to you like that, I would have given him a mouthful there and then. My other brothers are all cowards. They follow Ramu-*bhai* around like sheep.'

As Nirmala and Varun settled in for the drive, Nirmala reflected on the difference between Suparna and herself. She would be too afraid to confront someone like Ramu. Suparna, however, clearly had no fear.

As they drove through a quiet residential area, Nirmala reflected on Suparna's name, and how it tied in with the name of the mansion she'd known all her life.

'Were you named after the mansion or was the mansion named after you?'

'According to the dates, I was born just before completion of the building in 1952. So I like to think the mansion was named after me.'

'My father was also born in 1952,' said Nirmala.

'Was he? What month?'

'February. Twenty-sixth February.'

'Really?' Suparna looked delighted. 'Just two days before me. My birthday is twenty-eighth February. Almost twins. You said he was mild-mannered and soft-spoken. There's no way anyone would describe *me* like that, would they?' Her eyes twinkled. Nirmala laughed and looked out of the window.

Pretty bungalows with neat and tidy gardens lined the quiet streets. Suparna turned the car into a gated complex with a long driveway flanked by tall trees. Up ahead Nirmala saw a beautiful brick structure with a large AUM sign above the wide entrance. She realised they had arrived at the Omkar Temple.

Going in, Nirmala marvelled at the beautiful interior, and as always, said a special prayer for Varun's health. Outside, Nirmala admired the beautiful grounds. Everything was clean and tidy.

'My father played a big part in fund-raising when they built this place.' There was no mistaking the pride in her voice whenever she mentioned Mohanlal.

Next, they went into the heart of the city, which was buzzing with traffic and pedestrians. Some of the older buildings were similar to many colonial structures in her own country. There were also a lot of modern office blocks and high-rise apartments. Some of them were well maintained, while others had seen better days.

'Now we're in Avondale. Behind that parade of shops, we have a flea market which is open every day. I'll bring you here another time so you can buy some souvenirs for home.'

The mention of home took Nirmala back to Navsari. She wondered what Hema and Ashvin were doing. They were probably waiting to hear from her. She resolved to send them an email as soon as she could.

'Are we in the countryside now?'

'No. We're in a suburb called Mount Pleasant. See those trees there? They are jacarandas. In October, they look amazing, with bright purple flowers on every branch and twig. When they fall to the ground the streets are covered in an incredible carpet of purple.'

'We have them in India too. But I wish I could see these in all their glory.'

'I'll show you some photos. You know, at one time, these residential areas were for white people only.'

'Yes. I did read about the apartheid system.'

'There were a lot of restrictions. We couldn't choose where we lived or where we set up our businesses, and there were laws preventing us from going to certain schools, hospitals and restaurants. We couldn't even sit where we wanted in the cinemas and parks. If there were signs like *For Whites Only*, we had to steer clear.'

Nirmala was reminded of the stories she had heard about the racism and hardships endured by Indians during the British Raj. She was thankful those days were over.

Suparna swung her car through open gates and up a long lane to higher ground. 'We're entering the university campus now. I graduated from here in the early '70s.'

'What did you study?'

'English. I'm retired now, but I worked as a high school teacher for many years.'

Nirmala watched students strolling or rushing from one department to another. Some were sitting in the sun on the extensive grounds. They looked happy and carefree. She felt a sudden and unexpected pang of yearning. This was the kind of student life she would have shared with Sudhir if she'd had a chance to continue her studies.

'I wanted to go to university,' she murmured.

Suparna threw her a glance. 'There's no reason why you couldn't go when Varun is older.'

Nirmala gave her a highly sceptical look.

'Miracles do happen, you know. Look at you now. Did you ever think you'd get a chance to be here, so far away from home?'

Nirmala conceded that she did have a point.

'Now, come on. Let's get out of here.' Suparna headed out of the campus. 'Let's take Varun for some ice cream.'

She took them to a place called Borrowdale Village: a modern open-air retail complex with charming walkways between shops, restaurants and cafés. These were structured around beautiful courtyards with well-maintained flower and rock gardens.

All manner of shops circled the courtyards, selling everything needed for contemporary living: clothes boutiques, shoe shops, bookstores, furniture outlets and agencies for travel, sport and housing. Nirmala enjoyed window shopping under the blue sky and bright sunshine. She did notice, however, that there weren't many people around.

'Is it usually this quiet?'

'I'm afraid so. Most shoppers who can afford to come here have left the country or are leaving. They don't believe the economy will ever recover. It's sad really.'

They were walking towards a large supermarket where Nirmala could see trays full of fresh fruit and vegetables. As soon as they entered, she felt a surge of cool air from the air-conditioning vents above their heads. Stepping further in, she picked up a strong sweet scent from one of the wide shelves. Right in front of her, piled high on an enormous counter, she found herself facing the biggest and roundest and most dazzling oranges she had ever seen. Nirmala could almost taste the juicy flesh inside.

Looking around, she was amazed by the abundance and variety of different fruits and vegetables. Once again, she was transported back to Navsari, with its famous open-air market near the lake. There were mountains of produce all around her. Some she had never seen before, such as granadillas.

Picking up a few fruits, Suparna took them to the cashier. After paying and packing them into her own cloth bag, she headed towards a department store with rows of fashionable garments hung on rails for easy browsing. She encouraged Nirmala to buy warm clothes and trainers for their upcoming trip. Varun could barely conceal his excitement at having new things bought for him, and it gave Nirmala immense pleasure to see how happy he was.

The rest of the afternoon went smoothly, with lunch followed by ice cream at a modern café-cum-restaurant. By the time they were ready to leave the village, it was mid-afternoon. As they drove home, Suparna pointed out the potholes on the roads and broken streetlights.

'We face many challenges here. Power outages, water shortages, streetlights going off; they're all regular occurrences. We manage with domestic generators and boreholes for drinking water, but it's not easy sometimes.'

Nirmala nodded, thinking how similar this was to many villages in India which also lacked these basic amenities. The two countries had more in common than she would have thought.

Eventually they reached Suparna's house. It was a large bungalow with whitewashed walls and a black tiled roof. She took them through to the backyard where shady trees surrounded a wide stretch of lawn. There was a children's playground on one side complete with swings, slide and trampoline.

Varun immediately went for the trampoline. Nirmala sat chatting with Suparna on a bench under the shade of a tree. She found herself talking about Hema and Ashvin. She explained why they felt more like family to her than Jasumati did, and how lost she would have been without them. She missed them terribly and asked if she could send them an email.

'Of course. Come with me.'

They went into a small study which led to a large dining room. Suparna sat at the desk to start up her computer. Nirmala looked around and noticed a framed photograph of Suparna's parents, Mohanlal and Bhanu, mounted on the wall. It was the same black-and-white photo that Pramod had in his lounge. This one was hung at eye level, so Nirmala was able to have a closer look. Once again, she found herself drawn towards the woman in the picture. There was something arresting and familiar about her face. She reminded Nirmala of someone, but she could not work out who.

Her thoughts were interrupted by Suparna. 'You can log in now.'

'Would you mind if I used your email account? I don't have one of my own.'

'You can use mine, but we can create an account for you right now if you like. It only takes two minutes.'

Before long, Nirmala was all set up. Suparna patted her on the shoulder and left her to compose her email.

Dear Hema

I have been here for four days and already so much has happened. How are you and Ashvin? Varun has been seen by a specialist and is under new treatment. Please God he gets better.

My relatives are taking good care of us. There is someone here who looks exactly like Jasu-foi. I'm not joking. And guess what? Her name is Suparna. Yes. SUPARNA. She was born in 1952 and the mansion is named after her. So that's one mystery solved. I think the other mystery about why our families knew nothing about one another will take longer to solve. It's possible we may never find out, but I really hope we do. I can't help feeling that once that secret is uncovered, things will start to improve for Varun and me.

As you can see, I now have my own email account. I will try to email you regularly. I keep fretting about my problems back home. Any news of Ajay? I have a horrible feeling he will still be there when we return. The thought of him is a constant black cloud over my head. No matter what I do or where I go, he is always there, making me feel anxious.

Thanks again for everything. If I didn't have you, I don't know how I would keep sane.

Missing you.

Nirmala

No sooner had she signed off than she became aware of a commotion outside. She heard raised voices coming from the front garden. Nirmala moved to the window to see what was going on. To her surprise, she saw Pramod's Uncle Ramu striding up the driveway.

'You have some nerve coming here!' There was no mistaking Suparna's loud voice. From the porch, she bellowed at the top of her voice, bringing Ramu to a halt halfway up the drive.

'I want to talk to you about that girl from India,' he hollered. 'We need to knock some sense into Pramod.'

Feeling like an eavesdropper, Nirmala moved away from the window and beat a hasty retreat to the back garden. Her heart began to race and she sat down on the bench. Varun came over for a cuddle, then went back to play. Although muffled, Nirmala could still hear the angry voices of the siblings, who were clearly having a slanging match outside the front door. Shrinking into herself, she clasped her hands to stop them from shaking. She realised she was more than a little frightened to be the subject of so much aggression.

The voices grew louder and Nirmala began to panic. The back door opened and both Suparna and Ramu entered the garden. Alarmed, Nirmala stood up. Ramu took several steps towards her, looking fierce and threatening.

Immediately Nirmala thought of Ajay, scowling at her, holding the point of his tailoring scissors at her throat. Filled with fear, she stepped away to stand behind the bench. Holding her breath, she waited for her aggressor to come up close. With relief, she heard Suparna hold him back.

'Don't you dare go near her,' she screamed, making Ramu stop in his tracks. 'What kind of a man are you? Have you no shame? Leave her alone!'

Ramu stood still, between the two women, flashing his eyes at Nirmala in a glowering fury. Then, in a deliberate move to intimidate her, he spat on the ground between them.

'Ramu-*bhai*!' Suparna marched up to him, her fury matching his. 'That's disgusting. You need to go home right now.'

For a moment, they glared at one another. Then, drawing himself up, he blinked. 'I can see whose side you're on. But let me tell you something: I will win my case in court and this little upstart' – he pointed at Nirmala – 'will have to find someone else to swindle.' With that, he snorted in defiance and stalked away.

Feeling shaky, Nirmala walked round slowly and sank into the bench. Varun came running over and folded himself into her arms. Rooted to the spot, he had watched everything from the top of the slide.

'It's all right, my *dikra*,' she whispered, more to convince herself than him.

Suparna sat down beside them. 'I am so, so sorry. I had no idea he was coming today. Please don't worry. I won't let him come near you again. I promise.'

They sat like that for what seemed like an age. Eventually, the domestic servant brought out tea and cake, and Suparna urged them to have some.

'I can get you something stronger, if you like. How about a tot of whiskey?'

Nirmala smiled. 'No thanks. Ramu-*kaka* is really scary.'

Suparna nodded. 'He can be. But you mustn't let him get to you. He's a bully and you know what bullies are like. The minute you show your fear, they bully you some more. Don't ever let them smell your fear.'

Wise words, thought Nirmala. She could learn a lot from Suparna. Bullies like Ajay and Ramu had to be dealt with in a certain way. It was important to get a grip and be strong. Nirmala made a promise to herself that if in the future, anyone tried to bully her, she would stand firm and speak up for herself. That's what she used do when she was younger, but over the years, that spark of defiance had been slowly extinguished. She needed to bring back the old Nirmala.

Chapter 23

The next day, when she joined Pramod in the showroom, he took her straight up to the room with the safe. Inside, Nirmala looked at the mess of papers and decided to take charge.

'Let's separate the notes, letters and photographs and place them in different paper trays in date order. We'll start with the piles you've already made, then move on to the folders.'

'Sounds good. I'll fetch some trays.'

Nirmala sat down and began to tidy the mess of papers covering the desk. They were different shapes, sizes and colours, some very old and others, judging from the yellow Post-it stickers, fairly recent. Most were single sheets of information while others were lengthy reports of events, programmes, catalogues and much more. She arranged them into separate stacks.

Pushed to the back of the desk was the box full of photographs they had seen the day before. She picked up the box to move it to the shelf. As she did so, something toppled down. She looked down to see a white envelope stuffed with blue sheets of paper. Turning back to the desk, she noticed two similar envelopes which had been tucked under the box. Gathering them up, she saw that they were addressed to Mohanlal and they'd all been opened.

Nirmala held her breath. Was it possible that these were from Harilal, her grandfather? She placed each envelope on the desk and quickly checked the postage stamps. A wave of disappointment washed over her. All three were from abroad, but none from India. Silently, she cursed herself for getting excited prematurely.

Sitting down, she stared at the handwriting. They were all different. She pulled out the letters and went straight to the last page. The names of the senders meant nothing to her.

'Do you know who these people are?' she asked Pramod on his return. 'I found these three letters on your desk.'

Pramod checked the names and shook his head. He scanned through each letter. 'There's nothing relevant in any of them.'

'Never mind,' said Nirmala, looking at the open safe. 'We'd better get started with those folders. Should we start with those faded ones first? They look older.'

'Okay. But my goodness: it's going to take us ages to get through all of them.'

'Not if we are organised. I think it's doable.'

Pramod laughed. 'I like your optimism.'

For the next three hours, they worked quietly and methodically without stopping, speaking only when they came across something of interest. Nirmala soon realised that she was faster than Pramod at filling the trays because he was reading everything with care.

'I can't help it, Nirmala. It's all so fascinating. There are things here about Mohan-*dada* that I never knew. For example, here's a bundle of ticket receipts from journeys *Dada* made to India and back. He went loads of times when he was younger on steamships called SS *Karanja* and SS *Kampala*. He travelled overland to Mozambique and boarded at the Port of Beira. Look at the pictures on these leaflets. The ships look amazing.'

'The old ocean liners. That's how people used to travel before, didn't they?'

'And these are school reports and certificates from India. They're from the 1920s!'

'What do they say?'

'Well, they're all in Gujarati, but I can make out that he was doing well. That doesn't surprise me because I know he was very clever. My father told me that everything we have today is largely down to Mohan-*dada*. He went to school in India but left for Africa on his own before he turned twenty. He came because someone who knew his father had offered him a job. It was to run a shop like a mini supermarket near the railway station. At that time, there were only a handful of Indian families here and Mohan-*dada* fitted in well with them. He stayed and soon became a successful businessman himself. He obviously made enough money to return to India to build Suparna Mansions.'

'Sounds like he was much braver than my Harilal-*dada*.'

'Mohan-*dada* had a strong personality. He often came across as forceful and dominating. All his sons will attest to that. But with us, his grandchildren, he was fine.'

Nirmala continued to scan and sort, working quickly but taking care to place things in the correct trays. As she worked, she became aware that the stack of personal letters was growing rapidly. There were a few that were written on the old-fashioned aerogrammes which folded into their own envelopes. They were affixed with Indian postage stamps. But a quick check showed that none were from Harilal. She put them aside for reading later.

'Do you think Mohan-*dada* might have destroyed his brother's letters?'

'Unlikely. If he kept his friends' letters, he would have kept his brother's too. Look at these. They're from all over the world. South Africa, Fiji, India, Mozambique, East Africa, you name it. All from people he knew long, long ago. I don't know any of them.'

'Okay. We should keep going.'

Stopping only for a sandwich lunch, the two worked steadily through the afternoon. Both managed to speed up once they got into the rhythm of the process. It became obvious to Nirmala that Mohanlal had a wide range of interests. In his youth, he appeared to be keen on films, plays and musicals, both English and Hindi. He was also a sports enthusiast, especially of cricket. Judging from all the travel fliers and ticket receipts, he later did a lot of travelling around the world. A man with many interests.

Later in the afternoon, over tea and biscuits, Nirmala placed in front of Pramod the aerogrammes she had set aside earlier. They were from India posted in the 1950s and 1960s.

'We should read these. They are not from Harilal-*dada* but they're from the time Suparna Mansions was built. Want to take a look?'

'Definitely!' He unfolded one and let out a groan. 'Ach, it's written in Gujarati.'

'I thought you could read Gujarati.'

'I can but it takes me too long. I'm faster in English.' He leaned back in his chair and began to read.

Nirmala continued with her sorting, letting her mind wander to Varun who she'd left in the care of Kavita. She wasn't used to being away from him for so long.

'Oh my God.' Pramod was on his feet. 'There's something in here.'

'What is it?' Hearing the excitement in his voice, Nirmala stood up too.

'There's a whole page on our grandparents. Here. You read it. I want to make sure I've understood properly.'

Taking the letter from him, Nirmala read through silently. She raised her eyes to Pramod's.

'It's written by someone called Umagauri. Do you know who that is?'

'No.'

Nirmala drew in her breath, hardly believing what she was about to say. 'I think I do.'

Pramod's eyes widened in surprise.

'Seeing the name at the bottom has jogged my memory about a conversation I had with my mother when I was around ten years old. Umagauri is an unusual name. There was a girl in my primary school with that name. I remember my mother saying that she knew of only one other person with that name.' Nirmala paused for breath.

'So, who was it?' asked Pramod with impatience.

'My grandmother Kanta had a brother who lived in a town called Surat. It was his wife who was called Umagauri. I never met them myself, but my mother told me about them. This must be from her. She would know Kanta very well because they were sisters-in-law.'

'Wow! Imagine you remembering that.'

Nirmala read through the letter again. It was dated March 1952, and Umagauri was congratulating Mohanlal and his wife Bhanu on the birth of their daughter, Suparna. But the main thrust of the letter was about Nirmala's own grandparents, Kanta and Harilal, who had also had a baby around the same time. Nirmala knew that baby was Suresh, her father.

'It looks like Kanta was struggling with her baby boy. Umagauri is asking Mohanlal to help his brother cope with his wife. She says Kanta isn't bonding with her son and is angry all the time.' Nirmala paused. 'That baby she's talking about is my father.'

Dropping her eyes to the letter again, she read that Kanta was refusing to hold her son and not speaking to her husband at all, claiming that she hated him and his whole family.

Pramod jerked his head back. 'Whoa! She says she hates her husband?'

Nirmala nodded, looking dazed.

'She mentions Bhanu, my grandmother,' continued Pramod. 'What does she say about her?'

'That she never wants to set eyes on her.'

'I *thought* that's what it said. My God! I wonder what happened.'

Nirmala considered what was written about Kanta's behaviour. She was clearly very unhappy. She had just given birth to Suresh, the first son after two daughters. People normally celebrated when they had sons. What was going on? Was she suffering from postnatal depression? She reread the letter and thought it was a strong possibility. Her symptoms sounded very much like it.

'Looks like she was lashing out at everyone. Maybe she was depressed. That does sometimes happen to women after they give birth.'

'You could be right. But I don't understand why she said she never wanted to see my grandmother Bhanu again.'

Nirmala shook her head thoughtfully. She wondered if perhaps Harilal was comparing the two women, and his brother's wife Bhanu was being praised for coping better with her baby. Not understanding anything about postnatal depression, maybe he was saying all the wrong things.

'Let's read these other letters. We might learn more.'

There were four aerogrammes in total, each from different people and from different time periods. They all mentioned the two brothers, their wives and families, but none referred to any problems.

Pramod tapped at one of them. 'This one is from 1963 asking *Dada* why he has not visited India for so long. When I think of it, I can't remember him ever making a trip there. My father took us a few times on holiday to see the Taj Mahal and other places, but as far as I know, Mohan-*dada* never went. Except in his youth of course. I wonder if he stopped his trips because of a rift between the families.'

Nirmala was thinking of her poor father. She already knew that growing up, he was not his mother's favourite. And when he was older, he'd walked away from her. But now she was reading that he had been spurned by Kanta at birth. With an ache in her heart, Nirmala returned the letter to Pramod. Her father didn't even get the comfort of his mother's cuddles at a time when physical contact was essential for all babies.

Pramod was asking about Harilal. 'What year did your grandfather pass away?'

'Around 1965. Why?'

'Well. Mohan-*dada* must have heard from someone in that year, telling him about his brother's death.'

'Yes. There must be letters about that somewhere. Let's keep searching.' Nirmala moved to retrieve another folder from the safe.

'No, Nirmala. We should stop for today. It's nearly 5 p.m.'

Nirmala did not want to stop. She desperately wanted to know why Suresh was so unloved at birth.

'We have plenty of time. Don't worry. I'm just as keen as you to find out what happened. We'll come back to this tomorrow.'

Reluctantly, Nirmala agreed and followed him out, her mind filled with images of a new-born baby crying for his mother to hold him. Every child deserved that much, and she felt heartbroken for her kind and loving father.

Chapter 24

When she arrived home, Nirmala gave Varun an extra-tight hug. Running around in the front garden with the twins, he seemed completely at home.

'We went to a park, Mumma. It was so much fun.' Varun's eyes were shining.

Nirmala laughed. 'Guess what? We are going to see Victoria Falls tomorrow. And then a safari park with lots of wild animals like lions and giraffes.'

Kavita joined them. 'He knows a lot about wild animals, doesn't he? Especially elephants. He told me African elephants have bigger ears than Indian ones. I didn't know that.'

'It's true. I have some ancient ornamental elephant figures made of wood that I'm sure came from here because the ears are enormous.'

'We also have wooden figures like that, so they were probably bought at the same time. Someone must have sent one set to your family in India.'

'Or taken them over personally,' said Nirmala. 'It was those elephants that made me believe that I might have relatives in Africa. I didn't think it was true at first.'

Kavita smiled. 'Shall we go in? I came to tell you that Suparna-*foi* is coming this evening to discuss the details of your trip. We should go in now and wash up for snacks.'

When Suparna arrived with her husband later that evening, she swept in like a tornado, hugging everyone and talking non-stop. Pramod managed to sit her down to check the itinerary.

'Great plan. Yah. We can leave whenever you say.'

Nirmala marvelled at the way she made decisions without consulting her husband. There was no doubt about who was in charge in their marriage. Nirmala's mind shifted to Ajay and how he controlled everything in their married life.

'Nirmala?' Pramod seemed to be waiting for her to speak. She shook herself out of her thoughts. 'Shall we tell them what we found out today?'

Nirmala nodded and indicated that he should begin. She listened as he explained how they found the letters and what information they contained. When he spoke about Kanta's rejection of her baby son, she watched Suparna's growing consternation.

'That baby boy was your father, wasn't he?' she asked Nirmala, eyes wide open in shock. Nirmala gave a slow nod.

'And there's more,' Pramod continued. 'Apparently, Kanta was saying that she never wanted to set eyes on Bhanu, *our* grandmother.'

Suparna's eyebrows jerked up in surprise. 'My mother? What did she do wrong?'

Pramod shrugged his shoulders. 'We have no idea. But we're going to search some more tomorrow.'

Suparna tutted, shaking her head. 'Poor Suresh. And poor Kanta too. It must have been an awful time for everyone. We *have* to find out what was going on.'

'We'll have to do that when we get back from our trip,' said Pramod. 'We're off tomorrow.'

Nirmala pursed her lips. She almost wished they were not going away. Her heart was in those folders left behind by Mohanlal.

When they began their journey the next morning, Nirmala's mind was still on the events of 1952. She found it hard to push these thoughts aside and relax into a holiday mood. But seeing how excited Varun was, she tried to be more cheerful.

Pramod explained that they had a five-hour drive ahead of them. Suparna and her husband Ishwar arrived just as they were supervising the loading of their bags into the minivan. Pramod climbed in beside Abbot the driver, who drove slowly round the curve of the driveway and out through the gates.

For the next few hours, they travelled over good tar roads with little traffic. Nirmala noticed signs along the route showing a speed limit of 120km/hour and watched Abbot keep within this maximum.

They passed several small towns along the way. The first one seemed more like a village, the streets virtually empty. Nirmala looked at the whitewashed buildings on either side of the main road with its few retail outlets, one supermarket and one hotel.

'This is Chegutu,' said Suparna. 'An old mining town. Used to be gold mines, but now mostly copper.'

Pramod and Suparna pointed out places of interest as they went past, giving them a brief history. When in doubt, they asked Ishwar to confirm the facts.

'Ishwar is our walking Wikipedia. He knows everything about Zimbabwe.' Suparna patted his knee. He rolled his eyes but flashed her a brief smile.

Nirmala sat back and began to enjoy the scenic views as they travelled from town to town. She liked the place names on the road signs: Chitungwiza, Murombedzi, Lalapansi, Kadoma, Kwe. Every so often, they went past small round mud huts with thatched roofs set a little distance away from the road. A few families sat outside the huts idly watching the cars go by. Some had tethered goats nearby and chickens roaming freely around them.

'These villages remind me of India,' said Nirmala, observing the pretty round huts.

Suparna agreed. 'Just like in India, life is tough for these villagers. They have no water, gas or electricity. They walk miles to fetch water from nearby rivers which often gives them parasitic diseases like bilharzia.'

They stopped for lunch at a house-cum-restaurant on the outskirts of a town called Gweru. Abbot drove through an attractive brick arch then along a short gravel path to the side of a large rambling cottage. He parked under a leafy msasa tree alongside a few other cars.

'This is a home that has been turned into a restaurant,' said Ishwar.

They stopped at the entrance to admire the stunning garden with its freshly cut grass and sweet-scented flower beds. The sound of birds chirping filled the air. Nirmala breathed in deeply. The day was too beautiful to sit indoors. Clearly Suparna felt the same because she asked for a table on the veranda.

As they tucked into their pizzas, chicken burgers and chips, Nirmala looked at Varun's happy face. This was a far cry from their usual diet of daal and rice. She couldn't help thinking about Ajay who had been diverting money away from the basic needs of his own son. Silently, she cursed herself for being blind to his cheating ways.

After the meal, Nirmala took a stroll around the gardens with Suparna. When they returned to the table, she heard Ishwar giving Varun a history lesson.

'This restaurant is named after an Englishman called Cecil John Rhodes. When he died, he was buried in a beautiful place called Motopos Hills, not far from here.'

'Are we going there?' asked Varun.

'No. We don't have the time because it's still a long way to Victoria Falls.'

Nirmala was curious. 'Do people still visit the grave? I mean, since it became Zimbabwe?'

'Yah,' said Ishwar. 'It is said that the grave has never been desecrated out of respect for the dead. But I think it's more like respect for the money it brings in from tourists.'

Suparna patted her husband's cheek. 'Always the cynic, aren't you?'

~

They reached Bulawayo at 4.30 in the afternoon. The city looked beautiful in the sunshine, with its tree-lined avenues and colonial houses with verandas. The streets were wide with double car parking spaces in the middle. The main shopping area was busy with people.

The hotel was large and luxurious with an enormous reception area. Varun loved the family room so much that Nirmala had trouble coaxing him out for their evening meal.

After dinner, everyone except Nirmala and Suparna retired for bed. The two sat in the hotel lounge, sipping coffee and chatting.

'Tell me about yourself, Nirmala. What do you like doing? What are your interests?'

Nirmala sat back and rested her head on the comfortable armchair. She gazed at the crystal chandelier above their heads. 'I don't have much time for interests,' she said in a resigned tone.

Suparna studied her for a moment. 'What did you like doing before you got married? Did you enjoy going out with friends, watch films, read books?'

Nirmala paused. 'I stopped reading a long time ago.'

'Why?'

Nirmala looked away. 'I lost the joy of reading when I got married. Life changed so much.'

Suparna said nothing. Nirmala thought of all the times Ajay had raged at her for borrowing books from the library and becoming engrossed in them.

'Ajay didn't like me reading.' She pictured her husband scowling at her if he found her reading a novel. 'He argued with me so much over it that eventually I gave up. I think he felt neglected or something. I don't know.'

'Sounds like a killjoy to me. And a total control freak.' Suparna leaned forward, willing Nirmala to look at her. 'Tell me something.' She kept her voice low and gentle. 'Were you forced to marry him?'

This was not something Nirmala ever spoke about. It was too personal. But Suparna's warmth was like a magnet drawing her in, making her want to bare her soul. She felt safe with her. Sudhir's face flashed into her mind and her eyes immediately went soft.

'I was in love with someone else. His name was Sudhir. We were going to get married and live happily ever after.'

Suparna moved back in surprise.

'But no one lives happily ever after, do they?' asked Nirmala with a sad smile.

'What happened?'

'His parents put a stop to it. They made it clear I was not good enough.'

Suparna frowned. Nirmala sat back and looked at a spot in the distance. 'They came to my house to tell my mother that they would not agree to the marriage because we were too low caste for them. They are Brahmins, the highest caste in our Hindu religion, as you know. When Sudhir was out of the way they came to tell us that I was not welcome in their home.'

Suparna's frown deepened. She looked puzzled. 'Sudhir did fight for you, didn't he?'

'He didn't know. He was at university in Mumbai. We'd agreed to tell his parents after he graduated. Somehow, they found out what we were planning to do.'

'But when Sudhir learned about what they said . . . ?'

'It was too late. From the way his parents spoke, I knew they would never accept me. And I didn't want to be the girl who made Sudhir break away from his family. So, I didn't tell him.' Nirmala sighed. 'By the time he found out, I was married to Ajay.'

'What? So quickly?' Suparna looked shocked.

'I'd already had a marriage proposal from Ajay's family. Jasu-*foi* knew him from her husband's village and she introduced him to us. Funny, isn't it, how she didn't like us but was willing to arrange my marriage?'

Suparna's mouth was closed in a thin line.

Nirmala continued, 'I realised later that it suited her to have me married off to someone with no prospects. She didn't want me to move up in the world. Anyway, I knew things would be difficult for Sudhir if he married me, so I decided to set him free by marrying someone else.'

'But Nirmala. To marry a complete stranger?'

Nirmala felt a tiredness creep over her. 'I did meet Ajay once before the wedding. He was on his best behaviour and fooled me into thinking he was nice. Well, nice enough anyway.'

Suparna was speechless.

'My mother tried to talk me out of it. But I'd made up my mind. I knew we were not well-suited, but I was eighteen years old, young and foolish, as they say.' Nirmala paused to finish her coffee. Giving Suparna a sad smile, she shrugged her shoulders. 'It wasn't long before I realised my mistake. But it was too late to do anything about it.'

'How long have you been married?'

'Eleven years.' Nirmala let out a long sigh. 'Varun was born after two miscarriages. Two miscarriages! It was a distressing time. Then our miracle baby came along. I thought Ajay would be happy he had a son. But no. He says he's ashamed of Varun because he is weak. Varun is not weak; he's just a sensitive little boy.' Nirmala shook her head. 'You know, I was prepared to stay with him forever. But now . . .' She broke off, staring into the distance.

Leaning forward, Suparna prompted. 'But now?'

Nirmala lifted her chin and turned around. 'But now, I'm not sure.' In a flat voice, she told Suparna about Ajay's infidelity and about his other child. She watched Suparna's expressions change from shock to anger and then finally to sadness.

'In the end, my sacrifice was all in vain. Sudhir broke away from his family and left home because he was furious with them for what they said to my mother and me.'

'Did he marry someone else?'

Nirmala was silent for a while. 'No. He runs a pharmacy in Navsari and lives alone above the business.' Her eyes misted over. 'I tried to convince myself that I no longer loved Sudhir. The truth is, I have never stopped loving him.'

The two sat quietly for a while, sipping their drinks and thinking their own thoughts.

Eventually, Suparna patted her hand. 'Everything is going to be fine. Just keep thinking that and keep looking forward.' Nirmala's heart was too full of sadness to contemplate any happiness that might be awaiting her in the future.

Chapter 25

Pramod stood with his arms outstretched and face wreathed in smiles. 'This is it: Victoria Falls. Or to call it by its real name: *Mosi-oa-Tunya*, The Smoke that Thunders.' The roar of the waterfall behind him was so loud, he had to shout.

They stood face to face with the iconic view of the famous Falls. A powerful cascade of water plummeted down the cliff edge opposite them. The sight was awe-inspiring. Nirmala watched in wonder, lost for words, drenched by the spray coming up from the gorge.

'Cover your heads,' shouted Suparna. 'Use your raincoat hoods.'

Ishwar took out his camera. 'Stand together everyone. And say cheese!'

Varun screamed, 'Cheese!' He laughed and jumped about as the spray hit his face.

When they'd had their fill of posing, Pramod led them to a life-size statue of a stern-looking man gazing out to the Falls. He looked impressive but strangely out of place amongst the natural beauty of the Falls.

'This is David Livingstone,' explained Suparna. 'The man who *discovered* the Falls in the nineteenth century.' She air-quoted the word discovered.

They spent the morning walking around the National Park, seeing the cascade from different viewpoints. The damp soil gave off a pleasant earthy scent. Above them they could see and hear countless birds flying by, displaying brightly coloured wings. Nirmala looked up at the blue sky and allowed her mind to drift. She imagined she was a cloud, floating leisurely over the land, feeling blissfully happy and totally fulfilled.

'What are you thinking?' Suparna was walking beside her.

'Just enjoying the beauty of this place. I don't know why, but it makes me feel . . . free.'

Suparna puckered her brow. 'Is that unusual?'

Nirmala considered the question. Did she ever feel free? She had to admit that she didn't. There was always that sense of being held back from doing what she really wanted to do. Thinking of her marriage, she felt trapped, unable to leave for so many reasons; the main one being Ajay. He dominated her and made her feel inadequate. All the confidence she'd had before her marriage had ebbed away. She cursed herself because she had given him permission to bully her from the start.

'You look sad, Nirmala. What is it?'

Nirmala tried to shake off the feeling of gloom that had settled on her. It felt like she was falling into a sinkhole. 'It's anxiety. I feel anxious all the time.'

Suparna nodded, as if she understood Nirmala's churning emotions. She looped an arm through hers and gave her some advice. 'Be strong, Nirmala. Whatever life throws at you, remain strong. Things are going to change. They're going to get better; I just know it.' Nudging her gently, she spoke with a smile. 'Now, put all your sadness away and enjoy feeling free. Look around you. Isn't Mother Nature wonderful?'

In the afternoon, they took a short trip on a steam train crossing a bridge high above the Zambezi River. They looked out from the windows at the chasm below and the torrent of water plunging down. Craning her neck, Nirmala gazed in wonder at the billowing volumes of steam behind them as the train chugged along.

'See the footbridge running alongside the train tracks?' Pramod asked. 'When we get to the middle, you will see people jumping off the bridge with nothing but rope tied to their feet. It's called bungee jumping.'

Pramod laughed at Nirmala's expression of horror. 'Don't worry. We won't be doing that. It's for the thrill seekers who also go white-water rafting and zip wiring down the mountains. We'll be doing something much safer; we're going on a helicopter ride.'

It was a ride Nirmala would never forget. Looking down from the sky the next morning, the view was stunning, with the waterfall throwing a cloud of spray and mist high above it. The power of the water was incredible, and the noise was astounding. The pilot pointed out facts and figures, telling them that this was one of the seven wonders of the natural world.

Varun was so enthralled by the whole experience that he could not stop talking about it that evening. Nirmala gave him paper and a pencil to draw pictures of what he had seen. She left him in the room sketching away and went to join the adults on the terrace.

The hotel was an old colonial-style building, full of history and character, with arched verandas overlooking the bridge over the Falls.

'If things had been different, you might have grown up here with us and seen all this already,' said Pramod.

Nirmala smiled. 'My life would have been completely different. But I was happy growing up in Navsari. I went to an English-medium school and we had a lot of opportunities.'

'Did you grow up in the house opposite Suparna Mansions?' asked Pramod.

'Yes. And I still live there.'

Suparna looked curious. 'Didn't you ever feel hard done by? Jasumati and your cousins were living in such luxury just across from you.'

Nirmala grew serious. 'Sometimes I did. Especially after Pappa died and Mummy's treatment costs escalated. I had to give up my plans to go to university. It would have been nice if Jasu-*foi* had helped out a little.'

Suparna tutted. 'Do you have any idea why she shuns you? And what did she have against your father, her own brother?'

Nirmala sighed. 'I wish I knew. All I know is that both she and Kanta-*ba* treated my father badly. Now we know that even at birth, my father was pushed away.'

'But what grudge does Jasumati bear against you?' Suparna was becoming increasingly angry.

Nirmala shrugged her shoulders. 'It's possible that Kanta-*ba* turned Jasu-*foi* against my father. You know my other aunt, Pushpa, who drowned in the lake? Well, maybe Jasu-*foi* never stopped blaming my father for being the one who survived. And because I'm his daughter, she blames me as well.'

Pramod was studying her face. He hesitated before speaking. 'I have been thinking about Jasu-*foi*. How would you feel if we invited her to visit us here?'

Nirmala was caught off guard. She'd never considered the possibility of Jasumati coming to Zimbabwe. Frowning, she pondered the question before responding. 'I worry that she may cause problems for you when she finds out you own Suparna Mansions.'

'That's just it, Nirmala. I think she *has* found out.'

Nirmala raised her eyebrows. 'How?'

Pramod clicked his tongue in annoyance. 'Hemel phoned last night to tell me Ramu-*kaka* called him. He says he has written to Jasu-*foi*, telling her that she should start thinking about moving out.'

'What?' Nirmala was shocked. 'How did she react?'

'We don't know. He says he posted the letter a week ago.'

Suparna was furious. 'He's lying. I know my brother. Full of bullshit.'

'Maybe. But I can't help wondering what his legal team is getting up to. I wouldn't put it past Ramu-*kaka* to concoct a false story and present it as evidence in his favour. He wants Suparna Mansions, so he will try anything to win his case in court.'

'You don't really believe he could win, do you?' asked Suparna, looking surprised.

'Not really. But I can't ignore the fact that he will go to any lengths to get his way. I don't trust him.'

He looked at Nirmala. 'I wonder if it's time for me to tell Jasu-*foi* myself. I should make it clear she has no need to move out.'

Nirmala looked down, her mind racing. Jasumati was bound to put up a fight if anyone dared to tell her to leave the home she believed was hers. It was unthinkable. She would never accept that someone else owned it. How would she respond if Pramod told her she could stay? She would still fight. If invited, would she come to Zimbabwe? Maybe she would. But Nirmala did not want her to come to make trouble for these kind people. A feeling of dread began to creep up from the pit of her stomach.

'Pramod! Did you have to bring that up?' Suparna was irritated. 'You've got Nirmala all worried again.' Pramod looked contrite and Suparna tutted. 'Can we change the subject now?'

That night, Nirmala's thoughts were back in Navsari with Jasumati. She was probably aware by now that they were out of town. Maybe she knew where they were. It was possible, though unlikely, that Ajay had told her the whole story. And if she received Ramu-*kaka*'s letter, telling her to move out, she was bound to be furious with everyone, especially with her.

Realising that she was falling into a sinkhole again, Nirmala chided herself for wasting energy worrying about Jasumati. She made a conscious decision to park her concerns and try to enjoy the sightseeing. But it was hard not to let these thoughts cast a shadow over the rest of the trip.

The next day, they walked in bright sunshine through the main road of the town. Local Zimbabweans lined the street selling their handmade wares. They displayed wicker baskets, doilies, aprons, soapstone statues and many other artefacts. Shouting out their prices, the sellers competed with one another in loud voices.

The vendors were all desperate to make a sale. They were vying with one another to get the attention of the few tourists walking around. If this was the only way they could make a living, it was hard to imagine how they could survive. Once again Nirmala was reminded of the poor street vendors in her own country.

That evening, they enjoyed cocktails and soft drinks on the veranda. As she sipped her orange juice, Nirmala admired the beautiful African sunset. From their viewpoint, the sun was a glowing ball of fire in the sky, painting it bright orange and gold as it slowly sank into the horizon. For a brief moment, a feeling of calm washed over Nirmala and she sat back to enjoy it.

The next day, they travelled for two hours to the Hwangi Safari Park. When they reached their hotel, Suparna led them towards the back of the spacious reception area. Through a wide toughened glass wall, they were able to see far into the distance. What they saw made them gasp in wonder. Beyond a long stretch of lawn, they could see a small lake. And drinking at the lakeside were half a dozen elephants and a small herd of deer.

'Elephants,' breathed Varun. 'Can we go outside?'

Suparna shook her head. 'No. Those are wild elephants. You can't go close to them.'

'Why?'

'Because if we frighten them, they might attack us. We have to keep our distance.'

Over the next three days, they viewed an abundance of wildlife from the safety of their Land Rovers. The rangers took them to see lions, leopards, rhinos, buffalo, antelope and hundreds of elephants in their natural habitat.

Unfortunately, that evening Varun had one of his epilepsy turns. It was the first since he'd started his new treatment. Nirmala sat on the floor of their hotel room and gently placed his head on her lap, stroking his hair and waiting for him to come back. When he did, he lay tired and drained of all energy.

'It's all right, my *dikra*.' She kept her voice soft and low, doing her best to hide her own concern. Don't panic, she told herself. The new treatment will start working soon. She had to believe that. But gazing down at her son, she wondered if he would ever be free of this terrible condition.

Chapter 26

As much as she enjoyed seeing the sights of Zimbabwe, Nirmala couldn't help feeling relieved to be back in Harare and back in Mohanlal's room full of folders. At the earliest opportunity after their return, she'd asked Pramod if they could pick up where they had left off. He'd explained that she would need to continue without him as he had some pressing business matters to attend to.

Searching for the truth was becoming increasingly urgent for Nirmala. She had only two weeks left before her return to India. By discovering more about Mohanlal's life, she felt she was getting closer to finding out why he and his brother had been so secretive about their relationship. If they'd been open about that, her father Suresh would have known about his Zimbabwean relations, and they would all have met. She would have had people she could call family. Her aunt Jasumati had shown her no love whatsoever. But if their relationship could be mended by knowing what happened in the past, life would be so much better.

By meeting her new-found relatives, things were already much improved for her and Varun. But Nirmala needed to know why her father had gone through such difficulties in his life. What caused the argument with Kanta that resulted in him leaving Suparna Mansions to move into the small house across the road? Why did his sister Jasumati treat him and his family with such disdain?

Nirmala was convinced that knowing the answers to these questions would somehow lighten the burdens that were weighing her down.

Sitting at the desk with all the paperwork in front of her, Nirmala scanned through the items and sorted them into the appropriate trays. She paid particular attention to the letters. Although she found nothing revealing there, she did get an insight into Mohanlal's life over the decades. Disappointingly, there were no juicy bits of information about family relationships.

She decided to go through the box of old photographs again. She was curious about the collection amassed by Mohanlal. They must have been of some importance to him. There were dozens of black-and-white photos as well as more recent colour pictures of family, friends, Indian movie stars and even politicians. Faces of famous people like Mahatma Gandhi and Jawaharlal Nehru stared back at her from the time of India's independence. There was even one photograph of a young Mohanlal Dayal standing beside Prime Minister Nehru in an official-looking room. Clearly very interested in the politics and fate of his home country, he must have made a special visit to Delhi at one time.

Nirmala picked out all the family photos with names and dates scribbled on the backs. She held on to the ones from around 1952. She looked at each one, checking carefully to see if she could work out who they were, then put them back in the box. When she found one of three children posing in front of the camera, she scrutinised it closely, wondering who they could be. It was a grainy black-and-white, three-inch-square photo with a white border on all four sides. Turning it around, she tried to read the names scrawled in tiny Gujarati letters. The writing had faded over the years and she had difficulty in making out the words.

With a sudden jolt, she sat up straight. She recognised the names: Jasumati, Pushpa and Suresh: her father with his two older sisters. With a racing heart, she turned over the photo and peered at the children's faces. Her father around the age of four or five was grinning from ear to ear, holding his middle sister's hand.

With her heart pounding in her ears, Nirmala looked for more photos of the children and their parents, Harilal and Kanta. She turned the box upside down and searched through the whole collection. She found two more: one of the siblings with Kanta and another of the middle sister on her own. There were none of Harilal. He must have been behind the camera taking the pictures. All were taken on the same day: 27 June 1956.

Nirmala could not believe what she was seeing. She realised the little girl on her own was Pushpa, the sister who had drowned in the lake. The photos had been taken one year before her tragic death. On the back of Pushpa's photo, her name and date were followed by three additional lines. Nirmala focused her eyes on the words.

Even Pushpa has been taken from us.

Kanta has once again lost her mind.

Am I being punished for what I did?

Nirmala bit her lip. Her breath was tight in her chest. She read the lines over and over again, trying to decipher their meaning. *Even Pushpa has been taken from us.* Who else had been taken from them? Did they have another child that they never talked about? Perhaps Kanta had had a miscarriage.

Kanta has once again lost her mind. This must be a reference to the time Kanta experienced postnatal depression when Suresh was born. And what did the last line mean? It was probably Harilal who had written these lines. *Am I being punished for what I did?* What had he done? Nirmala sat staring at the words for a long time, trying to understand what this could mean. She had heard only good things about Harilal. What could he possibly have done that was bad?

Nothing was making any sense. Eventually, she gave up. Putting everything away apart from the three photos, she went to show them to Pramod. He was sitting at his desk, looking through some numbers on a report. Buzzing with nervous energy, she placed the photos in front of him.

'Look what I found!' She was breathless with excitement.

He glanced at her then studied each of the pictures one by one. Turning them around he shook his head as he silently read the names, dates and words. Nirmala waited impatiently for him to say something. When he finally looked up, she saw that his eyes were glazed and his face had lost some of its colour.

'How did we miss these?' he said in a hushed tone. He stood and held up Pushpa's photo. 'Can you read this one for me?'

Nirmala went round to his side and read it out loud. 'What do you think this means?' she asked.

'They must have lost another child. Maybe a miscarriage.'

'That's what I was thinking. What about the last line: *Am I being punished?* What could that mean?'

Pramod just stood there, shaking his head and thinking.

Nirmala let out a long sigh. 'It's so tiring trying to work it out. Something terrible must have happened.'

Pramod gave her a sympathetic smile. 'Look. Don't overthink it. It was probably nothing more than a father's guilt for not being there to protect his daughter. Any father would feel that.' He tutted. 'Go home, Nirmala, and have a rest. As soon as I can, I will get back to searching through the folders. Try not to worry about it.'

Nirmala shook her head. 'I can't help worrying.'

'I know. But you'll have to park this for a while. You're going on another trip. This is going to play on your mind, isn't it? Think of Varun. If he senses that you are anxious about something, he will also be anxious. Look, as I'm not going with you this time, I will make time to go through the papers. And if I find anything important, I'll call you. Okay?'

Nirmala sighed again. 'Okay. But you must promise to contact me immediately. Will you do that?'

'I promise, I promise.' Pramod laughed, putting both hands up as if she was holding a gun to him. 'Gosh. You can be as fierce as Suparna-*foi* sometimes.'

Chapter 27

With great difficulty, Nirmala set her worries to one side once again. This time, only four of them were travelling: Reena, Varun, Nirmala and Abbot the driver. Strapping herself in at the front of their Mercedes-Benz saloon, one of Pramod's many cars, Reena explained that they were heading for a place called Chinhoyi, about seventy miles away, famous for an ancient and mysterious cave.

Entering the mouth of the cave, they walked a few metres down a gradual slope, their eyes slowly becoming accustomed to the gloom. They headed towards a long, rectangular cavern with high rocky walls surrounding it. A steep flight of steps lay before them, leading deep down into the earth. There seemed to be some natural light filtering through from somewhere much further inside the cave.

Nirmala held Varun's hand and followed Reena. About halfway down, they stopped and stood to the side so they could take in their surroundings. Nirmala looked down and realised where the light was coming from. Way below, where the steps ended, part of the cave roof was open to the sky. Daylight was streaming onto a pool of water which filled the floor of the cave. The colour of the water took her breath away. It was an incredible deep shade of blue, highlighted by the sky which seemed to be shining a spotlight on it. All was quiet and atmospheric with the air cool on their faces. The water below was completely still.

'This is a very ancient site,' explained Reena. 'We think it was used by tribes as a hideaway from their enemies.' She moved closer to whisper in Nirmala's ear. 'Legend has it that people were murdered en masse and thrown into that pool, which is very, very deep.'

Nirmala widened her eyes in mock horror.

As they continued their descent, the silence seemed to intensify. When they reached the bottom, they stood quietly behind large rocks which acted as a barrier to the cobalt-blue water. They could see underwater rock formations many feet below the surface.

'It looks like blue glass,' said Varun. 'And there's fish.' He pointed to small silver-hued fish swimming near the top.

Nirmala peered in and couldn't help thinking of dead bodies lying at the bottom. Despite her earlier bravado, she shivered. All of a sudden, the place gave her an eerie feeling and she turned to start the ascent back to the top. But Reena wanted to take photos on her smartphone. As soon as that was over, they made their way carefully up to the open air.

Abbot was waiting patiently for them by the car. When he saw them approach, he took out picnic baskets from the boot of the car and laid out a sandwich lunch on a wooden table with bench seats. The weather was warm and the green open space was ideal for Varun to let off steam. He began to have a kick about with Abbot, who had produced a football from the car.

'He's a happy chap, isn't he?' said Reena.

'Most of the time. But sometimes he goes very quiet. It's usually when he's hungry or worried.'

'Worried about what?'

'About his father's anger, about how I will cope, about what will happen next. So many things. I try to be cheerful around him, but he can sense when I'm fretting.'

'You have a lot on your plate,' said Reena. After a few moments of silence, she continued: 'It's hard to understand why Jasu-*foi* doesn't help you. How is it that she stayed in the mansion and your father moved out?'

'My father walked away after a row with his mother, Kanta.' Nirmala thought of the image of her grandmother in the small photograph she'd found. Young, attractive and elegantly dressed in a sari, she had looked into the camera with a little smile. She didn't look like someone who would push her one and only son away. But that is exactly what she had done. Not just at the time of his birth, but later in life too.

'Jasu-*foi* sided with their mother?' asked Reena.

'She must have. When I was growing up, she had very little to do with us. My parents never really said much about her, except that she liked to keep to herself.'

'Jasu-*foi* was the lucky one.' Reena grimaced. 'Seems very unfair to you and your family.'

'It never bothered me when my parents were alive. My father had a good pest control business, and we were reasonably well off. It's only recently that I have felt the unfairness of it. I resent the fact that my son has to go without things when Jasu-*foi*'s children and grandchildren have so much.'

'It's not right that she inherited *all* the family fortunes.'

'But now we know that Suparna Mansions was never her inheritance.' Nirmala considered the possibility of Jasumati being forced to move out. 'Do *you* believe Ramu-*kaka* posted a letter to her?'

'No, I don't. He's full of hot air. And if he did, wouldn't we have heard from Jasu-*foi* by now? It's been nearly two weeks.'

Nirmala exhaled slowly. 'I'm beginning to think she might react in a different way. Instead of getting angry, she might just ignore the letter. It's possible she thinks no one would be able to evict her after so many years of living there. Maybe she's right.'

'Well, we don't have to worry about that because Pramod will not be evicting her.'

Nirmala said nothing. Her thoughts had moved on to Ajay. She wondered what he was getting up to in her absence.

Reena was watching her face. 'What is it that troubles you most, Nirmala?'

With a slow intake of breath Nirmala explained her fear of going home and finding her husband still there. 'I feel sick just thinking about it.'

Reena patted her arm. 'I know it's hard but try not to think about him. Don't let him ruin your holiday. You're going to love the next destination. You will see the incredible Kariba Dam and we will go on a cruise round Lake Kariba. There are so many incredible animals living in the wild.'

The boat cruise was definitely the highlight of the trip and seeing the look of fascination on Varun's face made all of it worthwhile. Starting in the afternoon, the tour boat seemed to float over the tranquil lake, like a swan gliding gracefully across the water. The size of the lake made it feel like an ocean. They passed a few luxury houseboats with tourists sunbathing or fishing from the decks.

The guide on board was pointing at something to the side of the boat. Two pods of hippos were surfacing with their huge mouths wide open to the sky. Above them, a group of large birds flew by emitting a high-pitched whistling sound.

Later, as the sun was going down, the boat went closer to the shore, and they were treated to exquisite sights such as elephant families and groups of impala having a drink. Nirmala wondered how safe the animals were and asked Reena if there were crocodiles hiding in the water.

'There might be. Sometimes the crocs lie quiet then suddenly leap up and grip with their sharp teeth. But you know, our elephants and rhinos have a more dangerous predator: man.'

'Poachers?' asked Nirmala. 'I thought that had stopped.'

'No. Parts of the world still pay a lot of money for elephant tusks and rhino horns.'

Nirmala looked at the magnificent creatures minding their own business on the shore and felt saddened that they could be killed so easily by human beings.

Varun was calling her, excitedly pointing at something further inland. The vegetation behind the drinking animals was low grass with thorny scrub. Beyond that was a wooded area with tall leafy trees. Eating those leaves from high branches were a tower of giraffes, at least twenty of them. They reached up with their long necks and stretched their tongues to pull in the leaves and buds from the treetops.

'Real giraffes!' Varun whispered as they all watched in awe.

Tired and happy, they returned to their hotel, ready to go back to Harare the next day. Nirmala was about to get into bed when there was an urgent knock on her door. It was Reena, looking flustered and a little out of breath.

'It's Pramod.' She held up her cell phone. 'He wants to speak to you.'

'Is he okay?'

'Yes, yes. He's fine. Here.' She thrust the phone at her. 'You need to speak to him.' Handing it over, she sat down on the bed nearest the door. Nirmala frowned and watched her for a moment before addressing Pramod.

'Hello?'

'Nirmala. I found something. Something really important.'

Chapter 28

It was a letter from Kanta to Mohanlal, written a few months after the death of her husband. She was informing her brother-in-law that Harilal had passed away. Holding the single sheet of paper in her hand, Nirmala felt as if Kanta's words were burning a hole right through her skin. They were tough, harsh and cruel. She read the letter twice in succession before looking up at Pramod and Reena, who sat opposite her on the porch swing. Looking shell-shocked, they waited for her to say something.

'When you told me about this on the phone last night, I didn't believe you,' she said to Pramod. Her hand trembled as she held up the letter. 'I still can't believe it. Can it be true?'

'It must be. Why would she write that if it wasn't?' Pramod's face was grim.

'It's not something anyone would make up,' said Reena.

Nirmala looked at the paper which must have been crisp and white at one time. It was pale brown and slightly crumpled, as if someone had scrunched it up then tried to smooth out the creases. The date at the top was 12 September 1965. There was no envelope.

'Was there anything else from her?' she asked Pramod.

'Not from her, but from her husband. There is a bundle of Diwali cards addressed to Mohan-*dada*. But apart from the scribbled greetings, there are no personal messages. These were all stashed in a tatty brown envelope labelled “Receipts”. I nearly tossed it into the miscellaneous tray thinking it was unimportant.’

Reena leaned forward. ‘Could you read the letter to us? Our Gujarati is not the best.’

Nirmala pressed her lips together. She stood up and walked to the front door and waited for a moment, looking out at the garden. Then she returned to sit on the wall seat, leaned back on the pillar and began to read, her voice tight and strained.

Mohan-bhai
I am writing to let you know that Harilal suffered a heart attack and passed away three months ago. You can inform your mother that her younger son is dead. You didn't hear about it sooner because I did not want you to turn up at the funeral. The reason should be obvious.

When you and your wife Bhanu took my baby away from me, I vowed never to speak to either of you again. People are obsessed with having sons and all of you assumed I would be happy to exchange my daughter with your baby boy. But I wanted my own blood, not yours.

You were the main instigator, but I blame Harilal too. Your brother died knowing that I never forgave him. I know all about the secret pact you both made on a drunken night before Bhanu and I had our babies. You were desperate to have a daughter, and without talking to us, you brothers agreed to swap babies if the genders did not suit you.

You should know that I hate your mother almost as much as I hate you. She should have understood. But no. A man must be obeyed by his wife. Convenient for you that Bhanu and I were in India, in the same house at the same time. Was it your mother who arranged the home births and bribed the midwife to falsify the birth certificates?

Bhanu was too scared to go against you, or maybe after five sons, she also wanted a daughter. But it is MY daughter you stole and ran off with before I could stop you, and before Harilal could change his mind.

Your brother forced me to give up a piece of my heart. And you held him to his promise, even though you must have known he would come to regret it. He is gone now, and I am closing the door forever, so stay away. Don't ever try to contact me or my family.

Kanta

The letter sounded even more shocking when read aloud. Pramod and Reena were struck dumb by the power of the words. After Pramod had read it to her over the phone, Nirmala had been unable to sleep. A baby exchange! How could that have been allowed to happen? Her father had been swapped with Suparna almost as soon as they were born. Swapped! It was unimaginable.

If that hadn't happened, Suresh would have lived in Zimbabwe and Suparna would have been in Navsari with her sister Jasumati. They were real sisters, not cousins. No wonder they looked so alike. But something was not adding up.

'Pramod-*bhai*? Wasn't Suparna-*foi* born here in Zimbabwe?'

'She was. I mean, that's what I assumed. But maybe she wasn't. I know one or two of my uncles were born in India, so I guess she must have been too. I never really paid much attention to all that.'

Reena agreed. 'We should ask Mum. She will know.'

'Hang on a minute,' said Pramod. 'We can't say anything about this yet. Suparna-*foi* needs to know first.' He whistled through his teeth. 'Just how are we going to tell her?'

They fell silent again. Nirmala was thinking about her grandmother Kanta. 'My father was not her real son. That's why she didn't love him.' Her voice quivered. 'He probably sensed that all his life.'

Pramod slapped a hand on his forehead. 'Nirmala! Those words on the photo make sense now. What was it?' He screwed up his eyes to remember.

Even Pushpa has been taken from us.

Kanta has once again lost her mind.

Am I being punished for what I did?

He exhaled through pursed lips. 'There was no miscarriage. The two children they lost were Pushpa and Suparna.'

Nirmala nodded. 'And Harilal-*dada* was thinking that because he had agreed to the baby exchange God was punishing him by taking Pushpa away too.'

Pramod put his head in his hands. 'This is blowing my mind. Suparna-*foi* is going to go crazy!'

Reena blew out her cheeks. 'You two should go and see her straight after breakfast tomorrow. I'll look after Varun.'

Later that evening, when Pramod's mother was chewing her after-supper *paan*, he affected a casual tone and asked, 'Mummy? Were all of Daddy's siblings born in Zimbabwe?'

'Not all.' His mother was similarly casual. 'Three of the six were born in India. Suparna was one of them.'

Nirmala looked down at her hands as Pramod continued with his questions.

'How come?'

'I was told that at that time, your Mohan-*dada* and Bhanu-*ba* were staying in India for a few years to oversee the building of the mansion. They took your great-grandmother, Godavari-*ma*, with them. This was all before my time, of course.'

So that explained it. Nirmala got a sudden mental image of the two brothers in the same house, waiting for their wives to give birth. Over a couple of drinks, they had made that fateful pact without any consideration of their wives' feelings.

Pieces of the jigsaw puzzle were fitting together nicely, creating the picture of Kanta and Bhanu giving birth in the same week in one house. Nirmala recalled her conversation with Suparna when they'd discussed her date of birth. She was born only two days after Suresh. She imagined Mohanlal's disappointment when Bhanu gave birth to their sixth son, and two days later, his joy at knowing that Kanta had a little girl. A terrible thought came to mind; that of this baby girl being picked up by Mohanlal and taken away while Kanta slept. Nirmala rubbed her eyes, trying to wipe away that sickening image from her mind.

Armed with the letter, Nirmala and Pramod set off the next morning. 'Does Suparna-*foi* know why we're going to see her?' she asked.

'No. She thinks it's a social visit. I'm pretty sure there'll be snacks laid on and we'll be pulled straight into her dining room.'

That was exactly what happened. 'I made your favourite, Pramod. *Patudi.* Hope you like it too, Nirmala.' She piled at least ten little chickpea flour rolls onto her plate.

'I do, but . . .' Nirmala looked at Pramod. They both became serious.

'What is it?' Suparna pulled her eyebrows together.

'I think you should sit down, *Foi*. We have something to tell you.' Pramod paused as she pulled out a chair at the head of the table. She looked expectantly from one to the other on either side of her. 'We found a letter in one of *Dada*'s folders that explains what happened all those years ago.'

A smile animated Suparna's face. 'Really? Tell me.'

Pramod pursed his lips. 'It's not good news.'

'Oh.' Suparna's face fell. She turned to Nirmala. 'Who is the letter from?'

Nirmala glanced at Pramod then reached for her bag to retrieve the folded sheet of paper. She handed it over, saying, 'You should read this for yourself. It concerns you more than anybody else.'

Looking puzzled, Suparna searched their faces before unfolding the letter. Then she placed it on the table, took off her spectacles and bent her head forward to read. Within seconds, her head shot up. She looked furious.

'What the hell is this? Who took whose baby away?'

Pramod put his hand on her arm. 'Read the whole letter before you say anything. Please.'

Looking even more puzzled, Suparna continued with her reading. Strange sounds came out of her mouth as she read: gasps, groans, yelps and hisses. She raised her head once then lowered it again to read the lines for a second and third time. Finally, she looked up.

Nirmala saw that she was horrified. Her mouth was a big round 'O' and her eyes were open wide. She reached for Suparna's hand and squeezed it. 'I know it's shocking. Hard to believe. But . . .'

'Are you sure it's true?' Suparna's voice was barely a whisper.

Nirmala nodded. 'We know that you and my father were born within two days of one another in February 1952. And we learned yesterday that you were born in India.'

Pramod gave her a questioning look. 'We didn't know that.'

Suparna gave an indifferent shrug. 'People assume I was born here because I've been here all my life. Well, most of my life. My parents were in India at the time of my birth.' She looked at the letter again and shook her head slowly. 'I don't know what to make of this. I really don't.' Her voice shook with emotion.

Nirmala tried to make sense of it. 'I've been thinking . . .'

Suparna stared at her, looking stunned and perplexed at the same time.

Nirmala continued. 'In India, you hear all sorts of weird reports. Like poor families killing their daughters at birth because they prefer sons. And rich families having designer babies where they select the gender and appearance they want. Six decades ago, who knows what was going on.' She paused for a response. When neither of them spoke, she ventured further.

'I know of cases where couples have given up one of their children to a member of the family unable to have any of their own. This is not uncommon. People see it as a kindness.' Again she paused. This time Suparna's expression changed. A flash of anger crossed her face.

'A kindness? How is that relevant to babies being exchanged and taken away thousands of miles?'

'It's not the same,' said Nirmala quickly. 'It's not the same at all. But what I meant to say is that maybe, just maybe, and there's no excuse for it, the brothers felt it was acceptable to do what they did because they were keeping the children in the same family.'

Suparna put her elbows on the table, resting her chin on her fingertips. 'Acceptable,' she said quietly, her eyes glazed with sadness. 'I was torn away from my mother's arms as soon as I was born, and your father was given in my place. Because of that, my birth mother suffered deeply and held a grudge against her husband all his life.'

Nirmala felt her throat constrict. 'She also held a grudge against the baby boy who took your place. My father. He suffered too.'

Immediately Suparna grabbed her hands. 'Of course! Suresh suffered more than me. I was the lucky one because I never felt unloved.' Her eyes filled with tears which began to roll down her cheeks. Nirmala found that she was crying too. She cried for her father who grew up knowing that his mother never loved him, and she cried for *his* mother whose baby had been snatched away from her.

After a while, Nirmala realised that Pramod was no longer at the table. Looking up, she saw that he was standing by the window, looking out, deep in thought. Suparna fetched a box of tissues and they both blew their noses.

'What are we going to do?' Suparna asked.

'I don't know. I keep thinking of Jasu-*foi,* who is not my father's sister after all. And she now has a sister. You.'

Suparna gasped. 'Oh my God. And my brothers! They're not my brothers anymore. They are cousins. I've been living a lie all my life. What am I supposed to do with all this?'

Pramod returned to his seat. 'It will take some time to digest. Don't think about what comes next. Just let all this sink in first.'

Nirmala took Suparna's hand again. 'Talk it through with Ishwar-*fua*. We won't do anything until you are ready.'

Suparna nodded, still looking lost.

'Do you want me to stay with you today?' asked Nirmala.

Suparna closed her eyes, then she shook her head. 'It's okay. Ishwar will be back soon.'

Pramod sat back in his chair. 'We'll stay until he comes home. I know he will give you good advice. Sleep on it tonight, and don't make any hasty decisions. We've got a bomb in our hands and if we're not careful, it could explode and hurt a lot of people.'

Suparna held up the letter. 'This bomb has already gone off in my head. It's shattered everything I ever knew or thought about myself.'

'I'm still reeling from it too,' said Nirmala.

Suparna pointed to the date at the top of the letter. 'Kanta's husband died in 1965. I was thirteen years old then. Why didn't she come for me then? Her husband was no longer there to hold her back.'

Nirmala pressed her lips together. 'We don't know what was going on in her mind. Maybe she didn't want to open up old wounds. Or she didn't want to cause you any distress.'

'It's also possible she was afraid of *Dada*,' said Pramod. 'We have to admit he could be very intimidating.'

Suparna dismissed that with a click of her tongue. 'She doesn't sound like the type of woman who would be afraid of anyone. And anyway, *Dada* was a big softie on the inside. He would have understood if she came for me as my birth mother.'

Pramod fell silent and Nirmala saw that he was feeling uncomfortable. He cleared his throat. 'I don't think he would have given you up without a fight.'

Suparna looked startled. 'What do you mean?'

'It would have been difficult for Kanta to prove she was your mother. Her name is not on your birth certificate.'

Suparna covered her face with both hands and gave a low moan. Nirmala reached out to comfort her. At the same time, they heard the front door open and footsteps approach.

'Good. You're still here.' Ishwar looked pleased to see them.

Pramod stood up. 'We're just going.'

'No, no. I just got here. Sit, man, sit.'

Pramod shook his head. 'We have to go. *Foi* has had a terrible shock. She needs to talk to you.'

Nirmala gave Suparna's hand one last squeeze then stood up to leave. 'Call us when you're ready. Take as much time as you need.' Turning around, she greeted Ishwar, but he looked right past her and locked eyes with his wife. Nirmala followed Pramod out of the house.

On the drive home, they sat in silence, both pondering Suparna's reaction. Guilt crept into Nirmala's mind. She hated seeing Suparna so upset. If she had never answered Pramod's first email, none of these painful revelations would have come to light and Suparna would not have been so hurt.

Nirmala focused on Pramod's remark about Mohan-*dada* being intimidating. She'd heard that he was strict and authoritative, strong-minded and possibly a little dictatorial. Was it possible that he was more to blame for the baby exchange than his younger brother? She had to ask. Choosing her words carefully, she questioned Pramod.

'In Kanta-*ba*'s letter, she accuses Mohan-*dada* of leaving the country with her baby before her husband could change his mind. Do you think she was suggesting it was all his idea?'

Pramod was quiet for so long that Nirmala worried she had offended him.

Eventually he replied, 'She possibly did think that. What we know is that Mohan-*dada*, who, you do realise, is *your Dada* too, had the stronger, more dominant personality. Whether or not the swap was his idea and he put pressure on his brother, we will never know. But we have to consider this: after two daughters, Harilal probably wanted a son, and maybe he thought Kanta wanted the same. But without discussing it with her, he made a pact with his brother and allowed the exchange to take place. He had a choice, and he chose his brother over his wife. In my book, they were both at fault.'

Chapter 29

It was three long days before Suparna got in touch. For Nirmala, it seemed like a never-ending wait. She was impatient to do something about the secret they had uncovered. She felt tense, as if there was a tightly coiled spring inside her needing to be released.

'You seem agitated, Nirmala-*foi*,' said Kavita, who knew nothing about their discovery. 'Are you worried about something?'

'No. Not really. Well. Maybe a little worried about Varun.'

'Has he had another fit?'

'No. Not since the one last week.'

'Don't worry, *Foi*. I'm sure he's going to get better.'

Nirmala was grateful for her kindness, especially to Varun. She kept him busy with the twins, keeping them happy doing different activities each day. Varun was so content he never once mentioned India.

'You know we'll be going home soon,' she reminded him.

He looked crestfallen. 'Can't we stay longer?'

'No we can't. You'll be starting school in a few weeks.'

'Can I go to school here?'

'No. We have to go back. But don't worry. We still have another week.'

'Mumma? Will we ever come back?'

Nirmala was surprised. 'Do you like this place so much?'

Varun nodded.

'Then we will try our best to return one day.'

A broad smile lit up his face. It was as if the sun had suddenly come out. He looked so happy. She realised he had changed in the last few weeks. His skin had a healthy glow and he had put on some weight. Nutritious food and fresh air had done him the world of good. Surely this would help keep his epilepsy away. Nirmala hoped with all her heart that this would be the case.

When Suparna telephoned, she asked them to visit her as soon as they could. They went in the evening after Varun's bedtime. Reena went with them so there were five around the table. Suparna sat beside her husband with a solemn expression on her face, her hands clasped in her lap, Kanta's letter on the table in front of her. There was no friendly welcome, no snacks and no loud, excitable chatter. Nirmala had never seen her so quiet and serious.

'Are you all right?' she asked.

Suparna gave her a weak smile. 'I'm better than I was.' She looked down at the letter for a moment. Then she glanced up at Ishwar. Nirmala saw him give a nod of encouragement, as if to say go on; you can do this. Suparna pressed her lips together, then turned to address Pramod.

'When I first read this, I didn't know what to do or how to think. I went into denial, certain there could be no truth in such a wicked act. Then I felt angry. Angry with my parents, angry with Kanta, angry with everyone involved. I read the letter again and again. For the past three days, I have flipped back and forth a hundred times. Finally, I've had to accept it as fact.'

She glanced again at Ishwar. 'I felt a sort of grief, as if I'd lost someone very close. My emotions have gone through the whole cycle of shock, denial, anger, depression and acceptance.' She paused before continuing.

'I couldn't understand why Kanta didn't come to find me when her husband, my father, died. I was thirteen years old. But Ishwar has helped me realise that she must have felt it would be too traumatic for her, for me and for both families. I need to think of this as another chapter in my life. A difficult chapter, but one that I have to finish and move on. I think I'm ready to move on.'

Turning to Nirmala, she smiled; a soft, apologetic smile. 'If your father was alive, I'm sure he would be feeling the same. I wish so much that he was still alive.'

'If he *was* alive, what would you do?' asked Nirmala, looking Suparna in the eye.

'I would apologise to him for taking his place. I would apologise on behalf of my father, or rather *his* father, for leaving Kanta so traumatised that she couldn't be a loving mother to him.'

Nirmala felt a lump growing in her throat. Tears threatened to escape her eyes. Reena reached for her hand under the table and squeezed it.

'It's going to be fine,' said Suparna with a determined nod. 'We're going to make it fine.' She exchanged another look with her husband. 'Let me tell you what I think we should do. If you disagree, we can think again.'

All eyes were on her. 'We need to tell Jasumati that she is my sister. We have to tell her everything.' She paused. 'I don't like the way she treats Nirmala and how she was with Suresh. She sounds mean and selfish. But I badly want to meet her. I have many, many questions for her.'

'What about your brothers?' asked Reena.

'My brothers are now my cousins. But yah, they do need to know. Not immediately though.'

Ishwar spoke for the first time. 'We believe that we should tell Jasumati first, and in person.'

'You mean, go to India?' Pramod sounded surprised.

'Yah. You and Suparna should join Nirmala when she goes back.'

Pramod and Nirmala gaped at one another.

'And one more thing,' continued Ishwar. 'It would be better not to say anything about the trip, not even to Jasumati.'

'Why?' Reena and Nirmala asked together.

'Because if someone tells Jasumati you are going to visit her she will start asking questions.'

'Does that matter?' asked Reena.

'I think it does. Remember what Ramu-*bhai* said? He said he wrote to Jasumati and told her to vacate the property. If she did receive that letter, you might not get a good reception.'

Pramod had been listening quietly for a while. 'Whether she knows already or not, we need to tell her that she's not the owner of Suparna Mansions. It was Mohan-*dada*'s property and now it's mine.' He paused. 'Well, it's mine as long as Ramu-*kaka* doesn't win his court case.'

Ishwar tutted. 'Oh, he won't. Don't worry about that.'

Pramod shrugged. 'We'll have to wait and see. In the meantime, as I've said before, I have no intention of asking Jasu-*foi* to move out. But I am going to make sure she knows that Nirmala is the rightful heir to the mansion.'

Nirmala shifted uncomfortably in her seat. 'How will you explain that?'

'Easily. Your father Suresh was Mohanlal's son, not Harilal's. And the mansion was built and paid for by Mohanlal with the money he made here in Zimbabwe. You have a direct bloodline to Mohanlal, so you are one of his heirs. Currently, the property is in my name. But it's a straightforward business to get that changed.'

'You have a good heart, Pramod,' said Suparna. 'That's why my father left the property to you. He knew you would do the right thing. I am sure he deliberately left Kanta's letter for you to find.'

Nirmala picked up the letter. 'There are creases in here as if it's been scrunched up. Mohan-*dada* must have considered destroying it. But he didn't.'

Suparna agreed. 'He saved it for a reason. You were meant to find it, Pramod. He even gave you the key to his safe.'

Pramod was biting his lip. Reena looped her arm through his and patted it. Suparna placed the letter in front of her again and sighed. With overwhelming sadness, she spoke directly to Nirmala.

'My father was a difficult man in many ways. But I loved him. When he died in hospital last year, I was at his bedside. He looked at me for ages before he closed his eyes for the last time. Now I wonder what he was thinking about at that time. Was he remembering what he'd done when I was born? Was he regretting it?'

She closed her eyes and shook her head slowly. 'He shouldn't have done it. He caused so much pain.' Opening her eyes, she spoke with an edge to her voice. 'He caused heartache for my birth mother and for his own son. It was wrong.'

Nirmala didn't know what to say. She suspected that Mohanlal was definitely more to blame than his brother. Kanta's words flashed through her mind: *It is MY daughter you stole and ran off with . . . before Harilal could change his mind.* It did seem plausible that Mohanlal instigated the baby exchange. And perhaps Harilal thought that Kanta would get over it. At any rate, Mohanlal had wasted no time in leaving the country after the babies were born, taking his brother's newborn daughter with him.

Pramod was talking to Suparna, trying to make her smile. 'You were *Dada*'s favourite. We all knew that. Don't let this spoil your memories of him.'

'And remember what I told you,' said Ishwar. 'Things were different six decades ago. We shouldn't judge peoples' past actions by today's standards. Men used to think of their wives as their property and women were expected to be subservient.'

Suparna squared her shoulders. 'I know. And I will try hard to put this behind me. Let's move on. What do you think of our plan, Pramod?'

Pramod sat up and looked at his wife, who smiled and gave a slight nod. 'It's a good plan,' he said. Pushing his chair back, he continued, 'If we're going to India, we'd better start looking into flights and visas. Nirmala leaves in one week. There's not much time.'

They made their way to the front door. As they passed the study, Nirmala found herself automatically walking to the black-and-white photo of Suparna's parents on the wall. It was as if there was an invisible thread pulling her towards it. The photo had bewitched her from the first moment she'd seen it in Pramod's lounge.

'What do you see?' Pramod was looking over her shoulder.

'There's something in Bhanu-*ba*'s face.' Abruptly, she turned around and walked back to Suparna. 'Tell me, *Foi*. What colour were Bhanu-*ba*'s eyes? I can't tell from the black-and-white picture.'

'Her eyes?' Suparna gave her a quizzical look. 'A sort of grey-green. Why do you ask?'

'Because my father had grey-green eyes.'

Suparna pulled her head back. 'You're joking!'

Nirmala nodded, her face glowing with a sense of triumph. 'People used to comment on them all the time. We always wondered who he got them from.'

Suparna let out a sigh. 'Unbelievable! You know, Suresh is the only one who inherited those eyes. I always wished I had light eyes like her and wondered why none of us had her beautiful eyes. None of her children or grandchildren got lucky.'

Nirmala shook her head in amazement. 'What was Bhanu-*ba* like?'

Suparna's face creased into a gentle smile. 'Full of love. A wonderful mother.'

Nirmala leaned forward and gave Suparna a side hug. Returning to the photograph, she gazed into Bhanu's eyes and whispered, 'Your son was wonderful too. You would have loved him.'

PART 3

June 2016, Navsari, India

Chapter 30

With Suparna and Pramod for company, the flight back to India seemed much shorter to Nirmala than the outward journey. The hours flew by as they discussed the details of their plan and their concerns about how they would be received. The uncertainty surrounding Jasumati's reaction was uppermost in their minds.

Varun was delighted to have them as travel companions. Leaving everyone in Harare had been upsetting for him, so to have two members of the family join them was like having a special leaving gift.

'Where will they sleep, Mumma?' he had asked.

'They won't be staying with us. They are booked into the hotel near Hema-*masi*'s apartment.'

Nirmala had telephoned Hema to update her on their findings. She couldn't help smiling at the memory of her reaction when she heard about the baby exchange. She had been shocked and lost for words, which was so unlike her. Then she was delighted and excited to learn that things were going to improve for her friend. According to Ashvin, she had run around the flat like a girl gone mad.

Pramod had booked a taxi to take them from Mumbai airport to Navsari. It was just after midnight, yet there was heavy traffic on the highway, with cars and lorries speeding along, braking and overtaking in a way that terrified Suparna.

'Oh my God! We're going to be killed.'

Pramod gave a nervous laugh. 'I'd forgotten how people drive in India. We have to put our trust in the driver and just hope for the best.'

Nirmala looked out of the window and pictured her tiny house. It felt good to be going home. But the joy she felt was mixed with a feeling of dread. Despite his promise to be gone, she was still worried that Ajay might be there, waiting for them, refusing to leave. The thought of opening the door and finding him in the front room filled her with nervous tension.

It was 4 a.m. when they arrived in Navsari. The shops and apartment blocks were in darkness, but the streetlights gave off a warm and welcome glow. It was good to see the familiar roads and buildings. She had come home.

'Take us to the Star Hotel first,' she instructed the driver.

They stopped at the front door of the hotel. It was located on one of Navsari's busiest roads, but at this time of the morning, there were only a few cars and auto rickshaws going by.

'I will come for you later as we planned,' she said and watched them follow the driver up the few steps and through the glass-fronted double door.

Her house was in darkness. The porch was lit by the dim light coming from the street. While the driver took their bags to the front door, she shook Varun awake and walked him inside. Flicking on the light switch, she swept her eyes around the room. A huge sigh of relief escaped her lips. No Ajay. She allowed herself a moment to enjoy the sense of freedom. A burden had been lifted from her shoulders.

Like a homing pigeon, Varun walked sleepily into the back room and went straight to bed. Not having slept a wink since leaving Harare, tiredness caught up with Nirmala too. Pushing the bags to one side of the room, she unrolled her sleeping mat and curled up under her cover sheet. Exhausted slumber took over as soon as her head hit the pillow.

After the long and tiring journey, Nirmala slept deeply until almost midday. She woke up to the sound of soft music. Varun was listening to some nursery rhymes on the iPod Kavita had given him as a leaving present. Stretching her arms and yawning, Nirmala savoured the feeling of being back home.

Feeling rested, she went to join Varun. 'Go and brush your teeth and have a wash. We're going to Hema-*masi*'s in an hour.'

Varun stopped the music and stood up. She was surprised to see a nervous look on his face. His eyes darted to the wardrobe.

'What's the matter?' she asked.

'Is Pappa coming back?' He spoke in a hushed voice, as if Ajay might be around to hear.

Nirmala gave him a reassuring smile. 'No. He won't come back. Remember what I told you? He is going to live separately from us.'

He was silent for a while. Then he pointed to the wardrobe. 'But his clothes are still here. And his sewing machine.'

Nirmala moved quickly to check. Sure enough, the shelves still held his shirts, *kurta pyjamas* and few pairs of trousers. With a sinking heart, she walked into the front room. There, pushed to the back, was his sewing machine, complete with saris, blouse pieces and the tailoring scissors. She'd been too tired to notice the previous night. Her eyes were drawn to the large scissors and the image of Ajay holding them to her throat flashed through her mind. Anger flared inside her. If he thought she was going to roll over and let him stay, he was very much mistaken.

Nirmala felt Varun take her hand and walk her back to the wardrobe. 'Whose clothes are those, Mumma?' He pointed to the bottom shelf, which she had neglected to check.

She could hardly believe her eyes. Stacked neatly and pushed to the back were a couple of *salwar kameez* sets that did not belong to her. And beside that stack, she saw shorts and tee shirts that were definitely not Varun's.

An involuntary cry of anger escaped her lips. She slumped to the floor, knowing exactly what this meant. While she'd been away, Ajay had brought his mistress and child to stay in her house.

'What's wrong, Mumma?' Varun was kneeling beside her, pulling at her hands which she realised were clamped across her mouth. With a deep intake of breath, Nirmala managed to stand up and give him a smile of sorts.

'It's all right, *dikra*. Your father will come and take all this away. He's not going to live here, so don't worry about anything, okay?'

Varun stared for a moment then gave a wide grin. She knew that he was happy to see the back of Ajay.

She herself was far from happy. She was fuming. How dare he? Did he really think she would put up with this? Her blood was boiling, and she wished he was there at that moment so she could tell him exactly what she thought of him. Without any fear or concern for how he would react, she was ready to confront him.

Putting her hand on her heart, Nirmala forced herself to calm down. She needed to release her burden by talking to someone, and Hema was just the person.

~

An hour later, they were standing outside her best friend's apartment. Hema opened the door and stood motionless for a moment. Then she tutted and pulled Nirmala in to give her a rib-crushing bear hug. Hugging her back, Nirmala felt as if she had returned from another world. So much had happened since she had last seen her friend.

Varun pushed past them to get to Ashvin, who was standing back wearing a wide grin on his face. He lifted the boy off his feet and swung him around.

Hema led Nirmala to the sofa. 'Ashvin took the day off work. He couldn't wait to see Varun. So tell me. How are you?'

'I am furious, Hema. Ajay hasn't left yet.'

'What?' Hema was surprised. 'We heard he is living with the widow!'

When Nirmala told her what she found in her wardrobe, Hema was infuriated. 'The swine! He had the nerve to bring them to your house? You need to tell Ashvin. He'll go and sort him out.'

'Thanks, but I want to go to the widow's house myself right this minute to tell him what I think.'

'On your own? Right now?' Hema was astounded.

'Yes! I am not going to put up with this.'

'*Arey wah!* I've never seen you like this. Tell you what, let me call Ashvin. He needs to know what's happened. He wants to discuss a few other things with you anyway. I'll give Varun his lunch while you two talk.'

When Ashvin joined her on the sofa, Nirmala told him about Ajay's latest stunt. He whistled at the sheer audacity of the man, especially after he had personally warned him before Nirmala's trip, to stay away from her home.

'Ajay definitely needs another warning. Leave it to me. I will go over to the widow's house later and shake him up.'

'No!' insisted Nirmala.

Ashvin arched his eyebrows at her in surprise.

'I want to go myself. And I don't care if his mistress is there to hear me.'

'Okaaaay.' Ashvin paused. 'I don't think it's safe for you to go alone. I should be there with you, in case he gets violent, you know?'

Nirmala could see the sense in that. 'I was thinking of going over around six o'clock. Will you be free?'

Ashvin thought for a moment. Then, with a shake of his head, he suggested a better plan. 'Why don't we wait a little while? You just got back from your trip and you need time to sort things out with your Jasu-*foi.*'

Nirmala frowned. She was all fired up to face Ajay and say her piece.

'Don't get me wrong,' continued Ashvin. 'Ajay *should* be told in no uncertain terms that he has to stay away. But he also has to be told about your decision to divorce him. You need him to sign a petition to get that process going. Why don't we go to see him with that divorce petition?'

He reached over to the coffee table and picked up a clear plastic folder. Opening it, he handed her a sheaf of papers stapled together. 'These will explain the process of filing for divorce. You both need to sign this, then register it as soon as possible.'

Nirmala sighed, flicked through the first few pages, then put them aside. 'Once it's registered, how long will it take for the divorce to come through?'

'With mutual consent, just six months. You need to provide evidence of living separately for one year and appear in court a few times. Then it's all over.'

'Does Ajay have to give his consent?'

Ashvin nodded. 'If he doesn't consent, the process can take two years or more. But I'm pretty sure he'll agree. He committed adultery and threatened you with violence. He has a lot to answer for. Let me read you something from the relevant section.' He took the sheaf back from her. '*Extramarital sex remains a valid ground for divorce because it violates women's rights to equality and treats them like the property of their husbands.*'

Nirmala raised her eyebrows. 'It actually says that? Property of their husbands?'

'Yes.'

Nirmala sighed again. 'My grandfather and his brother were guilty of that. They treated their wives like property, as if they had no human feelings. I don't know how they could even think of doing what they did.'

Ashvin nodded. 'The sad thing is, that sort of behaviour still goes on today. In many parts of our society, women are still treated like that.'

Nirmala thought of the last time she had seen Ajay. It was a week before their departure for Zimbabwe. He had given her such a look of resentment that even the memory of it made her shudder.

'There is something else that has been bothering me,' she said. 'The house is in my name. But as my husband, does Ajay have any rights over it?'

'None whatsoever. In this country, marriage does not give you automatic ownership of your spouse's assets.'

Nirmala gave a sigh of relief. 'Okay. We'll go and see him later. You can make sure he signs the petition, and I will tell him exactly what I think of him. I'm also going to say that if he doesn't come to collect his things, I'm going to burn the clothes left in my wardrobe and destroy his sewing machine.'

'Wow. Fighting talk. What's happened to you, Nirmala? The waters of Zimbabwe seem to have changed you completely.'

'I just want him to realise that he can't bully me anymore. He needs to see that I'm taking back control of my life.'

Ashvin nodded. 'Good. Very good. Now tell me – do you need to borrow cash until you decide what you're going to do next?'

'No. I have enough rupees to get me through the next few weeks before Varun starts school. My plan is to go back to work as soon as he starts.'

'But if you need some . . .'

'I know.' Nirmala gave him a warm smile. 'I won't hesitate to ask you.'

~

After lunch, Nirmala left Varun with her friends and walked the few hundred metres to the Star Hotel. Suparna and Pramod were waiting for her in the reception area. She joined them in a cosy corner with comfortable armchairs around a coffee table.

'Ready to face Jasumati?' asked Pramod.

Nirmala blew out her cheeks. 'I'm not ready at all. You won't believe what I found when I got home.' She explained what Ajay had done while they were away and told them about her plan to confront him with Ashvin.

Pramod gave a low whistle. 'Unbelievable. He doesn't seem to have got the message. Would you like me to be there when you speak to him?'

'Yah,' said Suparna eagerly. 'It will be better if you go with two men. That way he will think twice before he thinks of getting nasty.'

'Thanks, but no. Ajay has always been intimidated by people of authority, and Ashvin can be very authoritative. With him by my side, Ajay won't dream of getting nasty. He's a coward, really, and a bully, like Ramu-*kaka*.'

Pramod nodded. 'Okay. Let me know if you change your mind. Now, let's think about Jasumati. This is an important meeting.'

Nirmala looked at Suparna. 'How do you feel about meeting your sister for the first time?'

'Nervous. And my stomach doesn't feel too good.'

Pramod tutted. 'There's no need to be nervous. She's not going to eat us up, is she?'

Nirmala smiled. 'No. But you just don't know with Jasu-*foi*. We haven't given her any warning, so she might be difficult and start lashing out at us.'

Suparna was playing with her sunglasses. She was wearing flattering dark trousers and a pretty white blouse. Her hair, which was usually held back with a clasp, fell freely around her shoulders.

Nirmala gave her an admiring glance. 'You look like a typical NRI, a non-resident Indian. Jasu-*foi* won't notice the resemblance. Not at first, anyway.'

'That's what I'm hoping. I want to size her up before she realises, or before we tell her. Are you sure she will be in?'

'She should be. People try to stay indoors at this time of day to avoid the heat.'

'Right.' Pramod clapped his hands together. 'Let's get going.' His tone was anxious now, his face tense. 'How long will it take us?'

'Ten minutes by rickshaw.' Nirmala led them out to the street.

Chapter 31

By the time they reached the fourth floor of Suparna Mansions all of them were breathing hard. Pramod and Suparna stood behind Nirmala, two steps below. They waited to catch their breath outside the metal barrier at the entrance to the apartment. Through the vertical bars, they could see the spacious balcony with white marble floor tiles and elegant parapet on the left. Bright sunlight flooded the area and glinted off the metal frame of a grand *jhula* swing at the far end.

'Glad I don't have to climb these stairs every day!' Suparna was panting.

Nirmala pointed to the doorbell on the side of the barrier gate. Suparna nodded to indicate she was ready. The button was pressed and a loud prolonged peel rang out. They waited. When no one answered Nirmala rang again. The first door on the right opened and there she was. Jasumati stood facing them from the other side of the bars.

She looked dishevelled, with hair untidy and sari creased as if it had been wrapped around her body in a hurry. They had obviously disturbed her and she didn't look too pleased. She peered at Nirmala first then beyond her, squinting. She focused on Nirmala once more. She was not wearing her spectacles. That was a bit of luck, Nirmala thought, because it meant she would not see that one of her visitors looked very much like her.

Jasumati's body was stiff and her expression cold and hostile. 'Nirmala,' she said with no hint of welcome.

'Namaste, *Foi*. Can we come in?'

Jasumati glanced at Nirmala's companions. 'I was sleeping.' She made no move to open the gate.

'Sorry to disturb you, but I have brought some visitors who would like to see you.' For a minute, Nirmala thought she was going to deny them entry. Then something shifted in her face. Nirmala caught her look of curiosity. She tried to hide it, but it was there. Sliding back a bolt across the bars, she pulled open the gate, turned her back on them and shuffled away, leading them to her front room.

It was a large bright room furnished with two brown armchairs and a sofa arranged around a glass-topped table on a fluffy white rug. A bowl of potpourri sat on the table, filling the room with a pleasant cinnamon and clove fragrance. The window was wide open but the air inside was hot and heavy. Jasumati gestured for them to sit down while she flicked a switch to turn on a ceiling fan.

Nirmala took the armchair and the others sat together on the sofa. Jasumati sat down heavily on the other armchair. She seemed tired and her breath sounded laboured. Nirmala began the conversation.

'How are you, *Foi*?'

'I'm fine.' Jasumati's hostile expression had changed to one of quiet interest. She turned to the sofa and gave the pair an enquiring look.

Nirmala sat forward. 'These visitors have come a long way to meet you.'

Jasumati screwed up her eyes again to focus her vision. Nirmala could almost feel Suparna holding her breath. She was sitting back with a fixed smile on her face.

Pramod greeted her. '*Namaste.*'

'*Namaste,*' replied Jasumati. She stared at them for a moment then clicked her tongue in annoyance. 'I'll just fetch my glasses.' Standing up, she walked away to the interior of the apartment.

Suparna blew out her cheeks, putting a hand on her heart. Pramod patted her other hand.

Jasumati returned with gold-framed spectacles on her nose. She sat down again and looked directly at her guests. Nirmala watched her take a good look at Suparna, then Pramod then Suparna again. She shook her head and turned back to Nirmala.

'I don't think we have met before.' Her tone was civil. They were guests in her house after all, even if they did come with Nirmala.

Pramod cleared his throat. 'You are right. We have never met before, but we are related to you. Closely related.'

Jasumati frowned. 'I don't think so.'

Suparna pushed back her hair from her shoulders and twisted it at the nape of her neck where it stayed. She sat forward, still with the fixed smile. 'Look harder, Jasu-*ben.*'

Jasumati stared with greater interest. Nirmala saw her expression change from open curiosity to something akin to disbelief. She knitted her brows and gave a slow shake of her head. Her eyes grew wide and her jaw dropped. She stood up suddenly and gave a loud startled gasp of shock. Now she looked horrified. With mouth open, she gaped at the woman who looked so much like her. She put out her hand and gripped the back of the armchair.

'What . . . Who . . .?' She uttered the words and stopped, unable to tear her eyes away from her double.

Suparna stood up, giving her a warm smile. 'Don't be alarmed. There is nothing to worry about. Have you guessed who I am?' No answer. Jasumati seemed to have lost the ability to speak. 'My name is Suparna and this is Pramod, my nephew. We have come from Zimbabwe to meet you.'

Nirmala caught a look of fear cross Jasumati's face. Suparna saw it too. 'It's okay. We have come with good news.'

'Yes.' Pramod offered a friendly smile. 'We are very pleased to meet you.' He looked at the armchair Jasumati was holding on to. 'Shall we sit down?'

Still looking dazed, Jasumati sank into her seat.

Pramod began. 'I can see you had no idea we were coming. You didn't receive any letters from Zimbabwe recently?'

Jasumati looked mystified. She cleared her throat. 'No.' She was showing signs of recovery from shock.

'My uncle didn't write to you?'

'Your uncle?'

'Ramu-*kaka*. He said he wrote to you about Suparna Mansions.'

Jasumati sat up straight. 'What about Suparna Mansions?' Now she began to look suspicious.

Suparna put a hand on Pramod's arm. 'We should start at the beginning.' Turning to Jasumati, she sighed. 'What I'm going to say will sound unbelievable. You'll think I'm making it up. But I promise you, it's all true.'

Jasumati looked even more suspicious. She sat ramrod straight, silent, waiting to hear what Suparna had to say.

'You are in shock because you can see how much we look like each other. The reason for that is we are real sisters. Blood sisters. We have the same mother and father.' Apart from a twitch in her jaw, Jasumati showed no reaction. 'I'm saying that Kanta and Harilal were birth parents to both of us. Also to our sister, Pushpa.'

Jasumati raised her head and gazed at Suparna studiously. 'And you have proof of this?' A note of aggression had crept into her voice.

Pramod took over. 'My grandfather passed away last year, leaving behind documents that prove you are sisters.'

'Documents.' She loaded the word with heavy scepticism.

'Yes. And a letter written by Kanta, your mother, after your father died in 1965.' Pramod hesitated, looking at Suparna for permission to carry on. She gave it to him with a slight nod. 'You see, my grandfather, Mohanlal, had a younger brother in India who we were never told about. He was kept secret from us all these years. That brother was your father, Harilal.'

Jasumati was listening but showed no emotion whatsoever. It was as if she had switched off. Nirmala wondered if she was taking it all in. Perhaps it was too much for her. They waited for her to speak. After a long minute, Jasumati answered Pramod. Her tone was flat, almost uninterested.

'My father never mentioned a brother.' Turning to Suparna, she added, 'My sister died in childhood.'

Suparna nodded. 'I know. She was my sister too. And Suresh is not our brother, but our first cousin. He and I were born within days of each other, here in Navsari in 1952, when this mansion was built.' She paused and closed her eyes for a moment before plunging into deeper waters.

'I was our mother's third daughter, and Suresh was his mother's sixth son. Without considering our mothers' feelings, Mohanlal and Harilal exchanged babies. I was taken away to Zimbabwe when I was just a few days old, and Suresh was left here to be brought up as your brother.'

There was pin-drop silence in the room. All eyes were on Jasumati. She was still sitting dispassionately, showing no emotion. She looked at each person in the room, then turned her gaze to the open door. Her breathing quickened and Nirmala saw her body start to twitch. The corners of her mouth turned upwards as if she was going to smile. Then her body began to shake, first her stomach then her shoulders. Strange sounds were escaping from her mouth.

Nirmala was alarmed. Flashing through her mind was the image of someone having a fit. Was her aunt going to collapse? 'Jasu-*foi*! Are you all right?'

When her aunt turned to face her, she looked like she was ready to explode with pent-up emotion. Her lips were firmly pressed together as if she was struggling to hold something back. Then, inexplicably, she opened her mouth and burst into laughter, a high-pitched fit of derisive laughter.

Astounded, Nirmala glanced at the others. They all seemed bewildered, watching Jasumati in stupefied silence. Her attention was on Suparna and her laugh was without any mirth. She ended it with an abrupt snort, her face wrinkled into a scowl.

'I know who you are.' Her voice was filled with aggression. 'I never thought I would see you in person.'

They all considered what she had just said. Suparna pulled her eyebrows together. 'I don't know what you mean.'

'I mean that I knew about you all along. And I have known for a long time about everything that happened in 1952.'

Suparna was dumbfounded. She leaned back, looking dazed. Nirmala thought she had misheard. Jasumati couldn't have known.

Pramod cleared his throat. 'Are you saying you knew about Suparna-*foi* and our family in Zimbabwe?'

'Yes. Especially Mohanlal, your evil grandfather. My mother told me what a cheating bastard he was. She hated him. He tricked my father into giving up his baby.'

Pramod flinched, visibly troubled by her words. Nirmala began to feel sick. Jasu-*foi* knew all this time. She knew about the baby swap and she knew Suresh was not her real brother. That was probably why she had been so mean to him. It was a crushing realisation. Forcing her nausea down, she turned to Jasumati and spoke through clenched teeth.

'When did you find out?'

Jasumati waved her hand in a dismissive way. 'After my father's death.'

Nirmala fixed her eyes on her and swallowed hard. 'Did my father know that he had been swapped?'

'No,' Jasumati answered in a matter-of-fact tone. 'My mother didn't want him to know.'

Nirmala cried out in anguish. 'You could have helped him! You could have shown him some love even if your mother didn't.'

Jasumati shrugged her shoulders. This single act proved too much for Nirmala. 'You pushed him away, both of you!' She gave a strangled cry.

Jasumati's scowl returned. 'No. He walked away. He went against my mother's wishes and married your mother, who was too low caste for our family.'

Nirmala put shaking fingers to her lips, too astounded to say anything more.

Suparna looked extremely distressed. 'Jasu-*ben*,' she said. 'I know we have shocked you, but why do you want to hurt Nirmala? And Suresh. What happened was not his fault.'

'That's easy for you to say.' Resentment was etched across Jasumati's face. 'You didn't grow up with a mother who was heart-broken because her baby was snatched away from her!'

Once again, they were left speechless. Nirmala raised her head and blinked. 'So you wanted revenge for your mother? Did it make you feel better knowing you were hurting your brother and his whole family?'

Jasumati tutted in annoyance, then rolled her eyes. Crossing her arms, her lips formed a hard line. It was clear she was not willing to speak again, even when Suparna called her name a few times.

They sat in uneasy silence for a long while. Eventually, Pramod inclined his head, indicating they should leave. Suparna got to her feet.

'This has been a difficult meeting for all of us,' she said. 'We will leave you to think about what was said today. But we need to meet again.' Her voice softened. 'We are sisters. There is so much I want to discuss with you.'

Jasumati ignored her. Pramod stood up and addressed her. 'There is another matter I need to talk to you about. But it can wait. We will visit you again at the same time the day after tomorrow. I hope that will be okay?'

For a moment, Jasumati said nothing. Then she nodded once, still not meeting their eyes. Pramod looked at the others and tilted his head towards the door. Nirmala was filled with mixed emotions of anger and heartbreak, but seeing the sadness etched across Suparna's face, she put an arm around her shoulders and walked her slowly out of the room.

Chapter 32

'We should have warned her before we went,' said Suparna when they arrived at the hotel. 'It was too much of a shock for her.'

Pramod shook his head. 'We had to do it this way or she might have refused to see us.'

Nirmala bit her lip. 'I can't believe she knew about your branch of the family all along. She's always been mean towards me so I should be used to her. But her cruel jibes hurt every time.'

Suparna shook her head. 'Some of the things she said . . . When she found out about me, she could have come to find me. But just like our mother Kanta, she didn't.'

'Come on, you two. Let's give her some time,' said Pramod. 'She might be completely different when we go to see her again.'

Nirmala gave a shaky laugh. 'Somehow I don't think so.' She looked at the clock behind the reception desk. 'I have to go. But I'd be really happy if you came for lunch tomorrow. Will you come?'

'Of course,' said Suparna. 'No need for the address. We know exactly where you live.'

~

'How did it go?' asked Hema when Nirmala went to pick up Varun.

'Don't ask.'

Nirmala took Hema aside and told her what had happened. As expected, Hema was disgusted, uttering one expletive after another, offering to go personally to give Jasumati a piece of her mind. Nirmala held up her hand and begged her to calm down.

'Can you come to babysit when we go to see Jasu-*foi* again?'

'I can. And, Nirmala?' She placed a hand on Nirmala's arm. 'Don't be upset by what the *daakan* said, okay? She's just a twisted old witch.'

~

By the time they reached home, it was almost dark and Nirmala was exhausted. They had stopped along the way to do some grocery shopping for lunch the next day. She lay down on Varun's bed for a rest. Jet lag was taking its toll, though it seemed to have bypassed her son. He amused himself while she took the weight off her feet. His request for supper was toast and jam, something he had learned to love in Zimbabwe. Reena had filled their suitcases with various tubs and jars full of food that she knew they would enjoy. Together with a huge quantity of chocolates and biscuits, they had tasty snacks to last them several months.

Before turning in for an early night, Nirmala unpacked their suitcases and tidied up the house, ready for her guests the next day. Her house was small, and it was not possible for her to offer them the same level of generous hospitality that they had shown her. But she hoped they would feel the warmth of her welcome and see how much she cared for them.

Pushing the empty suitcases under Varun's bed, Nirmala thought she heard voices outside her front door. Then came the unmistakable sound of a key turning in the lock. Alarmed, she hurried to the front room. The door opened and with a shock, she watched Ajay step across the threshold.

He was talking to someone over his shoulder. But he stopped mid-sentence when he locked eyes with Nirmala. He froze, the key still in the lock. A little boy pushed past him and a woman stepped up to stand beside him. The boy stopped a few feet from Nirmala.

For a moment, everyone stood still, in shock. Ajay was the first to recover. A dark scowl came over his face.

'What are you doing here?' His voice was low and full of menace.

Nirmala gave him an incredulous look. 'What am *I* doing here? This is my house! What are *you* doing here?'

'It is *my* house also!' His sudden roar made the little boy run back to his mother's side. She held him and stepped behind Ajay, as if to hide from Nirmala.

Ajay lifted his chin and sneered. 'Why did you come back? Didn't your rich cousins want to keep you?'

Varun was standing behind Nirmala, peeping out at his father in fear. Ajay shot him a glare of contempt then scowled at Nirmala again.

'You and your weak-minded son should have stayed in Africa.'

'Ajay!' screamed Nirmala. 'How dare you. How dare you come here and bring them with you. Get out. Get out right now!'

'No, I will not!' He moved forward to grab Nirmala's arm. Instinctively, she moved out of his grasp and with both hands on his chest, pushed him backwards with force. Her sudden and unexpected action caught him unawares. He stumbled awkwardly, his heel landing on the little boy's foot. Crying out in pain, the boy buried his face in his mother's sari.

'Ajay, *nah*!' the woman cried out. She took his arm and pulled him onto the porch. Nirmala heard her upbraiding him for going on the attack and pleading with him to leave. He was arguing with her, telling her not to worry.

Nirmala was shaking with fury. She marched into the back room, opened the wardrobe and gathered an armful of their clothes. With the trio still on the porch, she threw the bundle at their feet. They looked at her, astounded. The woman seemed distressed, but Ajay had a look of complete disbelief on his face. Dumbstruck, he stared at her, open-mouthed.

'Take your things and go. All of you.' Nirmala was seething, but she refrained from raising her voice again, conscious of the noise they were making. 'Don't ever come back.'

Ajay straightened up and was about to approach her again. Nirmala held out a hand as if to say 'stop'.

'It's over, Ajay. Accept that. This house was never legally yours and I am taking back your key.' With calm confidence, Nirmala removed the key Ajay had left in the door. He watched in stupefied silence. 'And be warned,' she continued. 'I have filed a petition for divorce.'

She watched Ajay's face darken and his mouth compress into a hard line. Then it was her turn to be surprised. With a curl in his lip, he growled at her, 'I want nothing more to do with you or your stupid son.' He inclined his head towards his mistress and the boy. 'This is my woman now and this is my real son. The sooner the divorce comes through, the better.'

They eyed one another for a long minute. Astonished by the way he was backing down, Nirmala watched him with suspicion. She saw the widow tug urgently at his *kurta*. Clearly, she wanted to leave, and she wanted Ajay to go with them. Eventually, he turned his gaze to the back of the room.

Wagging his finger at Nirmala, he spoke in a threatening voice. 'Don't touch my sewing machine. I will be coming back to fetch it.'

'No!' screamed Nirmala. 'You will *not* be coming back.' With anger boiling inside her, she glared at him and thought for a moment. Then, with icy finality, she told him that she would arrange for it to be delivered to him.

'When Ashvin brings you the divorce petition to sign, I will ask him to bring you your machine.'

Ajay was still scowling, but the anger and menace seemed to have faded from his eyes. He opened his mouth to say something, then closed it, hesitating. After a few more silent seconds, he said, 'Just make sure he comes soon. After that, I am finished with you. You hear that? Finished.'

Abruptly, he turned on his heel and without a backward glance, walked away. The widow bent to pick up the clothes, grabbed hold of her son's hand and hurried after Ajay.

Nirmala watched them go, hardly daring to breathe. With Varun by her side, she waited for a full minute before closing and locking the door. Overcome with relief, she sank to her knees and wrapped her arms around her son.

'Don't worry, *dikra*. He's gone now. I think he's gone for good.'

As she uttered those words, Nirmala wondered if this time, Ajay really meant what he said. Was it possible for him to walk away? Only time would tell.

~

In the morning, Nirmala tried not to dwell on her troubles as she prepared lunch for her guests. She wanted to make them feel special after all that they had done for her. When they arrived, she went to receive them with a smile. 'Welcome to my little house.' She waved a hand at the *jhula* indicating where they should sit. For herself, she brought out a chair from the front room. As soon as they were seated, Varun came out carrying bottles of mineral water.

Suparna drank thirstily. Then she patted her tummy and chuckled. 'I think I have Delhi belly even though we are nowhere near Delhi.'

Nirmala sympathised. 'It's a common problem for travellers. You have to drink bottled water only and never eat food from street vendors.'

'Talking of food, something smells wonderful.' Pramod breathed in the aromas coming from inside the house.

'I've made a local specialty which I hope you will enjoy. But before we eat, there is something I need to tell you.'

Without getting emotional, she gave them an update on Ajay's visit the night before. They were both alarmed to hear that Ajay had tried to use violence again. But when they heard how she had stood up to him, they beamed.

'Well done, Nirmala,' said Suparna. 'I'm so proud of you.'

Pramod looked thoughtful. 'Do you think he's finally going to leave you alone?'

Nirmala bit her lip. 'Last night was the first time he said he wanted nothing more to do with me. And I got the feeling he meant what he said about wanting a divorce.'

'Do you know what I think?' Suparna smiled. 'I think he wants to marry this widow.'

Nirmala gave a little laugh. 'I've been thinking that too. Isn't it strange that this widow might actually become my saviour?'

Pramod nodded. 'I have a good feeling about this, Nirmala. Your problems with Ajay might finally be over.'

A quiet calm settled over Nirmala as she visualised her life without the black cloud of Ajay hanging over her. She sat quietly with her guests, happy in the knowledge that she had their love and support. They were her family. She watched them look up at the tall building across the road.

Suparna was staring straight ahead at the towering mansion named after her. She seemed to have disappeared into another world. Nirmala watched her eyes move up and down the building and then across to read the words etched on the balconies: her name and year of birth in both English and Gujarati.

Pramod was looking at it too but his eyes were roving over the facade searching for structural positives and negatives. He whistled softly. 'That must have been some building in 1952!'

'I was told it was unique in Navsari at that time,' said Nirmala.

Pramod looked at the premises on either side of the mansion. 'It's still one of the tallest. But it's in dire need of TLC.'

Nirmala puckered her brow. 'TLC?'

'Tender loving care.' Pramod laughed. 'Something Jasu-*foi* definitely isn't providing. She can easily use the rent money she receives to prevent this deterioration.'

Nirmala nodded, gazing at the mansion with sadness.

'Never mind,' said Pramod. 'We will fix that. It might take a while and be expensive, but we'll do our best to restore the building to its former glory.'

Nirmala smiled. 'That would be mind-blowing. I am always picturing my father in that building. I would love to see it as it was.'

Pramod's tone grew serious. 'Nirmala. You won't just be picturing things. You'll be living there. Haven't you worked that out yet?'

Nirmala drew her eyebrows together. 'You can't ask Jasu-*foi* to move out.'

Pramod looked surprised. 'Is that what's worrying you? I am never going to do that. I told you from the start. She can stay there forever. But you are going to live there too.'

'What do you mean?'

Pramod fell silent for a moment. He looked up at the mansion again. 'By my reckoning, there are six apartments in that building without counting Jasu-*foi*'s on the top floor. Do you know if they are all occupied?'

'They are. Jasu-*foi*'s older son lives with her and the other son lives in one of the flats on the third floor.'

'So there are five apartments let out. Well, one of the tenant families will have to be given notice to vacate as soon as possible. I am going to ask Jasu-*foi* to move down to that apartment so that you can have the fourth floor.'

'What? No!' Nirmala was aghast.

Pramod's voice was firm. 'You are the rightful heir to that property. I inherited it from our grandfather, Mohanlal, but I will be transferring it over to you. We'll find an agency to ensure all the rent is collected and deposited into your account every month. All you have to do is move in and start to enjoy the life that you and Varun deserve.'

'Look, Nirmala,' said Suparna, speaking in a gentle tone, her face as soft as melted butter. A smile touched the corners of her mouth. 'Suparna Mansions is yours. My father would have wanted you to live there. You have nothing to feel bad about.'

Nirmala looked across the road and remembered her father telling her how much he loved growing up in the mansion. Would Varun like it there? She cast her eyes over him playing in the tiny front room. A far cry from the spacious apartments in Suparna Mansions. Why shouldn't he enjoy a little luxury? Nirmala gave herself a pep talk. She needed to be bold and give him what he deserved. Smiling at Suparna, she nodded her agreement to move in.

Pramod shifted his weight on the *jhula* and craned his neck to see the ceiling. He looked impressed. 'This is a solid *jhula*. Very strong.'

'Yes. My favourite part of the house.' Nirmala stood up. 'Would you like to see the back?' Suparna did, but Pramod said he preferred to stay where he was, cool in the shade.

They walked through the two rooms and kitchen before re-emerging into daylight at the back. Aware that Suparna would find the house extremely small, Nirmala was keen to let her know how much she loved it.

'I never wanted to live anywhere else, not even in Suparna Mansions. This was a happy home.' Her smile was filled with nostalgia. Then she thought of Ajay and her smile disappeared. 'That changed after I got married.'

'Ajay is a stupid man. You are well rid of him.'

Nirmala sighed. 'I regret being so meek and mild with him. I should have put him in his place long ago.'

Pramod was standing at the back door, calling them in. 'Can you two stop talking now? I can't hold out much longer with all these tantalising aromas.'

Suparna laughed. 'You go,' she told Nirmala. 'I need to pay a visit to your bathroom!'

~

With lunch over, Nirmala left the tidying up for later and led her guests back to the porch. She sat with them on the *jhula* and talked about her parents, neighbours and friends. Outside the ground-floor apartment in Suparna Mansions, she saw the old storyteller watering his potted plants. When he noticed Nirmala, he waved.

She waved back. 'That's Saleji-*dada*. He was one of the first tenants there so he knew my grandparents personally.'

'Really?' Suparna was surprised. 'How old is he?'

'I'm not sure. Probably ninety-something. We are all very fond of him. I know he was very helpful when Pushpa-*foi* drowned in Dudhiya Talav.'

'I wonder if he knew Mohanlal.'

'No, he didn't. I asked him. All he knew was that years ago, letters used to arrive with postage stamps from Southern Rhodesia.'

Moving gently with the rhythm of the *jhula*, they each sank into their own thoughts. Nirmala marvelled at how much had happened since the old man had mentioned the letters. She'd been completely ignorant about her extended family in Africa, yet now here she was, sitting with them, and fully aware of the terrible secret that had kept them apart.

The heat and dust from the street filled the air, as did the noisy sounds of scooters and auto rickshaws. Cows ambled by and children, still on school vacation, shouted to one another. A call to prayer rang out from the mosque nearby. It was the mid-afternoon *namaz*.

Pramod leaned forward. 'Are we ready for tomorrow?'

Suparna nodded. 'Jasumati has had enough time to digest everything. Let's hope she's in a better mood.'

Chapter 33

The afternoon sun was blistering when Hema arrived at Nirmala's house the next day. She kicked off her sandals and went straight to the *jhula* to cool down. Suparna and Pramod arrived soon after.

'Phew! This heat is too much,' said Pramod. 'Must be at least 40 degrees.'

Hema laughed. 'It is. This is the height of our summer. The monsoon rains will be here soon and it will cool everything down. You should stay to see that.'

'No thanks,' said Pramod. 'I've heard about your monsoon floods.'

Nirmala noticed that Suparna had not said a word. She seemed deep in thought. When she caught Nirmala's eye, she shook her head and tutted. 'Guess who called me last night on my cell phone: my brother Ramu.'

Nirmala frowned. 'Did he upset you?'

'It was the other way around, actually. I upset him. He started off with his usual threats and bluster, but then he calmed down. He rang to say he found out Pramod and I were in India with you, and he was angry that we hadn't told him. He wanted me to persuade Pramod to do the right thing; and by the right thing he meant put the mansion on the market.'

Pramod and Hema were sitting quietly on the *jhula*, listening to Suparna.

'I let him rant on about his court case for a while, then I asked him to shut up and listen. Without going into too much detail, I told him about Kanta's letter and the baby exchange. He wouldn't believe me at first, but when he finally realised we had evidence to prove it all, he fell silent. Very silent. Suspiciously silent. Then he rang off.'

Pramod took over the story. 'He didn't say much to Suparna-*foi*, but as I expected, he called me later on *my* cell phone. He surprised me by speaking to me without shouting and swearing. I was able to explain everything to him without any interruptions. In case he hadn't worked it out, I stressed the fact that Suresh was Mohanlal's son, not Harilal's, and you were Mohanlal's real granddaughter.'

'How did he react to that?' asked Nirmala, when Pramod paused.

'He was surprisingly calm about that. But when I told him I was going to transfer ownership to you, he called me a stupid fool.' He paused again.

'What about his court case?' Nirmala asked.

'That's the strangest part. He told me that he was so disgusted with me that he was going to wash his hands of me. Then he put the phone down on me too.'

Nirmala and Hema both stared at him, waiting for him to explain what that meant.

'I think it means he's actually going to stop harassing me about Suparna Mansions. I believe it means he won't go ahead with the court case.'

Nirmala blew out her cheeks. She looked at Suparna for confirmation. She gave a slow nod. 'I think Pramod's right. He's giving up the fight. He's probably realised there is little chance of him winning, and with all of us against him, it's not worth the trouble. And now with this turn of events, with you being a direct descendant of Mohanlal, he's less inclined to go into battle. Don't get me wrong. I don't think he's suddenly become Mr Nice Guy. He will just find something else to be cross about.'

'Yes well, we shouldn't let him take up any more of our time,' said Pramod, holding up a black briefcase. 'We have another difficult meeting with Jasu-*foi* to think about. I have all the paperwork in here to prove that it's me and not her who owns Suparna Mansions.'

Hema was looking across the road. 'Looks like the old *dosi* has company.' They all followed her gaze. Three unsmiling faces were staring down at them from the top-floor balcony: Jasumati and two younger men.

Pramod cursed under his breath. 'Who the hell are they?'

'The one without the beard is our cousin Raju, Jasu-*foi*'s son. I don't know the other man.'

'What is Raju like?'

'He's all right I suppose, but totally under his mother's thumb.'

Pramod tutted. 'So we can't expect any help from him! And now we have to wait until they are gone.'

Hema disagreed. 'Your auntie probably called them to attend your meeting. You should go now if you are ready. I'll be here with Varun.'

Nirmala turned to Suparna. 'How do you feel?'

'To be honest, a little nervous. I just hope we can settle things without any nastiness.'

Pramod inclined his head. 'Don't worry, *Foi*. If there's any trouble, I will handle it. I'm prepared for whatever she throws at us.'

~

Jasumati opened her gate to let them in without saying a word. She looked only at Pramod before walking ahead. They followed her to the living room where the fan was already whirring. The potpourri was still there giving off the scent of cinnamon and cloves.

The two men were sitting on high-backed chairs, speaking to one another in lowered tones. They were both dressed in smart-casual office clothes with dark trousers and white short-sleeved, open-necked shirts. The older man was stocky with flat black hair. He sported a moustache and goatee beard. Raju was a small, neat man in his forties with a thick head of hair. They sprang apart and stood up when the group walked in.

'*Namaste*.' They bent their heads over joined palms, their faces grave. Raju's eyes became saucers as he stared at Suparna. She gave him a warm smile.

'Yes, I do look like your mother. We are real sisters, didn't she tell you?'

Raju seemed to have lost his voice. He looked at his mother. In a terse and edgy voice, she addressed Pramod.

'I asked Raju and Jagjivan Ram to be here.' She sat down in an armchair and gestured for everyone to take a seat. 'Jagjivan is our family lawyer.'

The atmosphere in the room was tense. Nirmala thought it was like a house of mourning. And yet, no one had died. Pramod gave the lawyer a friendly smile.

'I'm guessing you are here to see evidence of our claims. You want to make sure we are related.'

The lawyer seemed surprised. 'I . . .'

'He is here as our friend and adviser.' Jasumati's tone was aggressive.

Pramod nodded. 'Okay. Well, it's nice to meet you all. Jasu-*foi*, I want to begin by apologising for turning up unannounced the other day. I hope you understand why we had to do that. We needed to make sure you would see us. When we learned about you and our family connection, we wanted to meet you and get to know you. We still do.'

Jasumati had her lips pressed together in a firm line, and she looked back at him with a deadpan expression. She had not even acknowledged Suparna, who was now fidgeting with the edge of her blouse. Nirmala could see that she was agitated and becoming increasingly so as Jasumati continued to ignore her. Sounding tortured, Suparna spoke out.

'Look at me, Jasu-*ben*! Do you blame me for what happened? It wasn't my fault they took me away.'

Turning to face her, Jasumati narrowed her eyes, looking irritated. Then she seemed to thaw a bit. 'I know that. But you are a stranger to me.'

'We have the same blood running through our veins! We can be sisters at last!'

Jasumati closed her eyes for a moment, then with a dismissive shake of the head, she replied, 'It's too late for that. There has been too much pain and suffering.'

Suparna looked crushed. Nirmala stared daggers at Jasumati, but she had already returned her attention to Pramod.

'You said you had other matters you wanted to discuss?' She looked at him with an expression of cold haughtiness, her eyebrows raised.

Pramod cleared his throat. Opening his briefcase, he removed two tan-coloured manila envelopes and held one up.

'In here, you'll find all the letters and a few of the Diwali cards your father posted to Mohan-*dada*. The letter from your mother, which left us reeling, is also there.' He leaned forward to pass it over.

At first, she ignored his proffered hand, staring at the envelope as if she had no interest. Then she almost snatched it and put it on her lap. Making no attempt to open it, she fixed her eyes on Pramod's other hand.

He stole a look at Nirmala. Biting her lip, she wondered how he was going to explain the next bit. He sat up and squared his shoulders. His face took on a professional expression, ready to discuss business.

'When your mother told you about Mohan-*dada*, did she say anything about the ownership of Suparna Mansions?' He paused. Jasumati looked back, straight-faced and silent. Nirmala noticed Jagjivan Ram lean forward a little to pay closer attention.

Pramod continued. 'I ask because last year, at the reading of my grandfather's will, we discovered that *he* was the sole owner of this property, which none of us knew anything about. We were given all the legal documents to prove this. Things like the title deeds, land registry, records of plot purchase, planning permission and contracts with architects, builders, tradesmen and others. This envelope contains some of those documents and a few relevant receipts from workers dating back from before and after 1952.'

He raised the envelope but kept it close to him. Nirmala noticed a flicker in Jasumati's eyes and her mouth gave a slight twitch. But she uttered not a word.

'I'm here to tell you that I have inherited Suparna Mansions, so I am the legal owner.'

The hush in the room seemed to intensify. No one spoke but everyone waited for Jasumati to react. She was sitting up straight in her armchair like a statue, staring fixedly at a point in the distance. After a long minute, she breathed out and let her shoulders drop. Putting her hand out, she spoke in a calm steady voice.

'I would like my lawyer to have a look.'

Pramod hesitated for a moment, then passed the envelope over. 'Of course.' He watched her hand it to Jagjivan Ram, who accepted it with a slight nod. Ram then pushed his chair forward to place the envelope on the table. Moving the bowl of potpourri out of the way, he opened the top flap, pulled out all the papers and began to inspect them one by one. He seemed to scan through them quickly, then stack them in a neat pile on one side.

From her armchair, Nirmala looked at Suparna. She could tell that despite the fan moving air around the room, the heat of the day was uncomfortable for her. Her eyes were closed and she seemed to be breathing faster than normal.

'Are you okay?' she asked. Suparna opened her eyes but did not answer. Concerned, Nirmala turned to Raju and looked at him accusingly. Where were his manners?

'Could you bring mineral water for Suparna-*foi*?'

Raju stood up immediately. 'Of course.' He gave her an apologetic look. He walked away quickly and returned with three glasses on a tray. He gave Suparna a smile when he offered her the water, and he did have the decency to apologise to Nirmala when he held out the tray to her.

The water was ice-cold and Suparna drank it in one go. She leaned back on the sofa looking revived and more in control. They all sat quietly, waiting for Ram to complete his inspection. It wasn't long before he put the papers back in the envelope and reported to Jasumati.

'The documents appear to be in order. But I would like to take them to the office for a more thorough inspection.'

Pramod shook his head. 'Not today. I'll bring them to your office in a couple of days when I've finished with my arrangements.'

Ram and Jasumati exchanged brief but knowing nods and the papers were returned to Pramod. Jasumati lifted the other envelope from her lap. She seemed undecided as to what to do with it.

Pramod encouraged her to look inside. 'Take your time. Your mother's letter is in there. We are in no hurry.'

Jasumati blinked. She flipped it around a few times, then handed it back to Pramod. 'I don't need to look.'

Nirmala stifled a soft gasp of surprise. How could she not want to read Kanta's letter?

Pramod nodded knowingly. 'You have seen the letter already, haven't you? You were with Kanta when she wrote it.'

Suparna was sitting back quietly, observing her sister's reaction. With a calm control that surprised Nirmala, she directed a question at Jasumati which finally got her the attention she was seeking.

'Why didn't our mother come to fetch me? She knew where I was.'

The whole energy in the room seemed to shift. Jasumati's arrogant mask fell off and all of a sudden, she looked tired. She sighed and shook her head slowly. Holding Suparna's gaze, she answered in a weary voice, 'Because *Ba* didn't want to uproot you from your home. She was a kind and loving mother who suffered all her life because of what happened. She thought you were better off where you were.'

Suparna's forehead creased into a frown. Her heartbreak was in her voice. 'I don't understand why she wouldn't want me back.' The sisters locked eyes with one another, not speaking. Nirmala held her breath, looking from one to the other, wondering what each was thinking. She didn't have long to wait. Jasumati jerked her gaze away and lashed out at Suparna, turning aggressive again.

'I don't know, okay? Maybe she wanted to forget the past.' Her raised voice triggered a short coughing fit which made her even more aggressive. 'Everything was going well. But you had to come and spoil it, didn't you?'

Suparna recoiled as if she had been slapped. 'Why are you saying that?' She looked astounded.

Jasumati lifted her head high and refused to respond. Pramod gave her a shrewd look. Without taking his eyes off her, he answered

Suparna's question. 'Because you have exposed Jasu-*foi*'s secret, that's why. She's been pretending to be the landlady of Suparna Mansions, and now she won't be able to do that.'

A flash of anger and scorn crossed Jasumati's face. She curled her lip in disdain.

'That's the truth of the matter, isn't it?' he asked.

Her lips twisted into a sneer. Raju and Ram exchanged worried looks.

Pramod continued in a steady tone. 'You have known all along that your father was only looking after the mansion for his brother. You thought you would always be here living on income from the tenants. You were so sure no one would ever know that Suresh and Nirmala were the true heirs. But now your plan is scuppered because I have come with Suparna-*foi* to claim my inheritance. You should know that I will be taking over the full management of this property, including the collection of rent. And if I wanted to, I could ask you to move out of this building.'

He let that sink in for a while. Jasumati sat in stony silence and the two men gaped at Pramod in utter stupefaction.

'As it happens, I have given my word to Nirmala that I would not ask you to leave. She wants you and your sons to remain here.'

They heard an audible intake of breath coming from Raju's direction. Nirmala sensed his eyes on her, but she could not look away from Jasumati who was still giving Pramod a contemptuous look.

Pramod softened his tone. 'Jasu-*foi*, you are family. And you have taken care of this place all these years. I will not be asking you to leave. Of course, you can continue to live here with Raju and his family. But . . .' He became assertive again. 'You will have to move down one floor. I will be giving notice to the tenants below. When they leave, you will have the chance to move in.'

Jasumati's face was inscrutable. The only sign of emotion was in the movement of her chest as her breathing became more laboured. Raju spoke for the first time.

'What are you planning for this apartment?' There was no aggression in his voice, just concern.

Pramod gave him a smile of satisfaction. 'Nirmala will move here with Varun.'

Jasumati let out a short derisive laugh. 'You must be mad!' Giving Nirmala a sidelong glance, she wrinkled up her nose as if she could smell something disgusting. Feeling out of her depth, Nirmala shrank back into her seat.

'I can assure you I am perfectly sane.' Pramod's smile was almost playful. 'In the next few months, I will be transferring the property over to Nirmala. She will be the new landlady. As Mohanlal's rightful heir, she is entitled to Suparna Mansions.'

'What?' Jasumati looked incredulous. 'You can't do that!'

Her face whipped across to Jagjivan Ram, who looked startled, his jaw dropped in stunned surprise. Hastily he collected himself and spluttered, 'But, but . . . That is not correct. There are certain laws that . . .'

'I know all about the laws. I have done my homework so I know this can be completed in quite a short space of time. I will be seeking advice from property experts to make it all legal.'

Jasumati was on her feet. 'How dare you! You come to my house and order me about. Get out! All of you.' She was spitting fire as she growled at them, her hand pointing at the door. Her growl became a grunt which developed into a cough. Very quickly she went into a full-blown coughing fit. But still she tried to talk. 'Get out!' she rasped.

Raju rushed over to her. 'Mummy. Calm yourself.' He pulled back her outstretched arm and rubbed her back as he helped her sit down.

'Water. Bring her some water.' Suparna was clearly concerned.

Between further bouts of coughing, Jasumati drank some water and eventually recovered. She sat back with her eyes closed.

'My mother suffers from a lung complaint,' explained Raju. 'It bothers her sometimes.'

Pramod stood up. 'I'm sorry to hear that. We should go.' He motioned to the others to follow and began walking away.

Nirmala got up but Suparna remained seated, staring anxiously at Jasumati. 'Will she be all right?' she asked Raju.

'Yes. She will be fine,' Raju assured her.

Suparna sighed, then walked over to Jasumati and placed a hand on her shoulder. Jasumati opened her eyes and the two looked at one another for a long moment.

'I'm sorry,' Suparna whispered. 'For everything.'

Nirmala saw Jasumati narrow her eyes then pointedly look away. She was clearly not going to reciprocate Suparna's desperate need to connect with her. It was distressing to see the hurt on Suparna's face, and Nirmala put a gentle hand on her arm to move her away. Feeling weary and emotional, Nirmala walked away with a heartbroken Suparna.

Chapter 34

Hema was waiting for them by the front door. In response to her arched eyebrows, Nirmala shook her head. Hema looked at Suparna's forlorn face and tutted. 'Why don't you all sit down and I will make some nice *masala chaa* for everyone. I bet the *dosi* didn't offer any.'

Pramod rolled his eyes. 'Not even water. We had to ask for it. I would love a cup of *chaa*, thank you.' Hema retreated to the kitchen.

Nirmala sat beside Suparna on the *jhula* and put her arm around her shoulders. 'I'm sorry you had to go through that.'

Suparna lifted her shoulders and let them drop. 'It's my own fault. I shouldn't have come with such high hopes.'

'Don't blame yourself, *Foi*.' Pramod sounded annoyed. 'You did nothing wrong. Any normal person would have been overjoyed to find their long-lost sister. I think Hema is right; Jasu-*foi* is not normal.'

'Did I hear my name?' Hema popped her head round the front door.

Pramod laughed. 'Yes, you did.'

'I told you she's a *daakan*. Nirmala doesn't like me saying that, but she is a very nasty person. She was like that with Nirmala's parents too.'

Suparna shook her head. 'I can just imagine. It is so sad that while I was enjoying a happy family life in Zimbabwe, poor Suresh was suffering over here.' She gave Nirmala a tight squeeze. 'I wish so much that he was still with us.'

Hema brought out steaming cups of *chaa* for them. While they sipped, Pramod told Hema about the meeting. Looking across the road, Nirmala noticed Jagjivan Ram hail a rickshaw and leave. She raised her eyes to the top floor and saw Raju gazing down at them. Not wishing to acknowledge him, she turned away to listen to Pramod, who was giving vent to his feelings.

'She knew for so long that Suresh's father was Mohanlal and that it was he who owned the mansion,' continued Pramod. 'Yet she watched Nirmala struggle without money right in front of her eyes, doing nothing to help her. I'm determined to get them out of that apartment. And both sons will have to pay rent. They won't be able to squirm out of it.'

Hema leaned back, a triumphant look on her face. 'Good! I'm going to enjoy watching them live like the rest of us.'

Pramod regarded her with a steady gaze, looking thoughtful. 'I wonder if you could help me. I need to find a tenancy management agency with a good reputation. One I can trust to handle everything to do with looking after residential property. Can you recommend one?'

Hema grinned. '*I* can't, but I know someone who can.' She turned to Nirmala. 'Someone who will be very happy to help you.'

Nirmala's face softened into a smile. 'Hema's husband, Ashvin. He's the best lawyer in town.'

Hema laughed. 'I have to agree, though I might be a little biased. Ashvin knows all the right people and he'll do anything for Nirmala. He is right now working on Nirmala's divorce petition.'

Suparna put her teacup aside and twisted round to face Nirmala. 'I'm glad you are taking that step. You deserve to be happy with someone who loves you and treats you well. Maybe someone who is waiting for you?'

Suparna's empathy made Nirmala's throat constrict. Her mind flashed back to the conversation they'd had about Sudhir during the trip to Victoria Falls, sipping coffee in the lounge of the luxury hotel in Bulawayo.

She swallowed a few times and blinked. 'It's been eleven years. He might not be waiting.'

'Of course he's waiting!' Hema clicked her tongue with impatience. 'Come on, Nirmala. You should have divorced Ajay a long time ago.'

'It wasn't easy, Hema, you know that.'

Pramod inclined his head towards Hema. 'Could you let your husband know that I would like his help? I need advice on the legalities of property transfer and management of rental income.'

Hema looked delighted. 'At last Nirmala will not have to worry about money. This is such good news.' She looked over at Nirmala's frowning face. 'Nirmala? You have to be happy about that!'

Giving her a weak smile, Nirmala replied, 'It's hard to take it in. Too much change happening too quickly.'

Pramod laughed. 'You are going to be a wealthy young woman. Better get used to it.'

Suparna broke into the conversation. 'Nirmala, you have a visitor coming.' She was looking across the road.

When they turned their heads, they saw Raju approaching the porch, looking solemn. He appeared ill at ease as he stood looking at Nirmala. Getting off the *jhula*, she went towards him.

'Come and sit down.'

Hema jumped off her chair. 'Sit here.' She moved to stand by the front door as he took her seat and Nirmala returned to hers. They were all curious to hear what he had to say. He cleared his throat, darting glances at each one in turn. His eyes settled on Suparna, his expression full of regret.

'I'm very sorry for my mother's behaviour. She should not have talked to you like that.'

Suparna's whole body seemed to sag with relief. Sitting beside her, Nirmala could feel the emotion pour out of her as she gazed at Raju.

'You look just like my mother, but you are very different from her. A thousand apologies for what she said.'

Suparna seemed unable to speak.

Raju turned to Pramod. 'Please know that I had no idea we were only caretakers of the mansion. My mother never said a word. You can rest assured that we will be complying with all of your terms. Everything will be handed over to you and we will move apartments whenever you say.'

'Really?' Pramod had put on his professional voice. 'Your mother did not seem too happy about that.'

'You don't have to worry about my mother.' Raju was suddenly very firm and authoritative. 'After you left, I made her understand that she has no choice in the matter. We *will* move, whether she likes it or not.'

Nirmala regarded him with some scepticism. In all the years she had known him and his brother, they had always come across as 'Mummy's boys', at their mother's beck and call. Jasumati ruled her family with an iron hand, and that included her late husband. It was hard to imagine any role-reversal in their household.

'Are you sure about that?' Her tone was heavy with disbelief.

Raju offered her a tight smile. 'My mother is over seventy years old and not as strong as she used to be, mentally and physically. She has trouble climbing all those stairs. One flight less will be better for her health. She is my mother, so I try not to upset her, but I do stand up to her when necessary.'

He fell silent for a moment and gazed at her with a sorrowful expression. 'I never understood why my mother treated you like an outsider. You may not believe it but I did try to persuade her to offer you help. Many times. But she would never listen. I'm . . . sorry . . .'

Nirmala looked away, not convinced by his apology. If he had really cared, he would have made more of an effort.

Raju continued, his voice less faltering. 'Suparna Mansions is *your* home, not ours. I can't speak for my mother, but when you move in, I promise you will have no trouble from my brother and me.'

He turned his attention back to Suparna. 'I must go now,' he said, standing up. 'But I hope that we can spend some time together before you return to Zimbabwe.' Nirmala saw that he was trying to control his emotions. Surprising everyone, he walked forward and bent down to touch Suparna's feet with respect. Before she could give him her blessing, he turned around and strode away.

'Well,' said Pramod, 'I wasn't expecting that!'

Hema gave a strangled snort. 'Too little too late. He should have done something about his mother ages ago.'

Pramod laughed. 'Like what? Shake her until she came to her senses?'

'Something like that. Why didn't he take control years ago?'

'Well, he seems to have done that now.' Turning to Nirmala, he asked, 'Do you believe him?'

'I don't know. He sounded genuine but we'll have to wait and see.' Nirmala was looking at Suparna. 'Would you like to see him again? Maybe with his family?'

Suparna considered. 'It would be nice. I had hoped that Jasumati and I could have a close relationship, but she wants nothing to do with me. As painful as that is, I'm going to have to accept that. If her son wants to see me, I would love that.'

'Leave it to me, *Foi.* I will arrange a gathering with Raju and his family. And maybe his brother's family too.'

'Right,' said Pramod. 'I have an idea. We should all go out to a restaurant and we can ask Raju to suggest a nice place in town.'

'Make sure he pays for the meal!' Hema snorted, making Pramod laugh.

Nirmala invited everyone to stay for supper but they all declined and began to take their leave. The three of them squeezed into one auto rickshaw as they were going in the same direction.

With people returning home from work, the street was busy and noisy. Nirmala sat for a long time looking out but seeing nothing as she thought about the events of the day. Ramu's surprise phone calls, Jasumati's hurtful words followed by Raju's remorse. The thoughts echoed in her head, like waves crashing on the shore then ebbing away.

Suparna's sadness tugged at her heart. She thought of her kind, loving face, glowing with hope of a happy union with her sister. And her hope for Nirmala to be reunited with Sudhir. *Someone who is waiting for you.* In her heart of hearts, Nirmala believed that Sudhir *was* waiting for her. But how could she run to him now after the way she had broken his heart. She wanted to be with Sudhir, but she couldn't tell him that. If something went wrong with her plans to divorce Ajay, there would be no reunion and they'd both be hurt again. She simply could not let that happen.

With a sigh, Nirmala stood up and went inside. It was time to tell Varun what was going on.

Chapter 35

A few days later, they all met again in Hema's apartment. Within minutes of meeting one another, Pramod and Ashvin were chatting as if they were old friends. They settled down on the sofa in the apartment and began to exchange stories on a range of topics including cricket, politics and Ashvin's favourite hobby, electronic devices. The women left them to talk while they sat around the dining room table with Varun. He was telling Hema how he felt about moving to Suparna Mansions.

'Will you like living in a big house?' asked Hema.

'Yes!' His eyes were shining. 'It's a very big house. Like in Zimbabwe.' He began to describe the different villas and mansions they had stayed in during their holiday.

At the other end of the table, Suparna asked Nirmala if she had noticed a difference in his health since the start of the new treatment.

'He hasn't had any episodes recently, but I know that doesn't mean it's over. I'll keep an eye on it and take him to the doctor regularly.'

'At least you won't have to worry about his treatment costs anymore. Your money worries are all gone.'

Pramod called her name and Nirmala went over to join the two men. They told her that Ashvin was going to open a new bank account for her and arrange for all the rent money from Suparna Mansions to be sent directly into that account. Ashvin had also given him names of reputable property lawyers and residential agents. But there was a problem.

'It won't be possible for me to have everything concluded before we fly back home. Finalising the business arrangements will take several months so I'll have to leave some things for the two of you to sort out.'

Ashvin nodded. 'Everything takes time in India. There is always a lot of red tape, and you have to expect delays.'

'I'm in no hurry to move into Suparna Mansions,' said Nirmala with a smile. 'And in any case, my divorce will take some time to come through.'

'There won't be any delays with that,' said Ashvin. 'I will make sure of that. When I took the sewing machine to the widow's house the other day, Ajay signed the petition without any argument. So I don't think he'll give us any trouble going forward.'

Pramod was biting his lip, looking thoughtful. 'At least we don't have to worry about Ramu-*kaka* contesting the will anymore. When I get home, I will ask him outright and let you know what he says.'

Ashvin shrugged. 'In the meantime, we can start getting the agencies ready and prepared for the final sign-off. I'll get started next week on the property transfer process.'

Nirmala knitted her brow. 'What if we need you to authorise certain things?'

Pramod waved his cell phone. 'I can do that with this. Or online. We are living in a digital world, and even from two different continents, a lot can be done.'

Ashvin laughed. 'That's true. And, Nirmala? You wanted to study computer science. You can do that now and become an expert yourself.'

Nirmala rolled her eyes. 'It's too late for that.'

'No, it's not.' Pramod gave her a steady look. 'There's nothing to stop you from going back to your studies, if that's what you want.'

Nirmala allowed herself a moment to consider all the possible experiences she could now have. Experiences she could only dream about before. Smiling at the thought, she nodded. 'Maybe I will one day. Who knows.'

~

The next few days flew by, and Nirmala spent every spare moment making sure Suparna and Pramod had all they needed and wanted before they returned to Zimbabwe. The evening spent with Raju and his family had gone off without a hitch. His younger brother had joined them. They paid a lot of attention to Suparna, making her feel welcome, telling her about their families and life in India. It was clear they were going to keep in touch.

Pramod insisted on buying Nirmala a cell phone and laptop computer so that they could keep in constant contact. He called in an expert to set up the connections and made sure everything was in working order.

The night before they were due to leave Navsari, Suparna and Pramod came to Nirmala's house to say goodbye. They had booked a taxi to pick them up very early the next morning. Although she had not known them long, Nirmala felt a deep attachment to them. Suparna folded her into her arms as soon as she entered the house.

'We will meet again very soon. I promise,' she whispered.

Pramod gave Varun a quick squeeze, then pulled Nirmala into an affectionate bear hug. 'I'll phone you when we reach home.'

Suparna gathered Varun and Nirmala into a group cuddle. 'I will miss you. Look after yourselves, okay?'

They followed their guests out of the house and into the sunshine. Pramod stopped a passing auto rickshaw and helped Suparna climb aboard. She leaned out and clasped Nirmala's hand for the last time.

'Goodbye, Nirmala. Stay strong.'

Choking back tears, Nirmala stood waving until they were out of sight. Feeling despondent, she turned to go back inside her house. But something made her look over her shoulder. She turned around to face Suparna Mansions. Instead of the old crumbling building that it was, she saw a tall tower, freshly painted, and repaired. Closing her eyes, she made a promise to herself: Suparna Mansions would be returned to its former glory. It would be a beautiful and happy home once again. Varun would grow up in the mansion, just as her father had done when his father had been alive.

~

With a critical eye, Nirmala examined her reflection in the glass windows outside the pharmacy. She tucked a loose strand of hair behind her ear and adjusted the *odhani* around her neck. Varun waited patiently for her to take him inside to fetch his medicine. Wiping her clammy hands on her *kameez*, Nirmala glanced at the sign above her head: 'Sudhir's Chemist'. Just seeing his name in print brought a sudden fluttering in her chest, as if a tiny bird was trapped inside. She put a hand on her heart then laughed silently at herself.

Her mind was in a whirl of nervous excitement. Seeing Sudhir always did that to her. But this time she was going to speak to him about all the changes that were happening in her life. She wasn't sure how much, if anything, he knew. After so many years of silence between them, how would he react? Despite her new-found confidence, she felt unsure and anxious.

Taking Varun by the hand, she moved to the entrance and stepped inside. Immediately she was enveloped by the cooler air in the shop and the subtle clinical smells of antiseptics, medicines and chemicals. She paused for a moment to look around. There was a hum of conversation in the room, the staff busy with their customers.

Nirmala's eyes searched the back of the shop for the person she had come to see. A small crowd was waiting to have their prescriptions filled. Raising her head a little, she tried to catch sight of Sudhir serving from behind the counter. But he was well screened by the patients waiting to be seen.

Deciding to make her presence known, she walked with Varun past the huddle of customers to the front. When she arrived, the chemist looked up, and with a crushing disappointment, Nirmala saw that it was not Sudhir. It was another man in a white coat.

Frozen to the spot, she was struck dumb. The possibility of Sudhir not being there had never entered her head. After all her planning and rehearsing, she felt deflated, as if the air had been knocked out of her body.

Annoyed with herself, she was about to turn and retrace her steps when, from the corner of her eye, she saw movement in the dispensary. Looking up, she watched Sudhir make his way down the few steps. Nirmala held her breath, and something warm poured into her heart.

He saw her before he reached the counter. For a moment, he paused, clearly startled to see her. Then his face lit up. Hurrying down, he stood in front of her and leaned forward, a small smile playing about his lips.

'Nirmala,' he said, his voice soft and tender. 'I was hoping you would come by.'

ACKNOWLEDGEMENTS

Writing a book has been more rewarding than I could ever have imagined. From the moment the idea of the story first popped into my head to where the book is today, I have enjoyed the long journey. But this would not have been possible without the support I had along the way.

I am grateful to a lot of people, and none more so than my amazing agent, Kemi Ogunsanwo, from The Good Literary Agency. It was she who opened the door to a whole new world for me: the world of writing and publishing that I had always dreamed about. Her endless encouragement and belief in my characters gave me the confidence to bring them out into the light.

The whole team at TGLA have been extremely supportive. In particular, I am indebted to Arzu Tahsin, the development editor, whose attention to detail and keen insight are beyond impressive. Thank you also to Abi Fellows, literary agent, for requesting my full manuscript in the first place, thereby giving me the opportunity to become an author.

I owe a thousand thanks to my fantastic editor, Victoria Oundjian. I feel incredibly fortunate to have her as my champion at Lake Union Publishing. Her excellent advice has helped me bring greater colour and spark to my writing. Other professionals who have helped me polish my book include Jill Sawyer and Swati

Gamble. Thank you very much, and to everyone at Lake Union for your help and support.

Early readers who gave me excellent feedback include my daughters, Priyanka and Kaushal, and my beta readers, Lindsay Bamfield, Diana Jones, Carol Sampson and Chandralekha Mistry. They all gave me a tremendous boost.

Although I knew a fair bit about India, I made a special trip to Navsari to see the city and the mansion that was the inspiration for my story. Surendra and Hiral Tailor, my distant relatives, provided me with much-needed information about life in India today.

There have been huge changes in Zimbabwe since I was last there, and I must thank my friend's daughter, Beejal Madhvi, for getting me up to speed. It is still a beautiful country and I hope I have done it justice in my novel.

In London, I am indebted to so many friends for cheering me on. They include Rosie Canning and the Greenacre Writers Group, my Finchley travel buddies, Marcelle Akita, the North Finchley Library Book Club and members of the Mo Siewcharran Shortlister Review Group.

Finally, I want to thank my close family for their endless love and support. I wouldn't have been able to do this without them.

Supawala Mansion. Completed in 1954, Navsari, India.

Family Prayers at the start of construction in 1954, Navsari, India.

ABOUT THE AUTHOR

Photo © 2020 Jodine Rianna Williams

Vasundra Tailor was born in India and raised in Zimbabwe when it was called Rhodesia. She is a qualified pharmacist who completed her Masters in Pharmaceutical Microbiology at the University of Strathclyde. Based in London, she began her debut novel after obsessing about families currently living in a property in India which once belonged to her father. Curious about human relationships, she loves to meet people from diverse backgrounds and see how they connect with those around them.

Her novel extract won the second runner-up prize for the Mo Siewcharran Fiction Competition in November 2019.

@vasundrajay